WHAT LITTLE GIRLS ARE MADE OF

C.A. WHITTINGHAM

Print ISBN: 978-1-54399-799-6 | eBook ISBN: 978-1-54399-800-9

What are little girls made of?
What are little girls made of?
Sugar and spice and all things nice,
that's what little girls are made of.

—Excerpt from the poem *What are little
boys made of?* thought to have been written by English poet Robert Southey

PROLOGUE

"I know it's wrong. I do know. There's this overwhelming urge and I can't control it. I do, though, control it. I have done on many, many occasions. It's like the urge is always, always there and I fight it daily and hold it down. I even feel proud of myself, and then it comes roaring out; it takes me over. It's a sickness; people see me as a monster. I disgust people. I disgust myself. I try to imagine my life without this sickness, and I can't. I just can't." His voice drifted off, still searching for words that he felt would be effective enough but failing.

His eyes flicked between the austere woman and the obedient nodding older man sitting across from him, searching their eyes for some sort of reaction. There was none. He felt the distance between them, a gulf. He wanted to get closer, not so much to look into their eyes, but so that they could see into his, see his true desperation. It was clear to him that she was the leader, the drill sergeant, and he was the follower, the weaker of the two.

The woman carefully made her notes. Pausing, she cleared her throat. "So, this sickness, as you describe it, is not your fault?"

"No. It isn't. I don't want to feel this way, I don't want to hurt or ki... anyone. I can't help it." He shrugged his shoulders in supplication.

The follower interjected, never once looking in his direction, "So, who is responsible? Who should take the blame?" The follower's lack of interest in his answers was clear. Their questions were simply a formality.

"I don't know what you mean." He was confused somewhat by the follower's hollow tone, not the question.

"Mr. Mademan, if this sickness is not your fault, whose fault is it?" The question flew out of the woman's mouth and landed before him like a discarded handkerchief, sticky with unapologetic sarcasm.

Again, he shrugged his shoulders, unable to meet her stony gaze. She glanced up from her notes, ran a scathing eye over him, returned to her notes, and awaited his response. He shifted around in his seat, ran his hands through his hair, and peered up at her from lowered eyes.

"I've been doing a lot of reading. Nothing else in this hellhole to do. I read up about addiction. It's like an addiction to food, alcohol, or drugs. You have good days and bad days, but when those bad days come along, they ruin everything." His voice was almost lighthearted, a shift of focus hoping for some type of redemption. His eyes pleaded with them to understand, to show some sympathy. His desperation was almost tangible: he clung on to, his only life raft.

"So, you believe that raping, molesting, and murdering children is the same as stuffing your face with food when you're not hungry or consuming so much alcohol that you urinate on yourself and can't remember what's happened? Or sticking a needle in your veins?" She stomped on his fingers and pushed him out to sea.

Stefan knew how ridiculous his pitiful attempt at trying to justify his actions sounded, and not being one to accept sounding foolish, he leapt up out of his seat, hurled himself forward, and slammed his hand on the desk at which they sat, pointing an accusing finger at her. All this occurred before the silent statue of the prison guard had the chance to move from his position. The guard sprang into action, grabbed hold of Stefan, and pulled his arms roughly behind him. Stefan struggled, unleashing a strength that he had not used in years.

"You're supposed to fucking listen to me, help me!" His face inches from hers, he was shaking not with anger but with fear; she retracted only slightly. The follower drew back his seat and prepared to escape. Stefan felt little satisfaction in spooking the follower but he really needed to inflict fear upon her.

The prison guard dragged Mr. Mademan back to his seat. Mademan pushed his waist up high trying to avoid sitting in the seat like a petulant toddler, as the guard clicked handcuffs around his wrists.

"Sit down Mr. Mademan." Her voice calm, she unflinchingly glared at him with a blank expression, not at all fazed. Stefan realized for the first time that this woman was not only unafraid but was powerful, steely in her composure. He couldn't intimidate her. It was he who was intimidated. He slumped back down in his seat, defeated. Stefan ran his eyes over the follower—he was a coward. Not once had he attempted to defend her. Perhaps the follower knew something that he did not about this woman whose composure could not be rocked.

"I'm sorry. I'm sorry. I didn't mean..." Stefan felt the lump rising in his throat and gulped it back down. There was no way he could expose his total lack of control and fear. They all knew that she was in charge, that she called the shots, and Stefan was just having a hard time accepting that.

"Who told you that? Who told you that we are here to help you?" she enquired.

Stefan held his head low again, afraid to look at her. He knew she could smell his fear, see his hands trembling. Finally, clasping his hands together, he sighed. No one had actually told him that they were there to help; he simply felt that they should want to help him.

"We are here, Mr. Mademan, to decipher whether or not you are ready and want to be rehabilitated back into the community, and, more importantly, whether or not you pose a risk to children. That's our job. Do you understand?"

He nodded.

"We've taken account from your doctor, the warden, your probation officer, and psychologist, and we've also read your application. Think of it as a point system, and it is our job to score you on different areas of your progress, or lack thereof. We will then decide whether or not your parole is granted. It's all very scientific; there is no emotion or support here. I am not your therapist. Is that clear?"

Giving no time for him to respond, she continued, "From here, we will record our findings and make the relevant recommendations. If your score is high enough, a final decision will be made. You do not have to appeal to us or explain anything. Only answer the questions put before you."

Stefan nodded knowingly. He had said too much, crossed an invisible line. The anger and resentment emanating from the woman filled the room up to the brim. He felt claustrophobic and desperately wanted the assessment to be over. He wanted to move his feet or lick his dry lips—move in some way—but he couldn't. Instead, he sat paralyzed, motionless.

The woman quickly scrawled a few more notes in her leather-bound A4 pad. He could now feel her eagerness to leave the room and get away from him. He noticed her expensive diamond engagement ring sparkling against the dim light and wondered what kind of man could catch and keep a woman like her. Everything about her was perfect, which only added to his sense of inadequacy. Her perfume, subtle and light. Her neutral-colored manicure. Her hair held up in a bun—no straggles of hair lightly pulled loose. Her makeup understated. Confidence exuded from her.

The follower followed. Between the two people who sat before him, Stefan knew that it was she who would make the final decision.

As they whispered and wrote their notes, he felt as if he'd lost. There was no chance of his getting an early release. He felt utterly helpless. For the past twenty years, he had made sure that he had been a model prisoner, did everything by their rules, by their book. Everything had led up to this day, and he had blown it. He felt foolish and pitiful. He had lost. What would he tell Elise? She had waited five years; there was no way she was going to wait another ten.

The woman lifted her head. "We're all done here." She nodded, the two stood in unison, and they gathered their papers together. Stefan felt compelled to say something, try to get them on his side and smooth over his little outburst. He wasn't sure why, but he didn't want them to just leave without saying anything further. He thought to ask a question, but there were a million and one questions: which one first?

The follower hurriedly left the room, closing the door behind him. She shuffled a few more papers and collected them in her arms before taking several steps coolly past Stefan toward the door. He couldn't bear to see her exit. He sat quite still, not turning to watch her leave. She took a few steps, the sound of her pristine heels on the rubber-covered floor signaling finality, but then she stopped. She turned back and leant in closely over his shoulder. The guard stood unmoving, eyes to front. The subtle notes of her perfume wafted over him, the hairs on the back of his neck stood up in a shot as she spoke, her breath sending shivers down his spine.

"You see, Stefan, if it were down to me, if it were my job alone to decide what to do with you, I'd take you somewhere in the middle of nowhere and I'd chop your fucking balls off with a rusty axe. I'd put a stop to all that perversion. Then, I'd chop off your feet so you would never, ever wander near another child. I'd gouge out both of your eyes, so you would never again lay them upon another innocent child. Then, I'd chop off both of your hands, so you could never again touch another child."

She stood up straight, cleared her throat, and took a deep breath. "And finally, Stefan, I would throw what was left of your pathetic body onto a fire and I'd record your screams, so that every single time I'd see an injustice in this world, I would know that I dealt with this one and somehow, I believe, that would give me a small, tiny sense of peace."

She turned on her heels. He heard the door open and close quietly. She was gone.

"There can be no keener revelation of a society's soul than the way in which it treats its children."

—Nelson Mandela

CHAPTER ONE

Crimson red velvet and chiffon.

Charlotte loved the texture, the feel against her skin, the extravagance, the glamour. Turning heads was her aim; she needed to hear the hushed whispers as she passed. Never before had she been so incensed to make a mark, leave an impression. This outfit was the outfit of all outfits and she hoped it would remain in people's minds until the end of time. After handing her mother her housekeeping, she had spent a whole month's wages on this outfit, from the fire red lipstick down to her red patent stilettos.

Charlotte knew, as she made her way down the threadbare carpeted stairs, tiptoeing so as not to catch her heels in the sagging holes, what her mother's reaction would be. She could barely contain her excitement.

The silence in the lounge was everything she had hoped for and then some. She was a conversation stopper. Mouths agape, eyebrows raised, sherry glasses lowered, speechless.

"What in the name of…" her mother, Clara Hill, shrieked, propelling herself from her sunken burnt orange armchair, outraged at the spectacle.

"Why? How could you?" Auntie Millicent and Uncle Stan came to her aid, each coaxing her back to the safety of her armchair.

"She had to ruin this day, just had to. Selfish, ungrateful bitch!"

Charlotte preened, enjoying every moment of her mother's displeasure and humiliation. She scanned the room slowly, ensuring everyone got an eyeful of her splendor. Becky, her fourteen-year-old cousin, mobile phone in hand, was careful to get the whole scene in. Perfect.

Charlotte was the first to notice the three black hearses pull up through the off-white tatty net curtains.

"Let's not keep the cars waiting." Charlotte sashayed out of the room, collecting a large bright yellow umbrella from the hallway as she went. She was expecting rain. Hearing the tuts of disgust and disapproval only served to amuse her further. She ran her hand down the side of the fig-ure-hugging velvet dress and adjusted the collar of the chiffon wrap around her shoulders.

The entire service was centered around the disgraceful behavior of the deceased's daughter. How disrespectful, cruel, and thoughtless—atten-tion-seeking and spiteful. Charlotte lapped it up.

Charlotte, pleased when the drizzly rain came, had checked and dou-ble checked the weather forecast. She beamed brightly as the sun finally came out for her for the first time in her seventeen years. As they lowered her father into his final resting place, she lifted her bright yellow beacon into the air, and it sprung open none too quietly. The yellow frill twitched in the wind. The day couldn't get any better as far as Charlotte was concerned.

As the mourners finally turned to make their way back to the cars, Charlotte stood at the edge of the grave transfixed by the imposing mahog-any box adorned with the purest white lilies. He didn't deserve white lilies. He didn't deserve the expensive coffin which her mother had taken a loan to pay for. All these people here, paying their respects. Respect?

Albert Markham, the Hill's next door neighbor, poked her on the shoulder. "Make your own way home. You should be ashamed of yourself. Your mother's heartbroken, and your father, he'll be turning in there."

Charlotte didn't notice Albert; she had nothing to say to anyone. There were no words. She had done this. She had prayed since she could remem-ber that he would die, and now he had. She had prayed that he would die a painful death, and it had been. She believed that she had caused his demise and that power was only bestowed upon her to allow her to dole the retribu-tion she craved. She deserved it. She had been granted two wishes and they had both come true. Charlotte saw that people no longer believed in the power of prayer. Charlotte didn't just believe; she knew. Here was the proof.

She had asked Jesus Christ himself, and he had sent her her very own personal savior. She wasn't even sure how, but she didn't ponder on the how. God works in mysterious ways. They had been informed that her father had contracted a mysterious illness which had gripped him in three months of excruciating pain. Her mother had accepted her doctor's word and wouldn't dream of questioning such a well-respected professional.

At fifty-seven, Stephen Hill had been a healthy, physically fit man. Never a day sick. He smoked, had the occasional drink, but nothing had kept him from his job as concierge at the prestigious five star Hyde Hotel. He loved his job, his workmates, and, heck, he even got on well with his boss. He rarely socialized and, when he did, it was with his workmates.

Everybody saw Stephen, or Steve, as reliable, hardworking, and helpful. He was *the* right hand man and you could set your watch by him. Never late, not in the forty years that he had worked at the Hyde.

Charlotte pushed the tips of her pointed red shoes to the very edge of the grave and peered down. Death wasn't good enough.

She spat on his coffin, watching her saliva land on a white Lilly.

"Rot in hell you fucking pervert."

She no longer saw the lilies or the coffin. She saw him staring down at her as she lay in her bed as a seven year old. She was pulling the covers up over her head, and he was dragging the sheets back and telling her that she had to be a good girl or she would not have the blessings of baby Jesus. His big, doughy soft hands stroked her face, telling her that only good girls get to have a good life. "Don't you want to be a good wife to a good man?"

She spat again. She hated the word "good" and all that it was supposed to represent. It was such a pathetic word and meant nothing to anyone. Everybody, as well as his cat, believed that her father was a *good* man, who did a damn *good* job, he comes from *good* stock. What did they know?

Telling her mother of her father's nighttime visits had only served to create a huge distance between them. Her mother had slapped her hard and sent her away. It was never spoken about again. From that moment, Charlotte knew she should never speak a bad word against her father. She never did, but she longed to make him pay. She had to find a way to punish him and she had.

It had been way too easy, and though Charlotte was prepared to serve time, there didn't appear to be any comeback. So Jennifer Lloyd had promised. Jennifer Lloyd was the Francis Street Church's youth worker and Charlotte's oldest friend. Jennifer had been a prefect at Ladyswood school and a local in the neighborhood, taking the lonely Charlotte under her wing and introducing her to the church.

It had taken Charlotte years to confide in her, to open up to her, and tell her of the abuse she was suffering at her father's hand. Jennifer, being the true friend that she was, had told her there was a way to ensure that her father never hurt anyone ever again.

Jennifer knew someone who could help Charlotte find a way out. She was serious and adamant in ensuring Charlotte understood, that once she chose this path there was no way back, no cancellation, no regrets. It had taken Charlotte one day and one night to make up her mind. Steve, true to form, had taken her for the last time, and as she lay still, scrunching her eyes closed, cringing and holding her breath under his hard weight, she had no doubts, no qualms, no worries whatsoever. If she could do something to stop him, then she would, no matter the consequences.

Charlotte had never heard of the dark web before Jennifer had shown her a site called BVS, Buttercup Victim Support. "We save souls," it had declared. Jennifer had simply filled out a short form: the name of the abuser, date of birth, address, and his offences, and that was that.

They waited.

Seven months later, her father became desperately ill. The doctors had no clue as to the cause. Steve had fever, couldn't hold down his food, and eventually could no longer drink water. He became a shadow of his former self. He spent three months in the hospital and, finally, when the doctors gave him just days to live, Clara insisted on having him come home. Charlotte saw him only once, on her way to work, when the nurses carried him into the lounge on a stretcher. Charlotte stood on the stairs watching his emaciated shell—weak, desperate, hollowed. A skeleton with yellowing skin pulled tightly across his once strong bones. He had glanced up at her and she would never forget that look. A look that sought forgiveness: pitiful, look-at-me-now, I know what I did.

Charlotte was surprised at her own non-feeling: no elation, no sadness, no joy, no dismay. There he was, a man who had caused her so much pain, and he had returned home to die in her presence.

Charlotte had kept her word and followed Jennifer's instructions down to the T. "Keep praying and God will answer." And he had. Charlotte owed her life to the Lord and now that the monster was gone, she had to make sure that every day she gave of herself—and what better way to achieve that than to work in the church, giving back, paying her dues, which she knew she would be paying for the rest of her life.

Charlotte never asked about the organization BVS or how they had taken her father's life. She only knew that she was grateful to the organization and to Jennifer. She had heard rumors of this organization that sought out child abusers and pedophile rings, whose aim was to capture, torture, and murder the perpetrators of these crimes. She had wanted to say thank you, a personal thank you, to the people of BVS, but the only way to get in contact was via the dark web. You could donate to the cause, which she did and would always do—a small amount every month from her salary—and it was a very small price to pay for the peace in her heart. Now she was in a position to help other young people suffering at the hands of evil. That was her role in life. That was her duty.

CHAPTER TWO

Karen could barely see over the dashboard of the old Range Rover as it jostled up and up, and up further, following the narrow road's curve and the steep incline. Her laughter was loud and screeching alongside her best friends in the whole wide world, Michelle and Tessa. They rolled around on the passenger seat, clustered together, one big package: Siamese triplets, inseparable.

Dane, Karen's younger brother, was in the back, squeezing himself between the two front seats, not wanting to miss one joke or moment of fun, as always, craving to be included in everything his big sister did.

They'd never been camping before. Their parents never took them anywhere. Neither of them felt as if they were missing out, though. All the kids they knew existed as they did, spending their time either in school or on the forgotten estate they called home, always in search of adventure, but mainly getting in to mischief.

This year was to be different, though, with the arrival of Mr. and Mrs. Rosehill.

Mr. and Mrs. Rosehill were a couple in their late fifties from Wales, whom some of the community had dubbed Hilda and Jim Bloggs, a cute and cuddly looking couple whose resemblance to the cartoon characters was uncanny. They claimed to have taken early retirement after receiving an inheritance and had bought the old boarded up convenience shop in a row of other boarded up shops on the Bournbrook estate. They had erected a shiny new sign above the shop, announcing "Rosehill's Convenience and Post Office" in big red letters against a white background. The sign lit up at night, a beacon in the center of destitution and despair. They lived above the shop and owned two fat, lazy, ragamuffin cats that could be seen in the upstairs window, snoozing at all hours of the day and night. Outside the store, there were two bubble gum machines and a motorized ride-on, a small police car, which when a ten-pence piece was slotted in, would judder into action accompanied by a limp sounding siren.

Mr. and Mrs. Rosehill supplied everything: fresh fruit and vegetables, newspapers, alcohol, groceries, magazines, and, of course, the haven in the middle of the desert, the post office. Rosehill's Convenience and Post Office had the daily needs of the estate covered. There was no longer any need for the Bournbrook residents to travel out into the little town or yet further into the city.

The couple were loved by all, and everyone viewed them as the parents or grandparents they would have loved to have had: not for real sentimental reasons, but for the fact that they gave credit.

A full week's shopping could be had, including cigarettes and liquor, which could be added to a tab till pay day. For the single parents, this fell on a Wednesday. Wednesday mornings, come rain or shine, they would queue up outside, eager to get their hands on their wages and within minutes would spent those same wages, clearing their tabs and stocking up on their essentials, which always included cigarettes and more often than not, liquor.

No one ever stole from the Rosehills. They had no need to: they could have what they wanted when they wanted. All the kids loved Mr. and Mrs. Rosehill. They saw them as softhearted, some even softheaded. All the children were given free sweets, magazines, and comics, or anything they wanted, within reason. In return, they'd sweep the shop or the front of the store, run errands, and carry out small tasks. To the kids of the Bournbrook estate, Mr. and Mrs. Rosehill were their lifeline. The majority of the children barely had a decent pair of shoes and could not guarantee where their next meal was coming from, let alone pocket money and sweets.

Whilst the children on the estate lacked respect for any authority such as police, teachers, or even their own parents, Mr. and Mrs. Rosehill were granted a sort of get out of jail free card. The store was never robbed; they were never held up at knife point; they were untouchable.

One week before the schools were due to close for the summer holidays, Karen found Mr. Rosehill placing a sign in the window.

Free camping trip.

A three day adventure.

Includes travel and three nights in the Malvern Hills.

Learn to build a real fire and cook sausages and bacon for breakfast, hot chocolate, and toasted marshmallows at night.

Beneath the text, was a colorful little sketch of a bright green tent and four kids' happy, smiling faces peeping out. Mr. Rosehill waved encouragingly to Karen and Dane, who stood outside, hand in hand, peering up at the sign. Karen, being a skeptic of any good news or promises that seemed too good to be true based on her short life experience, clasped Dane's hand and thought it over. It was free; free is free. Eventually, she dragged him inside.

"Mr. Rosehill, I....."

"Hello, Karen. Hello, Dane." Mr. Rosehill, jovial and red cheeked, bent down to meet Karen's eye line and offered his hand. Karen hurriedly shook it.

"Hello, Mr. Rosehill," Karen uttered, trying to sound just as cheerful and yet disguise the excitement and urgency in her voice. She nudged Dane to speak up.

"Hello, Mr. Rosehill." He blushed, unused to such formalities away from school.

Mr. Rosehill pointed toward the far corner of the shop.

"Speak to Mrs. Rosehill. She's over in the fruit and veg section. She has all the details." Karen nodded and pulled Dane toward the back of the shop. They found Mrs. Rosehill stocking up.

Karen observed her for a moment before speaking, sussing her out. "Mrs. Rosehill?" she enquired.

"Hello, Karen, sweetheart, and what can I do for you?" Mrs. Rosehill carefully placed large red apples up on display.

"How old do you have to be to go camping?"

Mrs. Rosehill smiled cheerily and turned to face her. "How old are you?"

"Ten." Karen wasn't sure whether she should lie, wanting to be whatever age was acceptable. She decided on the truth.

"Well, you can go." Mrs. Rosehill tweaked Dane's grubby cheek and continued placing the fruit artfully on the display.

Karen mulled this this over for a second. "Can Dane go? He's five." Dane stood beaming up at Mrs. Rosehill, unsure of what camping was, but he felt Karen's excitement and anticipation. He was on his best behavior.

"Yes, of course, as long as you promise to keep a close eye on him." Mrs. Rosehill winked at Dane.

"And we don't have to pay a penny?" She had to be sure.

"Not one penny." Mrs. Rosehill handed them each a shiny red apple.

"Thank you." It was a Saturday morning, and Karen had planned on offering to sweep the outside of the shop today, with the hopes that Mr. or Mrs. Rosehill would offer them something to eat, and here they were getting an apple for doing absolutely nothing at all. The day couldn't get any better. Dane reached out his stubby little hands and accepted his apple.

"Say thank you, Dane." Karen tugged at his hand.

"Please. Thank you." Dane blushed and stood with the huge apple, eyes on Karen to see what she would do next. Karen took the apple, admiring it before she rubbed it hard against her worn, stained yellow t-shirt and took a huge bite. She crunched loudly, chewing hard, wiping the excess juice that escaped from between her lips with the back of her hand. Dane could barely hold the apple in his tiny hands and quickly followed suit.

He attempted a huge bite to fill the rumblings in his stomach, but his little mouth couldn't manage it, so he dug in and took a much smaller bite and broke through the tight red skin. The sweetness of the apple tingled on his tongue, and the juice trailed down from the tiny opening and trickled over his fingers. Neither of them had had breakfast.

"Can I put our names down? Me, Dane, Tessa, and Michelle." Karen listed the names out on her fingers.

Mrs. Rosehill's smile expanded across her face. She carried the box of apples to the counter at the front of the store where Mr. Rosehill was serving a customer, indicating for them both to follow. She placed the box on the counter and took a clipboard from a shelf stuffed with paperwork.

"You two are the first to sign up." Mrs. Rosehill turned the clipboard toward Karen. There was very little to the signing up form. It was simply entitled, "Summer Camping Trip," with a grid beneath. Mrs. Rosehill pointed out where Karen should fill out the names. Karen placed her apple on the counter and stood up on her tip toes to reach the clipboard.

"I have to check with Michelle and Tessa, but I know they'll come."

Mrs. Rosehill nodded as Karen carefully filled out all their names and slid the clipboard back toward her.

Mrs. Rosehill checked the form. "You have very neat handwriting, don't you, and you've put all the surnames too. Just fill out your ages here." Mrs. Rosehill pointed to a column of boxes beside each name. Karen filled the boxes in, each with a number ten and Dane's with a number five.

Mrs. Rosehill took the clipboard and the pen and placed it back on the shelf.

"We're taking all the names of those interested. Make sure to ask your parents' permission because we're going to need them to sign too. Then we'll arrange you all into little groups. The first trip is next weekend, leaving on Friday and coming home on Sunday evening."

Karen beamed brightly, a truly appreciative, wide smile, which she often hid due to her two front teeth being discolored. Despite her knowing the importance of brushing twice daily, sometimes she forgot. Moreover, she couldn't be bothered, and neither she nor Dane had ever visited the dentist.

She'd gotten used to people calling her names—"black tooth" or "Karen McBlack-tooth"—but she always had a comeback. She could defend herself, Dane, and her friends. Karen didn't mind. Just as long as no one upset or hurt them, she really didn't much care. Today, she shared her smile with Mrs. Rosehill, wanting her to see that she was so happy and grateful for the chance to escape and go on this amazing adventure.

A whole weekend away from home. Away from her parents. Away from the estate. She felt as if her heart would burst as she bid Mrs. Rosehill a cheery farewell. Pulling Dane along, she hurried from the shop. Dane did his best to keep up, holding his apple tightly toward his chest, galloping alongside her.

The closest they had got to camping was reading Enid Blyton's *Five Go Off to Camp* at school, and none of them had cooked anything on an open fire. The notice had said that they'd learn survival skills and learn how to look after themselves. Karen relished the idea of being able to cook for herself and Dane. A comforting picture formed in her mind that once she had learned these survival skills, she and Dane would be just fine. Learning to cook would ensure that she and her little brother would always have a hot dinner. Sausages and chips. The thought comforted her and warmed her stomach.

Karen didn't much like her parents, not because of their lack of care for her, but more for Dane's sake. They had always pushed him away and ignored his cries. He'd soon stopped requesting their attention and turned to her for his every need and had been doing so since he could crawl. She counted her blessings though, as they were free to do what they pleased. She knew that if she didn't go to school there would be no punishment or repercussion.

Though there was no chance of that, Karen loved school. She loved her friends, her teachers, and the hundreds of books she had access to. Karen and Dane had never missed a day of school: she saw to that.

Their parents passed through their home as if she and Dane were not in residence. When they came home from work, they holed themselves up in the lounge in front of the TV, barely acknowledging them. Karen and Dane were not allowed into the lounge once their parents got home from work. They were banned to their bedrooms or, if the fancy took them, to the streets. Karen had often found them having sex and would quickly withdraw herself from the room. She felt the love between them but never felt an ounce of this elusive love or warmth toward her or Dane. It was as if she and Dane did not exist. Her parents were so wrapped up in each other that, as far as Karen could see, if the house were on fire, their parents would save themselves. Karen and Dane never got a look-in.

Karen made sure Dane got to school, washed his hands and face, and brushed his teeth. If Dane was hungry, he complained to Karen. Their clothes were disheveled and often smelt stale, as they rarely got a spin in the washing machine. Often their shoes became too tight, so they wore canvas sneakers which she Michelle and Tessa would steal from the precinct in the town. Karen couldn't quite put her finger on it or understand fully the situation they were in, but she knew that Dane relied on her and there was no one else to look out for them. She knew that her parents didn't really care what happened to them, so she had no choice but to care. She dreamt and wished that she had a mom and dad like those she saw on the TV or, better still, Daddy Warbucks.

Today, Karen felt blessed, she had Dane, and her two best friends, Michelle and Tessa. She didn't need anyone else. Karen always knew where she could find her two best friends in the whole world, especially on a sunny bright day such as this: up on the embankment by buttercup path.

She ran hand in hand with Dane through the wild fields and a large expanse of green land, a full-size football pitch which the council kept neatly trimmed, surrounded by fields and bushes of every type. In the autumn, wild rhubarb, blackberries, and red berries could be found in abundance. And right through the middle of it all ran the canal, which lead to the River Rea.

Karen spotted her two friends in the distance basking in the sun, right where she had expected in the buttercup patch.

"Hey!" Karen couldn't wait to tell them the news. Her voice sounded distant and faint, but they heard her calling and sat up abruptly. They waved back vigorously. As she and Dane got closer, they jumped up into the air screaming at the top of their voices as if spectating at the Olympics.

The three were always overjoyed to see each other. Their friendship was a staple in each of their lives. They loved each other with a passion. No matter the gloom and monotony of their little lives, they found solace in each other's company. Together, they lit up the world around them and had promised to be friends forever.

Karen sped up, not for a moment loosening her grip on Dane's hand. Dane was used to being dragged around by his big sister and had become quite the little runner. He was almost as fast as she was, which had made him extremely popular on his first sports day. He had come first in every single race. Now, he threw one foot in front of the other as though his life depended on it, determined to not hold back his big sister, and grasped his apple which he noticed was beginning to brown around the bitten edges.

Tessa and Michelle squealed with delight as Karen and Dane drew nearer.

"Come on Dane!" Tessa bellowed.

Eventually, Karen and Dane flopped down on the ground at their feet. Tessa and Michelle threw themselves to the grass, held hands, and giggled as if they hadn't seen each other in a year.

"Good boy!" Michelle squeezed Dane toward her. Dane held on to her and stared at his browning apple. He was unsure whether he should take another bite. He turned the apple around and took another minuscule bite from the other side.

"We're going on a trip," Karen squealed.

"Where to?" Tessa was immediately caught up in Karen's excitement.

"A camping trip." Karen mustered up all the magic and delight she felt into her words.

Michelle and Tessa sat down. Karen had their full and undivided attention.

"To the Malvern Hills. We're going to set up tents and learn to cook."

Dane held his one hand over his ear as the girls squealed in chorus. Still studying his apple, he took another bite and laughed along with the girls.

"I can't go." Tessa's smile faded.

"You can, Tess. We can all go. It's free!"

"Free?" both Michelle and Tessa exclaimed in unison.

"Mr. and Mrs. Rosehill are taking us all on a camping trip for two nights next Friday."

Once again, the girls giggled with delight and rolled around on the grass, laughing. To them, anything that was free was the equivalent to winning a jackpot.

None of them realized then that Mr. and Mrs. Rosehill's camping trip was about to change the direction of their lives. This was a day that they would remember forever but for all the wrong reasons.

CHAPTER THREE

My Dear Stefan,

How are you? I miss you. I love you. I know it takes you a little longer to respond to my letters, but I've been waiting three days now—three days of waiting, and it feels like three months. You know I worry when I don't hear from you. I think about you all day and all night; the nights are the hardest. Do you think about me? Have you run out of stamps? You should have four first class stamps left. Have you misplaced them? I've enclosed more just in case.

I can never fully concentrate when I'm at work. I'm always wondering what you're doing and hoping that they aren't treating you too badly in there and that you're daydreaming of us.

I dream of the mornings when I can wake up with your big strong arms wrapped around me. I'll squeeze you so tightly. Just thinking about you now makes me feel tingly all over.

When we're together nothing else will matter, no one else will matter. It'll just be me and you. I don't know what I would do without you in my life now. Is that a strange thing to say? I don't care if it is: it's true. Everything I do, my whole future, is no longer about me. It's about us. You and me: we're a team. We're family.

Did you get the package I sent, the one with the summer socks and t-shirts? I hope you did. Let me know if you didn't and I'll call up and see what the holdup is. I want to know if everything fits okay. Sometimes Marks and Spencer's sizes are off. Please let me know—don't just keep hold of them. I can always collect them on my next visit and swap them; it isn't a problem. I want you to feel comfortable and look smart and be the best you you can be. Did you apply to write for the prison blog? I know you're nervous about it, but you shouldn't let nerves hold you back. You have as much right as anyone, and your opinions are valid. You could write under a pseudonym—you don't have to use your real name. People will be interested in what you have to say and, even if they aren't, I am. I'm your number one fan, remember that. Please think about it.

You mean everything to me and every day that passes gets me a day closer to you. The two of us will be together. I hope that one day you'll be able to understand just how much having you in my life means to me. Words don't seem to fit. I want to remind you that ever since I received your first letter, I knew it was destiny that we are supposed to be together. There is no force strong enough to keep us apart. No metal bars, no authorities, nothing that will prevent me from being in your life and I mean that with all my heart, every ounce of my being.

Write me soon, as soon as you can.

Always waiting,

Elise

* * * * *

Dear Elise,

Sorry: I got your package, and everything fits great. Thank you. I wrote you a letter the same day I received yours, but I was too late to get it in the post. They did it on purpose—you know how it is. I knew you'd worry, and I wish you wouldn't. Everything is okay. I miss you, too, and, yes, I dream of the days when I can hold you in my arms. You're a gift and a half and I wonder what you see in me, but I'm not going to look a gift horse in the mouth. If you believe in us, then so do I. You make me feel brave.

I'm still thinking about the blog. I might do that and use a different name. I'm not ready for any kind of backlash.

I wonder what I did to have someone so special in my life, but then I get paranoid. You brighten up my days here and the future looks bright, too.

Yes, we were meant to be together, someday soon, I hope.

Love,
Stefan

CHAPTER FOUR

The blood-soaked knife was slipping in her tiny hands. She needed to get a proper grip and all the while they were screaming, "Kill him!" A cacophony of children ordering her, egging her on, encircling her as she sat atop her prey, in the darkness of the cave. She couldn't see his face, blood-spattered and torn apart, a gaping wound where his face should have been. He was unrecognizable and yet they still called for her to keep going. She struggled to breath. There was no air in the cave.

Plunging the knife into his stomach over and over, stabbing and pulling, stabbing and pulling, she was exhausted. Covering her right hand with her left, she drove the knife down into his chest with all her might, over and over until the screaming stopped.

A beam of white light came from above, and when she looked up, the sun shone down on her face, so bright she shielded her eyes.

She pulled herself up, out of the hole from which she thought she would never escape. Up onto a lush green field, uncut grass for miles around, butterflies fluttered and birds sang. She could breathe again. She ran and ran: she would not stop, she could not stop.

Elise awoke with a start, immediately running her hand across her soaking-wet brow. She clambered from the bed and stumbled into the bathroom, pulling the light pull so hard it snapped back up and clipped her on the chin. Rubbing her chin, she stood in front of the mirror trying to regain her breath. The wetness was not blood as she had thought. It was sweat. She was soaked through. Relief.

The nightmare haunted her. She could never see his face and neither did she want to. Her greatest fear was that she might see his face. She turned the cold water tap on full, and icy water splashed up on her t-shirt. Shivering, she dipped her hands into the water. A sink full of blood. She pulled her hands from the sink and clamped her eyes shut.

"One, two, three, four, five. Please, please, please, please."

One eye squinting open. She peeked at her hands. Water, no blood.

The recurring nightmare didn't upset her, as such. It was the waking and what she felt she saw whilst she was awake that spooked her. Removing her t-shirt and leggings, she climbed back into bed and played the dream over in her mind. Dreams meant something, and since she'd had the same dream for years, she knew it had meaning. It was a message, a warning, a prophecy. She rolled over and slid her hand into the bedside drawer, snatching out a packet of tablets. She popped two into her mouth, realizing she had forgotten to take one the day before. She reprimanded herself for forgetting.

She had to be in top form for Stefan. What would he think? She couldn't tell him about her nightmares and hallucinations. He'd think she was some sort of nutter, and she was not about to give him any reason not to want to be with her, fall out of love, or distance himself from her. There was just no way. She had come too far. She had won his affections, and for now she wanted him to see her as the perfect little prospective wife, someone whom he desired and needed to be with. Her little quirks were not part of the picture, and, anyway, there was plenty of time for him to really get to know her.

She wanted to be perfect, which she knew was simply not possible, so appearing perfect was the next best thing.

CHAPTER FIVE

Shauna hated these dinners, schmoozing the fat cats. Smiling when she wanted to curse, laughing when she wanted to shout: it was all so false. She hated who she became when she was fitting in with the crowd. She was adaptable and found it easy to fit into a role, play a part, but when that meant going against everything that she believed in, more recently it had begun to irk her. It was her job, though, and in order to get ahead and to fulfil her ambition, this was all part and parcel. She had worked too damned hard to fall at this hurdle.

Two years at college, six years of studying for her law degree, a year for her Masters specializing in criminal law, two years working at the Crown Courts as the on-call legal aid solicitor before landing her job at Vincent & Church. She had had to fight to be heard and noticed, knowing that her voice would be loudest by putting in the hours.

The job at Vincent & Church had been a total victory for her, such a huge sense of achievement. More and more, she realized that since she had reached her goal and was now on the cusp of making partner and being in the position that she had coveted for as long as she could remember, she had become disenchanted by the whole thing. Did it really matter? One more step and then she would be free. Perhaps she could change direction?

Kent nuzzled her neck, whispering, "Chill. It's okay. We don't have to stay long." Shauna looked up at him, "Don't we?"

Kent grinned. He accompanied her to all of her work dos and found it amusing how much she hated them. Why she even attended and made the effort to look her very best was beyond him. He, on the other hand, loved socializing with his colleagues, though he had to admit there was definitely a different vibe. He was the sole proprietor of Sloane's Restaurant, the place to be seen, the most exclusive restaurant in the city. His colleagues were cool, laid-back, beautiful people. Shauna's colleagues, the legal pack from Vincent & Church, were mainly over sixty, overweight, and over indulged.

Shauna attended for one reason and one reason only: it wasn't just her job. If she wanted to get ahead, wanted to make her mark and prove herself, if she were to complete her lifetime goal, achieve what she had set out to accomplish, she had to show up and make good.

Mitchell Vincent appeared from behind her gently holding her elbow. "Ah, Shauna, Kent, how are you both? Enjoying your evening so far?"

"Good, good as always, Mitch." Kent always spoke in a mocking tone when he addressed Shauna's colleagues. It did not go unnoticed by Shauna and she found she enjoyed his little games.

"And you? Are you enjoying your evening, Mitch?" Kent surveyed the room. There was really nothing to enjoy: drinks, pomp and ceremony, a late stodgy dinner. It was not at all Kent's cup of tea, but he would make the best of it.

"Not at all. I can't stand these damn things. I'd rather have my feet up with a large scotch, to be frank, but I suppose needs must. I'm sure you'd rather be home with this lovely lady of yours?"

Kent was aware that Shauna was being appreciated from all angles of the room. He felt proud, as always. Tonight she was devastatingly beautiful, swathed in an emerald green silk dress, which was high at the neck and dangerously low at her back. She made him feel like a winner every single day.

Shauna watched as Mitch entertained Kent without quite realizing it. Kent, her man. He was so handsome and, despite his high-profile career, a minor celebrity by all accounts, his humbleness pleased her no end. He was a go-getter, a high achiever, and all off his own back. He'd set himself a goal, achieved it, and enjoyed all the perks that came along with it. Shauna envied his easy approach to life, though life had not been easy for either of them. Kent had a very optimistic outlook. Away from work, the smallest things satisfied and pleased him: a walk in the park; Shauna joining him on the sofa for the Sunday afternoon football match, especially because he knew she hated the game; or the first coffee of the day in bed together. Kent's whole world revolved around his work and Shauna. He wanted and sought nothing more. His life was complete.

Shauna wished she could find the same satisfaction and contentment. Oh, how wonderful it must be to rest your head on the pillow at night and actually sleep soundly. To get up in the morning full of energy and zest for life. Shauna's own sleep was fitful to say the least and her first thought every morning was "Oh, for fuck's sake."

Mitch took Shauna's hand and guided her toward his study. "Excuse me whilst we have a moment for shop talk. You help yourself to another drink." Kent took the instruction, kissed Shauna on the cheek, and made his way over to the bar.

Inside Mitch's study, Shauna relaxed, exhaling loudly as she locked the door behind her. She turned around to find Mitch loosening his belt and zipper. He allowed his trousers to fall to the floor and bent over; his oversized royal blue boxer shorts hung creased around his rotund posterior.

Shauna exaggerated her steps toward him, making sure her heels made as much noise as possible.

"Can I hear sniveling?" She was stern and in command.

"N-no, mistress."

"I believe I do, sniveling little piggy."

"I'm sorry, mistress."

Shauna slid her hand beneath Mitch's desk and produced a yard-stick. He flinched at the sound of her slapping the stick in the palm of her hand.

"Little. Piggy."

Shauna raised the stick and bought it down across Mitch's buttocks with force. He winced and gripped hold of the edge of his desk as he attempted to stifle his cries. He braced himself as the yard stick whistled through the air. This time she gave it a little more oomph. As the stick connected with his cheeks, he let out a small cry of delirious pain. Shauna gave him six of the best, rolling her eyes and chanting, "Little piggy, little piggy."

He was a harmless old man and a great advocate of Shauna's since she'd made the decision to follow a career in law. She owed Mitch nothing; yet, when she wanted something, she knew how to get her own way. Ten minutes of inflicting pain and humiliating a silly old man was nothing in comparison to what she needed to achieve, and when she put her mind to it, she found she could actually enjoy herself.

Mitch had never tried to kiss or touch her inappropriately; he had only ever asked her to punish and humiliate him, and of course asked for her complete discretion. No one, including Kent, knew of their little arrangement, and both parties wanted it to stay that way. No one needed to know. Shauna had, in the past, questioned whether it was her skill, hard work, and determination that had gotten her so far so quickly, or whether it was her ability to be the stern mistress with a firm hand. These thoughts only usually disturbed her on a bad day because she knew better than anyone there was no way she could have climbed so high without her graft. There was nowhere to hide in her field. She had represented and steered cases with the utmost professionalism, and she was renowned for getting the job done and being a hardball player. No one worked harder than she at Vincent & Church's.

Mitch had a keen eye for talent. Shauna had been just sixteen years old when they first met. Shauna knew from a very early age exactly what she wanted to do. Growing up with crime all around her, the community that was her home had taught her some tough lessons and she felt that being able to understand the law was her duty.

When she applied to Vincent & Church's for her two-week school work experience placement, she hadn't known what to expect but she knew for sure that making tea and coffee had not been on the list. She had made a great impression when asked to do the lunch run and told her supervisor to get it herself. She had confirmed that she was there to learn law, not how to shop. She could do that very well and had been doing so since the age of five.

Mitch had overheard the exchange and was not only amused but impressed that a little girl could state her case so eloquently; she was a shining star in his eyes. The very next day, he had told her that she would work alongside him in his office, helping him in sorting his paperwork, filing, a little typing, and reviewing cases with her. He loved her openness, fresh mind, opinions, and, above all, her no-nonsense attitude.

It had started with him deliberately calling her Sean instead of Shauna. She had bitten her tongue and let it pass the first couple of times, correcting him politely, until finally she had turned to him and asked him if he needed a hearing aid. He apologized profusely and said that he deserved to be punished as she was right: he of all people should remember her name, and because she had correctly put him in his place, she should give him a good whack, a ruler across his hands. Shauna had been taken aback, but followed instructions: to her it was a game, one she relished. She found herself wanting him to make mistakes so she could reprimand him, put him in his place, and ultimately inflict pain.

On completion of her two-week work experience, he had given her his card and told her that if she ever needed anything at all, he was only a telephone call away. When she had needed placements for both college and university, she had called him. He had often offered her money, which she had always refused: if she was to be paid, it would have to be for actual work and she wanted to be on the payroll. He had obliged.

Mitch had given her great advice over the years; from tips on studying for her exams to beating the competition, she always got a heads-up. He had been, and still was, an exceptional mentor. Although money had never exchanged hands, their agreement was always a favor for a lashing. Mitch would never contact her or ask; as and when she needed, she would go to him. Their arrangement worked perfectly for both of them.

When Mitch had asked what Shauna wanted to achieve in life, her answer had been simple: "I want to be a change-maker." Mitch had approved greatly and had supported her application for a parole board member, giving a glowing report of her work ethic. Being a member himself, of course, Shauna knew he had the right connections.

When Shauna had asked to make the final decision on a parole hearing, Mitch had no problem in allowing her carte blanche. He didn't need to know the details, just that she would attend the works dinner and give him the attention that he yearned for.

CHAPTER SIX

Elise wore isolating ear plugs as she ran, mainly to prevent people from trying to talk to her. There was no music, podcast, or radio that could entertain her on her morning run. She didn't want to hear the birds singing, the traffic, or the wolf whistles. The only sounds she focused on were her breath and her trainer-clad feet hitting the ground and lifting in uniformed succession. She listened and noted the rhythm and pace of her heart pounding away in her chest, reminding her that she was alive and kicking and that she had a focus, something and someone to live for.

She varied her route but never veered from the sixty-six minutes that she allowed herself before a whole twenty-four minutes to shower, dress, eat a small bowl of porridge, and head onto the busy Stanford Road at the end of her street before it became gridlocked. She took a full circle around the block. She passed shops, a garage, a running track behind a huge retail park, headed further past the small village, past the cemetery, the underpass beneath the dual carriageway, which led to the motorway, and re-entered her road from the Lane Brook Street side.

Picking up speed as she approached the shops local to her flat, her mind was clear, her body felt bionic: she could easily have run for another hour without tiring, even with the ten-pound weighted rucksack on her back. She had been running every single morning since she was thirteen years old: rain or snow, high winds or sunshine, sick or healthy, she ran.

Slim, wiry, all legs and graceful arms, ballerina like. There was a softness about her. She always wore a rather floaty expression, one which men found attractive and women found annoying.

It was clear, though, that this was not an attempt to garner attention, more one to distance herself from others. She never seemed fully in the room; there was always somewhere else that she would rather be.

She glanced down at her watch as she hit Lane Brook Street on time. She sprinted up to the main entrance to the block of the upmarket maisonnettes that she called home. Elise met the postman on her doorstep just about to deliver her letter. Elise held out her hand, slightly out of breath, and gave a brief smile. The postman ran his eyes over her, admiringly. Elise pushed her key into the lock, throwing the postman a killer look of disgust, stepped inside, and closed the door sharply behind her.

Elise stood behind the closed door, hands trembling. She hadn't received a letter from Stefan in almost two weeks and her stomach was in knots. She knew he was waiting for an outcome for his parole and that he was having difficulty dealing with how he would feel if he was turned down. She would also be devastated, perhaps more so. For the past five years, they had planned exactly what they were going to do. She more confident than he. He had his doubts and Elise dismissed them, swatting each and every protest and worry away like bothersome flies.

"If you want something bad enough—really want something—then there is nothing on planet earth that can prevent you from getting it," she had to constantly remind him. Some days were easier than others, Stefan wished he had Elise's determination, focus, and one-track mind. She simply assumed that he would get parole; there had been no question in her mind. He, after all, had been a model prisoner, never getting in to trouble and had always followed the rules; surely this must count for something. She pushed the fact that he had violently raped and murdered a young girl to a separate compartment of her mind.

Closing her eyes, she tore the letter open.

"Thank goodness." She exhaled heavily, followed by a broad smile. All her plans and preparations for Stefan's release could now begin. Once he was out, he would be all hers.

She made her way back to the kitchen of her small flat. The place was immaculately clean and tidy, minimalist. There were no photographs of family or friends, no notes on the fridge, newspapers, or magazines on the coffee table. Everything had a place, including her letters, which she kept in a small plastic filing folder, whose place was in one of the lower kitchen cupboards. She leafed through and, coming across the tab labelled M, she smoothed out Stefan's letter and slotted it in at the front. The M tab was crammed with his letters, filed in date order.

She gulped down a glass of orange juice, daydreaming about the next phase of her life, the big day, the day she had been waiting for all of her life.

As she showered, her plans filled her mind. Stefan being there in her flat with her, spending day and night in each other's company. Her life would start, and she would finally be able to truly live. She daydreamed all day every day about life with Stefan. At times, her mind would wander to the fact that Stefan was one of the most hated people in the country and that life was going to become increasingly difficult with him in it, but she always managed to allay her own worries. She wanted Stefan all to herself. No one was going to get in her way: she would make sure of that.

Dressed, hair brushed and neatly coiffed, lashings of mascara, a pink glitter lip gloss, she drained her glass of the last drops of juice, collected her keys, and left for work.

Elise had 15 GCSEs, four A Levels, and a degree in the Classics, yet she worked at one of the big five estate agents in the country as a property manager. She had left university with a distinction and immediately applied for a job as an administrator. Her intention had been to prove to the company that she was an asset. She had flown up the ladder, proving her reliability and talent for sales. She had never taken a sick day. She had the patience of an angel, deliberately and purposefully making friends with the right people, socializing—which she hated but recognized that in order to progress she had to be seen to blend in and be a real team-player. Within only five months, her first step up had been to sales negotiator and, more recently, the job she had been aiming for, property manager.

The salary and benefits were superb, but, above all else, Elise craved the connections and the power. She had contacts in real estate across the globe. She took her time paying attention to who the movers and shakers were and made it her mission to befriend them all. She had opened her role up to international property manager and the company loved her for it. They saw her as forward thinking and creative. She was known for brokering deals for properties that were not yet even on the market.

She knew every property coming onto the books, both in lettings and sales; moreover, she knew all the properties on their competitors' books and often took the time to do viewings, even though viewings were seen by other property managers within the company as beneath them. Elise loved meeting people on their moving journey. People changed their abode for myriad reasons: promotions, marriages, divorces, get-togethers, and break-ups. Elise was fascinated by people moving long distances away from what they were used to and admired people for taking big steps in their lives toward change. She respected that; she could relate to it.

Stefan's letter was brief and to the point. All of his letters were. Stefan was not, by his own admission, a very good writer or reader of letters. He kept his letters to a couple of paragraphs, whereas Elise wrote to him two to three times a week and more often than not her letters were three pages long, wordy affairs that at times read more like a personal diary.

Stefan, ecstatic yet afraid, very afraid, could not wait for his release. Of course, he wanted out. He couldn't wait to breathe in the fresh air, go where he pleased, when he pleased. To live again. His fears were born out of the unknown: sure, he knew that times had changed on the outside—advancements in technology, new buildings and roads. He had access to TV and had taken computer classes, so he had ideas about what to expect, but twenty years was a long time. What he would never admit to, however, was that which frightened him the most. The people.

He was thicker around the waist and his hair had greyed within the first six years of his incarceration. He had changed considerably over the past twenty years, but there were two identifying features which protruded from his face. The first, a dark red birth mark across his bottom lip and chin. The media had played up on this: the whole country knew his name and identified him by his birthmark. The second feature, his empty grey blue eyes, had been described as the eyes of the devil by all who had seen his image. There was no getting away from it: he would be easily recognizable. Elise had said that she knew how to mask his birth mark with make-up; he believed her, had to believe her, but he was still afraid.

Elise, ever the optimist, had suggested colored contact lenses or glasses. He could wear a cap. He knew she tried so hard to make him feel better, knew that she put more effort and time into him and his life than she did her own. No one had ever given a damn about him before; no one had invested their time and money into the likes of him in his entire life, and he loved her for it. He had fallen hard for her. He couldn't for the life of him work out why a young, beautiful, intelligent woman like her would even bat an eyelash in his direction, but she had, and she had stuck by him and encouraged him. For one so young, her words of wisdom had carried him through the past couple of years. She made him feel like a king.

At times, he felt uneasy that he relied on her for everything, but she loved him and they were going to get married and spend the rest of their days together; she had said so. Five years ago, he had received her first letter, a letter of encouragement, stating that she believed that people could change and that she felt he had been treated unfairly by the press and had genuinely a hard time of it all. He didn't understand why at that particular time she would even consider writing to him. Stefan believed the letter had been written and sent by some nutter trying to take him for a ride, a journalist trying to get the exclusive of the decade, and he had thrown the letter away. The second letter she sent omitted the fact that he was in prison doing time for his heinous crimes. Stefan felt human again; he had a friend in the world.

Elise persisted: she was sending two to three letters a week. Talking about the world, her life, her dreams, she never again mentioned his crimes. At times he wondered whether she had somehow been confused and mixed him up with some other inmate, an armed robber, terrorist, or the like. She skirted around his crimes, and it bothered him slightly at first but, because she never mentioned it again, he believed that her faith in humanity was what enabled her to push his crimes to one side and get to know him, the man. She made him feel good and no one had ever done that before. No one in the world had given him the time of day unless he had forced them to. She always wanted to know how he was feeling or if he needed money. She looked after him and had a soft, caring nature.

She wanted to know his thoughts and ideas on current affairs and politics. He could tell she was educated by the way she wrote, and she provoked his mind and thoughts into thinking and talking about subjects he had never even broached before, not openly anyway. After reading her letters, he would regularly request a visit to the library, so that he could respond intelligently to her. He carried around a pocket dictionary, learning new words with each new letter. No one had ever made him want to learn anything or improve himself. To him, these were signs that this was true love, someone who loved him from all angles, unconditionally and he wanted to bring his best self to the forefront, wanted to believe that he could be someone better and live like others. She made him feel as if all this were possible and more.

Her first visit was more like a visit from a mysterious princess. She had sat waiting for him, her back toward him. He had been hesitant: what if she saw him in the flesh and had a change of heart. Most people were repulsed by him and turned in the other direction. The prison guards and cleaners all kept their distance. Even his psychologist and doctor seemed to hold their breath when in his presence, as if inhaling the same air would somehow contaminate them.

She had turned to him and looked him dead in the eyes; her smile shone through him, brightening up the whole room, his whole life. She didn't take her eyes off him, nor him off her. They hadn't spoken for the first minute, but simply absorbed each other's energy. His worries were a far-off breeze that had come and passed, and now he had his prize, a beautiful bouquet of flowers that belonged to him. Her eyes never wandered from his; he felt special and important, as if he were the only person in the world that mattered to her, and that mattered greatly to him.

He would never forget how she had finally greeted him. "Hello Stefan." Quiet. Unassuming. Sweet. The way she spoke his name was intoxicating. Fluttering her eyelashes, she seemed a little shy. He was drawn in by her innocence. He couldn't take it all in. His heart pounded in his chest and, despite himself, he grinned from ear to ear. This mysterious princess had travelled some distance to visit him, the most hated person in the country, and she was beaming at him with the sweetest smile he had ever witnessed.

They spoke like old friends. She wanted to know how he was, if he was eating well, how they treated him. She wanted to protect him and he for sure wanted to be protected from a world which he believed had discarded him, thrown him away, was unforgiving and cruel.

CHAPTER SEVEN

The first surprise had been that it was just the four of them going on the camping trip that Friday. Apparently, the following weeks were fully booked, and each trip would allow only six children. The girls had been delighted. They'd be able to go back home and tell all the other kids on the estate about their wonderful adventures; they would be the first.

The consent forms had been a doddle. Karen's parents had ignored her request for a signature, so she squiggled one herself. Michelle's mother had happily signed. Michelle had deliberately caught her mother on her way in from her night shift, a time when Michelle knew that she could have asked for the moon and stars and her mother would have nodded and agreed, which she had done, before falling into bed besides her husband who was dead to the world. He would not stir until midday when he would arise and begin the process of ensuring that he was inebriated by early afternoon, and so his days were filled.

Tessa had told one lie, that the trip was being organized by the school. As soon as she had said that, of course, more lies ensued. She had no reason to lie, really: it was all the same to her father, but Tessa thought that the school would have more sway. Her father, Robert, was strict when it came to her education. He wanted her to do well. He had fired off a litany of questions, all of which she had answered as truthfully as she could. The questions she did not have answers for, such as how many teachers would be in attendance, she made up as she went along. Tessa was quite comfortable telling her father lies because she knew he would never find out the truth; he very rarely ventured outside. It wasn't as if he would pop down the shops and see the camping trip poster for himself. Wheelchair-bound and mostly depressed, he sat indoors watching TV, all day, every day. Tessa was his carer of sorts. He could move himself around the bungalow, he cleaned, he cooked, he was the king of his domain; but anything outside was off limits to him, or so he thought. Tessa did the shopping and collected his benefits, prescriptions, and anything that involved outdoors.

Robert Arnold had been a factory operative at British Leyland for nineteen years until his spine had been crushed in a warehouse accident. He'd received a healthy sum for his injuries, enough to buy the bungalow they lived in, and there should have been enough for him to manage on for the rest of his days quite comfortably. Lydia Arnold, his wife and the mother of Tessa, had decided that taking care of an invalid was not what she had planned for her life. After eleven months of putting up with his depression and mood swings, she had cleared out the bank account and fled. Lydia had never returned. Not a letter. Not a phone call.

A framed photograph of Lydia held pride of place on the mantelpiece. Robert held resentment for a very short while and then busied himself with the thought that one day she would return—she had to, if only to see how little Tessa was getting on. He kept the house pristine and would talk to her photograph when Tessa wasn't around. He ventured out into the small square of patchy grass they called their back garden to hang out the washing, and, for Robert, that was all the fresh air and exercise he needed.

The second surprise was that the kids weren't traveling in a mini bus. They had all assumed that the vehicle that would be taking them on their adventure would be a mini bus. They'd never travelled in a mini bus, but they had seen them leaving from the big comprehensive school just up the road for day trips and sports tournaments. No mini bus for them, just an old rusty clapped out mustard-colored Range Rover, which was caked in mud. The driver was Mr. Rosehill.

Mrs. Rosehill had ordered them to meet outside the shop not one minute past midday. They had arrived half an hour early. Karen clasped hold of a carrier bag stuffed with her and Dane's toothbrushes, a bar of soap wrapped up in a smaller carrier bag, one change of tatty clothes each, and their pajamas.

Michelle had thrown fresh underwear and her toothbrush in her coat pocket, and Tessa had bought her huge school duffel bag.

"What you got in there?" Michelle had stubbed her finger into the duffel bag to find it was densely packed. She couldn't work out what on earth Tessa would have packed for a two nights' stay out in the wilderness.

"My dad," was all the answer she need give. She sighed, embarrassed that he'd filled most of the bag with food, believing that she wouldn't be able to survive without some of his home-cooked Jamaican fried chicken, stew pea soup, fried dumplings, and salt fish fritters. He packed each meal into Tupperware containers, wrapped them individually in tin foil, and covered them all with cling film. There was enough food for all of them for a week. Tessa had already made up her mind to dispose of the food at the earliest opportunity. She wanted to learn to cook on an open fire like the rest of them.

Mrs. Rosehill had waved them off before tending to the few customers that stood waiting to be served at the counter. Mr. Rosehill wasn't his jovial self, but the children hardly noticed.

As the old rattling Range Rover juddered forward, the steeper the incline, the more it choked. Dane clapped his hands frantically. "Look, a motorbike!" Dane had a thing for motorbikes; fast sport cars didn't really grab his attention, but the bright green dirt bike that he saw trailing behind them had him squealing and clapping excitedly. The girls all turned around in their seats to see. The driver wore a matching bright green helmet with the visor blacked out and was dressed in black leathers.

Silence fell for the first time since the four children had climbed into the Range Rover.

Mr. Rosehill observed the dirt bike in the rear view. Tessa noticed the grave look spread across his face. She couldn't decipher whether it was anger or if he was upset about the bike following them.

The road was extremely narrow, even for the Range Rover, but the dirt bike driver sped up until he was level with Mr. Rosehill's window. He lifted his visor and nodded at Mr. Rosehill, and his pale grey, blue eyes scanned the children. Finally, he waved. Mr. Rosehill nodded acknowledgement but kept his eyes on the road.

Dane waved enthusiastically and, breaking the silence, screamed hello. The dirt bike rider dropped back a little and gave Dane his own special wave, winking. Dane was thrilled with himself. The girls remained silent, staring at the stranger as he sped up again past the Range Rover and disappeared round the next curve of the road.

The girls sat quite still. None of them knew why they suddenly felt uneasy. The mood had shifted, and Mr. Rosehill's face was set into a stiff mask. They all noticed.

"Is that your friend, Mr. Rosehill?" Tessa blurted.

Mr. Rosehill forced a smile and spoke through gritted teeth, which appeared to the children as more of a grimace, an expression none of them had witnessed before.

"I can't talk and drive at the same time. Hush, now." He cleared his throat gently.

Tessa was less than pleased for the first time, Mr. Rosehill actually reminded her of one of her teachers, and he had never spoken to her like that before, never.

She slumped back in the seat. Michelle and Karen followed suit. Only Dane was unable to read the tension in the vehicle and made loud noises emulating the sound of the dirt bike. They could still hear the sound of the bike ahead of them; it was steady, and it wasn't fading away.

Karen grabbed Michelle and Tessa's hands and squeezed tightly. They knew something was wrong, but they couldn't work out what exactly.

"It is easier to build strong children than to repair broken men."

Frederick Douglas

CHAPTER EIGHT

Elise had had a busy morning, fluttering along the high street, nipping in and out of shops, checking things off her to-do list. She popped into the florists to collect a colorful array of roses, the butchers for two juicy beef steaks, the gift shop for an elegant welcome home card, and a small New York cheesecake from the patisserie. These were Elise's little finishing touches. Crossing the road, she hesitated by the door of a run-down fast food shop and peered in the window. She glanced up and down the street before stepping inside. She purchased a bottle of water, collected a straw, and went to sit at the window. She ran the straw up and down her cream silk blouse, knowing that any germs that existed on the straw would not be dissolved by her actions. She placed her bags on the seat next to her and scanned the high street.

The little coffee shop opposite was more Elise's cup of tea. One side of the street was derelict and decrepit, a forgotten place where the homeless found refuge in the empty buildings, and just around the corner and reaching onto the high street, the opulence was spreading at an alarming rate. There were boutique coffee shops where a cup of coffee cost close to four pounds and shops where shoes were the equivalent to double the monthly minimum wage. The two would soon become one as the opulence reached out and swallowed every spare patch of land that existed.

Elise saw and understood what this street represented: change, the future, though she knew the future would not be bright for all, just a select few.

She observed the people traffic flowing by and for the millionth time, as she did whenever in a crowded place, wondered what sufferings shadowed the people who passed. Elise had always had a sense, a feeling, that everyone was dealing with some kind of suffering, that most people had something in their lives that they were trying to move past, push to the back of their minds, stomp out. Elise never felt alone, it gave her a sense of connection with the world, allowing her to believe that everyone was feeling pain, so her own pain was normal. This allowed her to blend in; she felt she was part of the bigger picture, and that comforted her. She had a great desire to heal people, almost as if just by wondering and hoping, she could in some way help.

She did not consider herself in any way religious, yet she said little prayers for each and every person. "Please let them be okay, let them find a modicum of happiness in their days. Let all their wishes come true."

At times, she caused herself great anxiety as the feeling that she couldn't help or pray or focus on all the people fast enough as they swept passed her and that would mean they were about to walk into some disastrous situation and it would all be her fault.

Her therapist had told her to close her eyes and imagine herself way above the kerfuffle, way above the city, way above the trees, high in the sky, floating on a cloud, and from there she could spread her loving thoughts and prayers and the world would be well. This little tip, more often than not, helped. Today, though, she was beginning to feel swamped by the energy she believed she was receiving through the window.

The people seemed mechanical, each one totally wrapped up in their own lives, their travels, where they had to be and where they were going. She scanned the street, running her eyes over as many people as she could.

The man in his cheaply made, ill-fitted suit, worn-down shoes and over-washed shirt, shuffled along zombie-like, his eyes underlined with deep dark circles. He appeared exhausted, yet it was so early in the day.

The pregnant lady bracing herself as if she was ready to go into labor, slowly massaging her stomach as she gazed dreamily around her, watching the world whizz by, an uneasy yet pretty smile held in place. Elise saw the truth, the worry, and the sadness.

The couple of teenagers sharing the earphones to one phone, trying way too hard to appear as if they had nothing and their appearance meant little to nothing to them, their clothes disheveled, holes in their sweater elbows and frayed jeans, hair uncombed and un-brushed, but Elise paid attention to their skin, their nails, and the expensive smart phone: she saw quite the opposite.

As a child, she had always felt that she stood out, that she could walk into a room and everyone could see her past etched into her skin. It took many moments of observing others until she began to see that no one was actually paying her any mind. Everyone was wrapped up in their own stuff. Once this information sunk in, she became much more relaxed and comfortable with herself. People only noticed her if she was somehow affecting their lives in some way. The only person's life she had chosen to affect was Stefan's and that suited her just fine.

"Get your fucking hands off me!" A deep throaty growl demanded everyone's attention. Elise spun round to see a woman being dragged out of the bathrooms by a tall lanky member of staff. Lady Godiva, or so the locals called her, had the reputation of strutting around the town center as if she owned the place. She was not of the belief that she, a homeless woman, was not welcome. She had rights; this was a free country; she was a law-abiding citizen. The boy struggled with the woman, her single solitary plastic bag, which didn't appear to have much in it, flapped around. She had long scraggly black nest of hair, with strands of grey running through it; her full length coat, which would have been quite expensive new, clearly had two functions, wearing by day and a blanket by night. Her patent shoes no longer shone, worn down and scuffed. Washed and scrubbed up, Godiva would have been quite elegant.

"You've been told over and over, this is not a public bathroom. You have to buy something." The boy pushed himself up against the bathroom door and held the woman at arms-length. "Just leave. Please." The boy's face reddened as he realized that the two of them were the main focus of the patrons. Elise made her way over.

"I'm sorry. She's with me." Elise eyed the boy, knowing there would be no challenge. The boy blinked between Lady Godiva and Elise.

"She comes here every day, trying to have a wash in the sink." He protested.

"I know. She has nowhere else to go." Elise's voice was soft but firm. The boy let go of Godiva. Elise gave him a smile, a smile that she knew he would savor for the next week at least.

The boy shrugged apologetically and watched as Elise guided Godiva back to her seat. Godiva sat upright opposite Elise.

"You're a godsend, you. Every time I need 'elp, you turn up, just like an angel."

"Would you like something to eat?"

"I'm starvin'. I'll have one of them meals, super-size me. Skip the pop—get me a big coffee instead, one of them posh ones."

Elise nodded and headed back to the counter to place the order. The boy served her nervously, worried that Elise was perhaps a mystery shopper or someone important checking up on him. As Elise paid and took the tray up from the counter, the boy spoke gently, "I'm really sorry."

Elise nodded.

Elise slid the tray in front of Godiva. Godiva's eyes lit up at the sight of the feast.

"Bless you, my little star."

Godiva carefully unwrapped just enough so a small section of the burger was revealed. She multi-tasked and spilled the fries out onto the tray. Ravenous but taking her time, she delicately bit in, closing her eyes momentarily as she savored the burger, chewing softly and slowly absorbing every morsel. She glanced over at the counter and caught the boy staring over at them. Sticking her middle finger up at the boy, she said, "Bloody cheek." The boy quickly turned away and busied himself at the fryer.

"He's only doing his job." Elise soothed.

"What kind of bleeding job is that then? He's supposed to be serving, not policing."

Elise took a sip of her water, not taking her eyes off the woman.

"You won't be seeing me much for a while."

The woman stopped chewing abruptly and placed her burger down on the tray.

"I'll miss you, little star." Godiva reached across the table and patted Elise's hand. The woman's gnarled fingers, still damp, her nails uneven but clean, were surprisingly soft and warm. Elise allowed the touch just for a moment before easing her hand away.

"Found an' husband for yourself, 'av ya?"

Elise shook her head. Godiva took another small bite. Swallowing, she leaned closer into Elise. The aroma of cheap soap and detergent wafted from her.

"Well, you should, and not one of those weak flimsy types, neither. A good strong man who can bear the weight of a whole family on his shoulders."

Elise nodded. Godiva took one French fry at a time and chewed thoroughly.

"I'll be alright. You don't have to worry about me, love."

"I can get you somewhere to stay and..."

"No. I told you before. The more responsibilities you 'ave, the more problems follow, and I've had me fair share of problems, girl. I don't need the headache."

Elise nodded slowly, trying to accept that there was nothing she could do for the woman, no matter how hard she tried. Elise slipped her hand into her pocket and pulled out a neatly folded wad of cash, placing it on Godiva's tray. Godiva continued eating and slowly pushed it back toward Elise without looking up at her.

"You don't have to sit here with me. I can take care of meself. You get off."

Elise nodded. Godiva watched Elise leave the fast food restaurant and waved cheerily to her through the window as she walked away.

The lump in Elise's throat grew and pulsed painfully. She knew that she should not turn back and look. She kept her head straight and thought of the next chapter of her life, the changes she was going to make; she was going to be a new woman. Godiva would be fine, she reassured herself. Godiva was an army wrapped up in a shabby black coat; Elise knew this. She was strong and steadfast, and she wouldn't go down without a fight. In many ways, Godiva had taught Elise everything she knew about fending for herself.

CHAPTER NINE

Elise had so much to do and so little time. Stefan would be arriving in three days and she wanted everything in place, perfect. She wanted to look good. She wanted the flat spotless and immaculate; everything had to be ready for him. She was determined not to mess up. She couldn't afford to mess up: this was her big chance, her only chance, to move forward, let go of the past and build a real future for herself, and she knew that everything rested on her shoulders now. There was no one else.

She had hoped to have one more visit with Stefan before his release, but it all seemed to be happening so quickly now. She knew she was overly anxious: her excitement, she had been informed by her doctors, was a trigger for anxiety. She couldn't allow her anxiety to ruin Stefan's homecoming. She wanted him to feel comfortable with her, as comfortable and as in love with her as he was in his letters and on her visits.

All of these thoughts tumbled over in her mind as she scurried around the flat, scrubbing and cleaning an already perfectly clean apartment. This was yet another sign of her anxiety and stress. She knew she had to calm down, but there was so much to get ready and prepare for. Elise had dreamt of this day for so long; it was all she had focused on for such a long time. She rarely thought of life before Stefan; she didn't want to think about life before Stefan. She wanted to occupy her mind with thoughts of the day that he would be released.

She had her hair done, a full manicure and pedicure. She had ordered the groceries online because she had no time strolling around the supermarket. She had purchased Stefan a whole new wardrobe so he would not feel out of place or lacking. She had upgraded her Sky package to include the sports channels, since he had said that movies were not his thing. The car had been valeted inside and out and waxed, too. She had simply requested the full works and they had worked their magic; the fire engine red 2010 Volkswagen looked brand spanking new. She was ready for him.

Communication from the prison with his parole officer, solicitor, doctor, and psychologist had all become normal to her. They had to check that she was genuine, that she had no existing or previous convictions, that her home was suitable. Elise felt that all these checks were not exactly necessary but understood their caution; they had to cross all their T's and dot all the i's so that if anything went wrong, they could prove they had taken all the necessary precautions and then some. Elise didn't mind one bit; in fact, she would have been worried if they were not so. All the officials in her life somehow made her feel safer, that things were above board and carried out correctly. There was always someone on hand to answer her questions and give her advice, should she request it.

She felt judged by them, knew that they wondered about her, even questioned whether she too were some sort of child predator, but she was not, so she rested easy in that fact alone. They would all see, soon enough.

Elise had thought about the fact that people would see them together and that Stefan might be recognized and how she would deal with that, should it happen. What should she do if confronted by an angry public?

Run! Was the only sensible thing she could think of. She had seen the news reports about how people wanted Stefan dead, their seething anger; they wanted him hung, drawn, and quartered, and she would be associated with him now and forever.

Elise knew that the moment she opened her front door to him and allowed him into her world fully, everything about her life would change forever. So far, there had only been visits and letters. People could forgive that to some extent, but to harbor him, protect him, live, sleep, and eat with him—that was a whole different ball game. She let out a deep sigh as she sat stiffly at the kitchen table staring out across the common, allowing her worries to flow. She battled with herself: what was the point of worrying now? It was happening. She had set the ball in motion, she had took it upon herself to allow Stefan into her life, and now she had to face the consequences. She was ready.

"The important thing is to teach a child that good can always triumph over evil."

—**Walt Disney**

CHAPTER TEN

Shauna sipped her peppermint tea, perched on the sumptuous champagne velvet couch as she waited to view yet another bridal gown. She was bored and disenchanted by the whole ordeal. Traveling all the way down to London, being followed around by the two pecking birds whose sales technique bordered on psychotic. They bustled her about, ushered her here and there, grabbing gowns from what appeared to be every corner of the room. Cooing, oohing, and ahhing until Shauna had insisted that she felt faint and needed to take a seat. They had continued chattering away incessantly, their main focus being to choose the most expensive dress that they could lay their hands on for Shauna: under Kent's direction, money was no object.

It had been Kent's idea. He had selected the store, a recommendation from one of his patrons and said she could pick any wedding gown she desired. Shauna had no desire. She did not crave the fairy-tale wedding that Kent thought she deserved. She did not want a whole bunch of people that she spent no time at all with, who knew nothing about her and whose only interest in her was her husband's wallet and notoriety. This was his fanfare. Between them, they had little family to speak of. Her side consisted of one person, her brother Lee. Kent had a few distant aunts and uncles, but he had drawn up a list of one hundred and fifty people, all of whom were mere acquaintances that he had met through Sloane's, his restaurant. A long list of ass-lickers, Shauna had thought when she had first read the list.

"But we don't know these people." She had handed the list back to him with a look of utter dismay that she didn't bother to attempt to conceal.

"Of course we do, there's..." He had been about to describe each and every person's importance in their lives when he noticed the look on Shauna's face.

"They're important for business. It's just what we do." His reasoning was weak and Shauna had little time for a debate. She had gone along with his planning for months, burying herself in her work, not really paying much attention, and now that the big day was drawing near, she felt nauseous.

What had she been thinking? She should have nipped it in the bud, insisted on a quiet day, just the two of them, Lee and Kent's best friend, Nigel. That's all they needed. The registry office would suffice, a celebratory meal at Sloane's afterwards. What else?

She sat back in the velvet couch and closed her eyes. She longed to be at home with her feet up. She was dreading the long trek home and was determined to catch the train before four o'clock to ensure she secured a seat to avoid the commuter passengers. That was the last thing she needed. Kent had booked her in for a lava shell massage at Harrods Beauty Salon. She intended to cancel the appointment; she didn't need a massage: what she needed was for the wedding preparations to sort themselves out.

"Oh for god's sake," Shauna heard one of the chirpy birds, no longer chirping but sounding distressed.

Shauna's eyes flashed open; she sat bolt up-right. What on earth were they doing?

The second voice was just as astonished.

"No, no, no." This was followed by consecutive tutting.

Shauna could hear the hushed whispers and figured they'd ripped one of their precious dresses and were planning on finding a way to force it upon her. She'd had enough. She was going to tell them that she couldn't make up her mind and would come back another day.

Shauna followed the sound of their voices and found them in a small kitchenette toward the rear of the shop. The door had been left ajar and she could see that they were both facing a small flat-screen TV, the sound turned down low.

An old photograph of Stefan Mademan flashed up on the screen. The newsreader announced that Stefan was due for parole and had successfully secured his release after serving twenty years of his thirty-year sentence. The news report went on to say that Mr. Mademan also had a fiancée who had been supporting him and, even though she had not been willing to be interviewed, had commented that Stefan had served his time and that they should be left alone to get on with their lives.

"They should bring back hanging," the elder of the chirpy birds announced. "What kind of woman takes up with the likes of him?" Her voice dripped with disgust. Both of them had lost their nasal tones and now sounded more human to Shauna; neither of them had noticed her hovering behind them, her heart pounding.

Shauna hurried back into the main shop. She scanned the room, finding the cupboard where her coat had been hung. She snatched it from the hanger and scurried to the front door. She paused, it was pouring with rain, a tropical downpour and she knew that once she opened the door, the little bell would alert the two birds. She yanked on her jacket and searched aimlessly through her handbag for her umbrella to no avail. Bracing herself, she pulled the door open and trotted from the shop without a backwards glance.

The image of Stefan was etched onto her memory. Everywhere she looked, she saw his face staring back at her. The sinking feeling of guilt pulled at her gut. Had she done the right thing? She knew the news of Stefan's release must be all over the papers and the TV. The sickening feeling in her stomach grew. Stopping abruptly at the end of the cobbled street, she paused, bent over, and threw up.

The street was full of independent boutique shops with shoppers all running for cover in the doorways. They were running for shelter, but Shauna saw this as a sign: people were running away from her, for what she had done, for her part in allowing that man to re-enter society. She had hardly eaten anything that day, and she wretched painfully and uncontrollably. A pitiful figure, soaked from the rain, hair plastered to her face, standing in the street vomiting. Shauna simply wished the day would end.

CHAPTER ELEVEN

Lady Godiva stood at the back door of St. Martin's Church. She was soaked through, though she hardly noticed as she clasped hold of a polystyrene cup of hot sweet tea. She stood at the doorway looking out at the graveyard as she gulped down the beverage, then crunched the cup in her hand and dropped it into the bin in the doorway. There was always tea and biscuits on offer at the church for the homeless, though Godiva only made the journey once a month or so. She didn't want to become a regular, didn't want her movements documented, didn't want to be the familiar face around the church. She disliked the church, the building, the people, the institution. There was no room for God in her life and, by all accounts, God had never given her and hers the time of the day.

She made the twenty-minute journey for one reason.

She headed out along the path to toward the graveyard, not bothered by the torrential rain that had soaked through to her skin. Her feet were sodden, squelching with each step.

"You weak bastard," she muttered over and over again, stopping at the broken-down, unkempt headstone of her late husband, Gregory Isaac Muller. The stone was plainly inscribed with his name date of birth and death. She glared down at the stone, wringing her hands, beside herself with anguish.

"Oh what a pitiful man you are. Waste of bleeding skin."

Godiva peeked over both shoulders in turn, ensuring there was no one around to witness her next move. She rolled up her coat, pulled her stringy panties down, squatted over his grave, and urinated.

"Bastard." Hoisting her undergarments up, she adjusted herself. Satisfied that she had accomplished what she had set out to do, she made her way back along the path. She'd take one more cuppa before she set out again and she wouldn't return for another six weeks or so. She made this trip every once in a while since his passing, just to remind her dear departed husband that she would not forget and she could not forgive, even if she tried.

"A person's a person not matter how small."

—Dr. Seuss

CHAPTER TWELVE

She plunged the knife deeper, harder, the blood ejecting across her face. She could taste his blood. She continued, plunging, grunting with the exertion it took to puncture between his rib cage; she so desperately wanted this to end.

"Kill him, kill him!" The chanting children's voices grew louder, stronger. She knew she had to continue and finish the job, otherwise the sun would not shine. Never in her dreams had she stopped stabbing the man to find out what would happen. She had always followed the other children's orders. She was more afraid of the other children than she was of the man.

As the pulp of the man became still with not a breath, on cue the bright sun shone above her head.

Elise flicked her eyes open. Her breathing heavy, physically exhausted. She checked the time: two thirty nine. She checked her tablets; she could have sworn she had taken it this morning. She had.

The dream was becoming more frequent, and she knew that she should contact her therapist but she was worried that by telling the truth, he would only up her dosage and request that she go back to their twice weekly meetings. She didn't have time for that. No, she knew that once Stefan was there with her, everything else would slot into place. She knew herself, her body, better than any doctor or therapist. This was her life, and she knew exactly what she needed to do.

CHAPTER THIRTEEN

Dane managed to unlock the heavy vehicle door and he leapt as if skydiving from a helicopter down to the floor. He ran around the dirty heap of junk they had arrived in and right up to the shiny bright green dirt bike. His eyes lit up and shone with excitement. He so wanted to touch it but instead gazed at its meaty tires and its alluring shiny chrome handlebars. The rider removed his helmet, revealing a mass of light brown spiral curls. He shook his head slightly, hunkered down in front of Dane, and held out his hand for a shake.

"Hello, mate." Stefan Mademan eyed the boy with keen interest.

The girls huddled together on the passenger seat, unmoving, waiting for Mr. Rosehill's instruction before getting out of the car. They had stopped at the summit, surrounded by a vast, lush green forest as far as the eye could see. They were parked in front of a building that reminded them of an upmarket version of their local community center. No graffiti here, all the windows were intact and sparkled in the early afternoon sunlight; the handle to the door appeared secure too.

The three girls had not taken their eyes off Dane and the scary-looking man swathed in leather. He had pale grey, ethereal eyes that were vacant and at the same time piercing, as if he could read minds and move objects with his thoughts alone.

As soon as Karen saw him shake Dane's hand, she forced the door open and hopped out, rushing to Dane's side. Tessa and Michelle followed.

Karen pulled Dane's hand from Stefan's grasp.

"He's my brother." She pulled Dane closer toward her, his shield and protector.

Stefan chuckled and stood up. At six foot three, he towered menacingly over them all.

"That's nice. And what are your names, then?" The girls surrounded him, which only served to amuse him further.

"Who are you?" Tessa was having none of it. This strange bike rider had followed them up the hill, upset Mr. Rosehill, and now he wanted to know who they were. They had all been taught at school not to give their names out willy nilly, especially not to strangers.

"You can call me Stef." Stefan showed his full set of pearly whites, but the girls didn't find the smile at all warming.

"That's a girl's name," Michelle whispered to her friends. They were interrupted by the sound of another car approaching. A dark blue Ford Escort pulled up beside the Range Rover, and out stepped a younger, much smaller, mean-faced looking man. He wore white decorator's overalls and black round-toed boots; spatters of yellow and white paint covered him, including his short blonde army cut hair.

He nodded toward Mr. Rosehill and Stefan as he retreated to the boot of his car. He pulled out camping equipment, three tents, a small stove, several rolled-up sleeping bags, and a huge rucksack. He shut the boot with some force and made his way over to the awkward group.

"Here's your bags." Mr. Rosehill placed the children's bags on the floor, to Karen's horror.

The smaller man stepped forward in a friendly manner.

"Hello kids." He rubbed his hands together in a let's get down to business sort of way. None of the children responded.

Two teenage boys exited the building rather quickly, not quite running but definitely in a rush and peering over their shoulders, as if being chased. They hurried down the three steps onto the car park, before the tallest of the two clapped his eyes on Stefan. Karen noticed how the boy's whole manner changed. He stopped in his tracks; the second boy collided into his back.

"We— we're just going to have a fag."

Stefan nodded, unsmiling, and watched as the two hovered around, the tallest digging in his pockets. It was clear they had no intention of having a cigarette; it appeared to all that their intention had been to hot foot it down the hill.

Stefan moved forward slowly, taking his own packet of cigarettes from his pocket, opening it, and gesturing for them to take one. Both boys cautiously took a cigarette. The smaller of the two's hands trembled, afraid to accept the seemingly friendly offer. Stefan lit each of their cigarettes.

The smaller one choked as he inhaled a thick plume of smoke. Stefan chuckled.

Stefan stood with his back to the four children. They could not see his facial expression, but Karen saw both of the teenager's expressions. She saw panic and fear.

Mr. Rosehill inched toward his car and slowly opened the door, attempting to depart without the children noticing. Michelle noticed.

"Where are you going?" Michelle questioned accusingly. Michelle did not miss the shiny glassy sheen in Mr. Rosehill's eyes.

"Now, don't you worry about a thing. Stefan here and Will are going to look after you; they're the experts at camping." His voice was a calm whisper.

Tessa stepped forward, grabbed her bag up from the ground, and followed Mr. Rosehill; the others followed in a little huddle. Karen gripped tightly to Dane's hand.

"But you said you were going to teach us survival skills?" Michelle's voice pleaded.

"Now, you go on, now. They'll look after you." Mr. Rosehill slammed the car door shut with finality.

Stefan sauntered over to Mr. Rosehill's window. Mr. Rosehill wound down the window and the two shared a few hushed words. Stefan dug deep into his pockets and passed something to Mr. Rosehill, who snatched it from his hands.

"I'll be back on Sunday to take you all home." Mr. Rosehill waved his hand around vaguely, then rolled the window up quickly and started the engine.

Tessa stood right in front of the vehicle, her eyes fixed angrily on Mr. Rosehill, who refused to make eye contact. He turned his head, and with a rapid reverse he spun the rusty heap around to face the opposite direction, threw a wave over his shoulder, and sped off down the hill.

Both Stefan and Will began collecting the camping equipment together.

"Don't worry, we're going to have a great time." Stefan's reassurance did nothing to alleviate the children's concerns or fears. They stood bunched together looking to Karen for some sort of instruction.

"We want to go home now." Karen's voice quivered. She was visibly shaken by Mr. Rosehill's swift departure.

Stefan approached the huddle. "Don't be silly; you'll all be fine. There's no scary monster in the woods."

He rubbed her shoulder. Karen stood frozen to the spot, unsure of whether to scream, run, or cry.

"Who likes ice cream?" Will was confident in winning them over.

Dane stuck his hand up in the air like a shot. "Me, me, me, me."

Will and Stefan laughed. Will placed the camping equipment on the floor and opened his rucksack, pulling out a huge flask. He held his paint streaked hand out and tipped the flask upside down. Four Tongue Twister ice lollies slid out. He turned to Dane, who took one, and he offered the others out. Tessa and Michelle tentatively took one each. Karen simply stared up at Will.

"We can save yours for later if you like." Will slid the last ice lolly back into the flask and twisted the lid back on.

"Come on. Let's go and find a good spot." Will and Stefan headed out in the direction of the forest.

Karen looked to each of her friends. "That Mr. Rosehill's a fat pig, I hate him. I'm never going in his stupid shop ever again." She stomped off following the two men, Dane's hand firmly clasped in hers. Michelle and Tessa followed.

The two teenagers stood behind the building, listening out for the voices to disappear.

"We should wait." The eldest boy suggested.

"No, let's just go." The younger boy wanted out immediately.

"What about them kids, they're only young?"

"Do you want to stay and look after them?"

The older boy shrugged. They remained in their hiding place, peering out, watching after Stefan, Will, and the children, as they marched off into the forest.

Karen sauntered slowly behind, glancing back over her shoulder at the two teenagers; she noticed their nervousness. As soon as Stefan and Will made it over to the woods, the teenagers ran toward the direction of the road. Karen said nothing. She didn't know why, but she wanted them to get away, escape. She had a strong urge to follow, flee with them. Questioning herself as to why she wanted to escape, she decided that she should keep her guard up. She didn't feel at all comfortable, though Stefan and Will seemed harmless. In Karen's experience, that didn't mean that the two men were harmless. On the one hand, Mr. and Mrs. Rosehill were the nicest people she had ever met; they would never allow anything bad to happen to them. On the other hand, Mr. Rosehill had just dumped them with two strangers and that didn't feel right. The children followed, deliberately hanging back.

"Do you think they're bullies?" Tessa asked finally.

"I think they're pigs, too," Michelle chimed in.

"Mr. and Mrs. Rosehill said they were going to take us camping. And they haven't, so they lied, so that makes them big fat pigs." Karen felt betrayed by the only two people apart from her friends that had seemed good, honest, and caring.

"Bastards," Tessa added.

"Ahhhh, you're swearing." Dane pointed accusingly at Tessa. The three girls laughed for the first time since they arrived.

CHAPTER FOURTEEN

The two men stopped at a small clearing. There were already pieces of charred wood arranged in the center, surrounded by stones of all shapes and sizes. There were a couple of huge logs, cornering the circular camp fire as makeshift seating.

"Here we are. This is our camping site." Will announced triumphantly. He and Stefan dropped the equipment to the ground.

"I want to wee wee. Karen, I want a wee wee," Dane whined, twisting and turning from side to side.

"Alright, come on then." Karen was reluctant to leave her friends, though she had no intention of venturing off too far.

She continued through the clearing to the other side. She pulled Dane along after her, turning every now and then to check if the others were looking. Satisfied when she saw the two men sorting through the camping equipment, she stopped.

"Go on, then." She knelt down beside Dane and pulled his shorts down. She peered toward the clearing, making sure no one was following. Once finished, Dane quickly pulled his pants and shorts back up and ran back to the clearing. Karen followed slowly. The fun had somehow deserted her, and she couldn't get back into her usual cheery self. This camping trip had been her idea and now everything seemed to be going wrong.

Michelle and Tessa stood their ground as Will and Stefan busied themselves, unpacking the camping equipment, laying everything out as if on display.

Will described everything to the girls as he unpacked.

"So these are where we'll be sleeping." He pointed to the three army green bundles.

"Are you two having a tent each?" Tessa enquired.

"It might be a bit of a squeeze with you four all in one tent."

"Well, me and Dane can have one, Michelle and Tessa share, and you and him can share the other." Karen had worked this out way before Tessa had asked the question.

Will nodded "Good idea." He lifted one of the bundles, undid the tie, and allowed the tent and poles to slide out.

Stefan sat down on one of the logs and lit a cigarette, watching Michelle intently. Tessa noticed but didn't say a word.

The sun beamed down on them as Will gave simple instructions and showed them how to set up the tents. Dane busied himself, digging holes with sticks that he was using as miniature shovels; his attention swayed between helping the girls and playing on his own. The children had relaxed somewhat and clapped with glee once they erected the first tent.

Stefan mainly watched, throwing the odd bit of advice to the children when hammering in the tent pegs.

"Karen, I'm hungry." Dane tugged at Karen's sleeve as she pulled one of the thin ropes out from the second tent, ready to attempt hammering it into the ground. Karen stalled, not wanting to ask either of the men for anything at all.

Tessa, feeling the tension, ran to her bag and began removing each foil and cling film wrapped container. "Want some chicken, Dane?" She felt useful and helpful; it was usually Karen that took charge and helped them all. She began un-wrapping the largest container. Dane crawled over to her cautiously, wanting to see what the containers had to offer.

Stefan immediately opened one of the bags at his feet and pulled out a carrier bag; placing it on the floor, he rolled the sides down and revealed a bag full of goodies. Tessa caught a glimpse of the treasure trove and quickly wrapped the Tupperware container back up and joined the others to see what was inside the bag.

All four of the children gasped: the bag was full of sweets, chocolates, crisps; their eyes lit up. The children stood back and peered down at the treasure laid out before them.

"Help yourselves, then." Will's invitation was warm and friendly. Karen didn't like it one bit.

Dane dove in." Dane, just one: you don't want to get sick." Karen wanted to dive in to; she loved marshmallows and candy floss and the sticks of Chewits in all different flavors, but she couldn't bring herself to take anything from them. She felt as if by taking their sweets, she was inviting them into her space and she didn't want to. She didn't know why, but she just didn't want to.

"Oh, come on. This is supposed to be fun. Fill your boots," Stefan ribbed. Karen threw him a filthy look and went back to the tent. She laid out the ground sheet, keeping a close eye on Dane.

Michelle and Tessa each took a packet of crisps and sat right at the mouth of the tent that Karen sat in.

"Want a crisp?" Tessa held her packet of crisps out to Karen. Karen's stomach was rumbling. She glanced over at Stefan who was lighting yet another cigarette and quickly took one of the crisps. Michelle offered hers, too.

She whispered, "We stick together ok?" The two girls nodded in agreement.

CHAPTER FIFTEEN

The evening sun burned as bright and as hot as it had done at midday. The heat was relentless, and only the thick forest protected them from the scorching sun. Will had instructed the children to collect what he had described as tinder and kindling. They had stuck together, working in their small huddle. Karen had relaxed a little but was still on her guard. She didn't trust either man. She was waiting for them to make one wrong move and she and her friends would run for it. She hadn't told her friends this piece of information as yet; she didn't want to scare them, but that was the picture she had formed in her mind, and that was the plan she was sticking to.

Karen noticed that Will and Stefan rarely spoke to each other, but everything was directed through them. Stefan kept a keen eye on Michelle and Dane, so Karen kept an anxious eye on Stefan.

CHAPTER SIXTEEN

The children gathered small twigs, dry leaves, fungi, and branches and placed them into a big pile next to Will.

Will was impressed. "That'll be enough now." Will showed the children how to get the fire to smoke and set it alight and allowed each of them to try for themselves. They had been promised a free camping trip and here they were, loving the outdoors and learning new things. Karen began to feel as if her initial response to the two men had been a little premature; they were all right really. Dane was having a fantastic time, and so was she. She allowed the protective guard to slide down, just a tad.

True to Mr. and Mrs. Rosehill's word, they learned how to cook sausages and bacon over an open fire, with Stefan declaring that tomorrow night would be their turn to build the fire all by themselves. They were thrilled at the idea but doubted he was going to let them have complete control.

With their bellies full, Will announced that they were all going to play a camping game. The children's suspicions and discomfort had slowly been erased, and they were excited and raring to go.

"What's it called?" Tessa asked, trying not to sound too excited.

"The bear hunt." Will's eyes lit up.

"Are there bears here?" Dane questioned, inching himself a little closer to Karen.

"Well, that's what we have to find out." Will grinned, enjoying the children's discomfort. The children gave each other slightly surprised looks.

"Not real bears?" Karen wanted the facts. She didn't like the idea of bumping into a big bear in the night.

"Yep, real bears. We have to find their tracks and see if there're any close."

"What if they are close?" Tessa had visions of them all being armed with shotguns and shooting at angry bears surrounding the camp.

"We lay bear traps. There're special berries that they don't like the smell of. We surround our camp with them, so they can't get in."

"Why can't we just put down the berries anyway?"

"No point if they're not close."

Will stood up and grabbed his rucksack. It was almost the size of him; he was small, squat, and sturdy. He swung it over his shoulder. "We'll split into groups...." Will flinched, not getting the chance to continue as his suggestion was met with screams of dismay.

"We stick together." Karen's guard flew up. Will was getting on her nerves with this bear hunt, a stupid game.

"It's quicker and easier if we split into two groups. You, Dane and Stefan and me, Michelle, and Tessa.

"No." Karen was the spokesperson and she did not take the role lightly. The children looked up at Will to let him know there was no way they were going to split up. Will looked over to Stefan who shrugged nonchalantly.

"This is not going to work if we don't split..."

Stefan stood and joined them. "We'll all go together, shall we?"

The children's silent relief represented their agreement.

"Children are like wet cement.
Whatever falls on them makes
an impression."

—Haim Ginott

CHAPTER SEVENTEEN

Once Karen closed her eyes, she fell immediately into a deep sleep, her arms wrapped around Dane tightly. The butterflies that had been fluttering around in her stomach since they'd arrived at the camping site had subsided. She felt calm and relaxed. She had watched and made sure that Dane had fallen asleep first. She could feel his little chest rise and fall, hear his tiny baby snores. He was her little baby; she had always looked after him and would continue to do so. She loved him so much it hurt. She wanted to protect him from the world that she knew. He had no one else, and neither did she. She actually needed him as much as he needed her. He made her feel grown up and in charge even though there were times when she didn't want to be in charge. Sometimes she simply wanted to play and run and let loose. She couldn't always do that with Dane around. Dane looked up to her, followed her everywhere, copied the way she spoke, admired her, adored her. It was like having her own little living doll and she loved that more than life itself.

All the children were exhausted and worn out. The bear hunt had turned out to be a lot of fun, and Will had confessed that there weren't any real bears in the forest when he realized that they were more frightened than playful. Once the children heard that piece of news, they threw themselves into the hunt wholeheartedly. Screaming and scattering through the forest when Will took on the role of the bear. Karen had warmed to him. He had told her that she was a great sister, looking after Dane, and wished he'd had a big sister like her when he was a kid. She had never received praise or been commended for looking out for Dane, and Will had made her feel proud of herself. He'd offered her the Tongue Twister ice lolly again, and this time she took it without hesitation.

Karen hadn't been able to sleep initially and only listened to Dane breathing and thought about the day's events. She couldn't remember a time when she had had so much fun. She tried hard to remember, but, after much consideration, she decided that this trip was the best thing that had happened to her and Dane ever. Finally allowing her heavy eye lids to fall, with a satisfied smile on her pretty face, she succumbed to deep and peaceful slumber.

Dane slept for a couple of hours and then woke with a start. He wanted to go to the toilet.

He fidgeted and held himself, hoping the urge would go away, but it was persistent and there was no way he was going to pee on Will's sleeping bag. Not wanting to wake Karen—she was so grumpy if he woke her up—he slid carefully out of her grip and made his way to the bottom of the tent. He could see the fire still burning and heard the men's voices. He undid the strings and popped his head out. Will and Stefan sat by the fire. Dane crawled out, and the sound of snapping twigs beneath his hands and knees caught the men's attention. Stefan beckoned him over.

Dane crawled over on his hands and knees.

"I need the toilet," he whispered urgently.

Stefan nodded and took him by the hand out to the nearest tree.

"Need a hand?" Dane shook his head, wanting to show he was a big boy. He pulled his pajama trousers down. Stefan waited until Dane was finished and, taking Dane by the hand, led him back to the camp fire.

"We said we'd wait till tomorrow, get them at ease first." Will's cool tone hid his anger to anyone listening, but Stefan could feel Will's unease. Stefan didn't answer.

"Hot chocolate, Dane?" Stefan brushed Will's comments aside as if he were no longer there, no longer mattered. Dane had his full attention now.

Dane nodded. Dane could see that Will wasn't happy with Stefan. He liked them both, but he preferred Stefan. Stefan had a dirt bike.

Stefan dug out some sweets for Dane, then placed the old battered kettle over the fire. He tipped water from a flask into the kettle and turned to Dane.

"Don't tell the others: they'll only be jealous." Dane nodded, pleased that he was being treated like a big boy with secrets. He loved his sister more than he could describe, but being with the two men made him feel good, more grown up. His own father never paid him any attention, barely spoke to him. Dane chomped down on his Wham bar and looked into the fire.

"We said..." Will attempted once again to assert some authority.

"We said nothing." Stefan glared at Will, waiting for a comeback.

"It's too early." Will spoke quietly. Stefan ignored him, his eyes and attention flicked back to Dane.

"Can I sit on your bike?" Dane asked, whilst trying to pull the soft sticky pink sweetness from his teeth with his nails.

"Yep. I'll take you for a ride in the morning if you like."

"I wish I had a bike like yours."

"You're a bit young yet, but I'll let you ride mine for now. I've got more chocolates in my tent."

Dane hesitated and looked toward the tent where Karen slept. He knew that he shouldn't be eating sweets and chocolate at night, but he loved chocolate. If Karen found out, he'd be in big trouble.

Dane got to his feet. Stefan took him by the hand and led him over to the tent.

Dane climbed in, and Stefan followed, Will gazed into the fire. Will was unsure: these kids were a tight little pack, and he knew the girls were going to be a lot more difficult to separate. He hadn't taken the weekend off work and paid five hundred pounds of his well-earned cash to come and sit out in the wilderness for nothing. He looked over to the tent where Michelle and Tessa slept. It'd be difficult to wake one without the other. The boy seemed much more amiable.

Will heard the rustling of wrappers and Dane giggling quietly. Will disliked Stefan, but Stefan's network of children all over the country kept him at bay. Stefan was taller, stronger, smarter, and this whole thing was his operation. Will wasn't about to look a gift horse in the mouth. It didn't make sense to cause problems or defy Stefan in any way, not whilst he had access to children of all ages, any day of the week. These had been the youngest ever and his excitement bubbled over. He was nervous and overwhelmed with desire. Michelle, with her delicate rose bud lips and frightened eyes, and Tessa's firm little body rolled over and over in his mind as he stared into the fire. Karen was a treat, too, but he knew that she would fight with all her might. He could see that the innocence had faded from her eyes a long time ago; she knew too much, and he wasn't up for the fight—that was more Stefan's game. Will couldn't contain himself a moment longer. He crept over to Michelle and Tessa's tent and slipped inside.

CHAPTER EIGHTEEN

Karen awoke to screams.

Loud, urgent, terrifying wails of desperation and fear. She shot up and realized to her dismay that Dane was no longer by her side. The panic rose up inside her body like a pulsating hammer, making its way through her veins, exploding in her head. She called out to him, loud and clear in her mind, yet only a weak and raspy whisper to the outside. Hurling herself from the tent, she saw frantic movement coming from Michelle's and Tessa's tent. She scrambled to her feet and threw herself inside. She gasped as she saw Will, on all fours, trousers around his ankles, gripping Tessa's wrist as she struggled and fought to free herself. Michelle was on his back, both arms firmly clasped around his neck, her small teeth digging into his skin voraciously. Karen took it all in in a heart-beat, and, without a second's thought, she ran out toward the camp fire, grabbed hold of the large frying pan and metal stoker she has witnessed Stefan using, and returned, full of venom and determination.

Re-entering now, the only word she managed to muster was, "Stop." Will, for the first time, noticed her, as he continued to struggle with Michelle, who was still making a meal out of his neck.

"Wait, hold on a second, I..." Karen smashed the pan down over his head. Once, twice, three times, six times, again and again, she dropped the stoker to the floor so that she could get a better grip on the pan. Michelle and Tessa scrambled to the top of the tent, teary and trembling. Neither uttered a word; they only watched on in terror. Michelle covered her eyes. Tessa's eyes began to widen to a wicked and sinister sneer; she reached for the stoker and began stabbing at Will's chest and stomach with all her might. The two girls slammed and stabbed relentlessly. Michelle whimpered, holding tightly onto her pajama trousers.

Finally the two blood-spattered girls stopped and studied Will, out of breath and shivering as if the blood covering them were ice drops. They watched as the pool of blood spread around Will's head and chest, still face down; they waited until there was no movement and he was still.

The sound came of twigs snapping, footsteps, heavy and sure. Karen turned to Tessa for the first time, noticing her little face covered in blood, her chest heaving as if she'd just run a sprint.

"Where's Dane?" The girls turned and waited. Karen pushed her head out of the tent. Stefan was upon them.

"Run!" Tessa followed Karen's shrill demand without hesitation. She ripped up the back of the tent and the two darted toward the forest. Michelle was too slow. Stefan grabbed her by her arm; the sound of her arm snapping, like a thin branch from the trees above them, echoed into the silence of the forest. Her scream stopped the two girls in their tracks. They turned to see Stefan, holding Michelle up by her arm, a lifeless rag-doll, against the moonlight and fading light from the fire. A werewolf about to devour his prey, his eyes fierce, he looked deranged.

"Get back here, or I'll break the other one." Stefan's voice was barely an octave over a whisper.

"Where's Dane?!" Karen shouted, wanting to assert authority. A sickening feeling crept up her body. Then she heard him, small whimpers and footsteps. Dane stepped out of Stefan's tent naked, eyes red-rimmed and sad. Karen had never seen him looking so pitiful. She ran toward him.

"Karen," Dane called out to her, lifting his arms awaiting her to pick him up and soothe him. Before she could get to Dane, Stefan simply leaned out and grabbed her by her hair. Dane sobbed mournfully.

"Stop it!" Tessa ran toward Stefan and began beating his stomach with her small fists.

"Cunts." Stefan flung his foot out, viciously kicking Karen to the floor. The impact sent her a short distance before landing in a painful heap. Stefan placed his right foot over her rib cage.

"Shut your fucking mouth right now!" Stefan slung Michelle under his arm and kept his foot on Karen's body. Karen felt the weight of his foot bearing down on her chest. Dane knelt down beside Karen.

"I want to go home now." Dane spoke softly. He sounded so tired.

"It's okay, Dane. It's going to be alright." She spoke knowing that her words did not ring true. The damage had already been done. She had not been there when Dane needed her most.

"Do you always lie to your little brother? Not a very good example, are you?"

Karen shook with fury and despair. Her hip ached where Stefan had kicked her. She was helpless: she couldn't move, and Michelle had stopped struggling, her tears dripping down on to Karen's face. Karen looked up at Michelle, exploring her eyes. She didn't look good. She was evidently in tremendous physical pain, but Karen also knew she was in another type of pain, a pain that was going to live within her forever. A pain Karen knew only too well.

"You little fuckers are going to do exactly as I say; do you hear me?" There was no answer. Stefan was unsure of what to do next. How could things have gotten so out of control? He prided himself on being experienced; he'd met all types of kids and there was always a way to win them around, especially kids like these, doing their own thing, no sense of rules and regulations, left to their own devices. He was the one who could open them up and have them dancing in the palm of his hand. All kids liked sweets, treats and money, fags and booze, all kids liked special attention. The younger they were, the more malleable. This trip should have been a doddle, but here he was, in the middle of the forest with these little feral bitches. The Rosehill's were going to pay for causing him so much aggravation. And as for Will— Where the fuck was Will?

"Do you fucking hear me?" Stefan pronounced his words slowly, almost growling. He was in charge. He would not be beaten by a trio of ten-year-old girls.

"Yes," Karen answered through gritted teeth, the weight of Stefan's foot bearing down on her. She knew this was bad, really bad. She couldn't think clearly. The only thoughts that echoed in her mind was that she knew they should have run off right from the start. She had known deep down that Mr. Rosehill had been frightened of Stefan and the look on those teenagers' faces, as if Stefan was the big bad bogeyman from their worst nightmares. She had seen it in their faces and still she had taken her friends deep into the forest with him. She was beside herself.

Dane lay down beside Karen and held her face.

"It's okay, Dane. It's okay." She spoke gently and tried to pull a smile of comfort across her face.

"You three are going to come and sit by the fire and be good little girls."

Tessa stepped forward slowly taking a seat at the camp fire obediently though a look of defiance shone in her eyes. A deep-set hatred for the man giving them orders. The man who was hurting them, the man with the big bag of sweets who now reminded her of the devil. Stefan slowly lifted his foot from Karen's chest. Karen rolled over and grabbed hold of Dane.

"By the fire." Stefan pointed in the direction of the fire. Karen pulled Dane over to the fire, wincing at the pain in her chest. Stefan lay Michelle down in the tent nearest to the fire. Karen saw Michelle lift her head and stare right back into her eyes, pleading and desperate. Karen felt helpless. She could see Michelle's chest rising and falling, panicking and frightened, allowing only small whimpers to escape from her lips.

Stefan approached the tent where Will's size-nine paint speckled boots were sticking out. Peering inside, he let out an annoyed sigh. It was a mess. How had he got himself into this? Stefan crouched down beside Will, and he rested two fingers on his neck. No pulse. Stefan shook his head in disgust. Will was a liability in life and now more so in death. Stefan couldn't stand Will, why hadn't he followed his gut instinct. Will was inexperienced and lacking in more ways than one. Stefan had known in the first moment of meeting him and he had been spot on, just as he had thought: the man had messed things up for him. How was it possible that the thick shit couldn't handle three little girls?

Stefan turned to the three children sitting on the log. Tessa and Karen stared right into his eyes. A look that he would never forget, they made him feel uncomfortable. Murdering little bitches. Maybe it was the moonlight, maybe he hadn't had enough sleep, but the darkness and danger that emanated from them sent a shiver down his spine. He turned back to Will's lifeless body, covered his face with one of the sleeping bags, and crawled backwards out of the tent. Making his way across to the girls, he stood over them. Their gazes were fixed on his every move. Was he losing it? They looked as if they were possessed, anger, hatred, disgust, and sheer defiance etched in their faces. He had to pull himself together.

"You kids are in a whole lot of trouble." The three pairs of eyes rested on the tent that housed Will's body.

"Call an ambulance." Tessa's flat and cold voice ran right through him.

"If you do as you're told, I can sort all this out." Stefan knew exactly the best way to play this out.

"It was an accident. You were all asleep, weren't you?" The girls' expressions remained cold and hard.

"There's no need for anyone to find out what happened here." Stefan waited for a response, figuring that they were in shock. They were unmoved, not bothered; his words held no gravity. He changed tack.

"The police are going to want to know exactly what you did, and you will go to prison. But I can help you."

Karen inched her hand toward Tessa's and held on tight. Tessa lifted her head up, and knowing Karen was right there beside her gave her the encouragement she needed.

"You stay there, and you don't fucking move an inch." Stefan pointed at them, firm and strong, again looking for a response. The children sat and watched Stefan climb into the tent with Michelle. Karen squeezed tighter onto Tessa's and Dane's hands. All three of them sat still, barely breathing, listening and hearing Michelle's muffled cries against Stefan's grunting and growling. The three sat waiting for the sounds to stop. Karen went over and over the day when she had seen the sign for the camping trip, wishing that she hadn't seen it, wishing that Mrs. Rosehill had said that she and Dane were too young to go camping, and mainly that the old couple had never moved to Bournbrook in the first place.

"Let's go," Tessa whispered, not moving her head an inch.

"We can't leave Michelle." Karen had been thinking exactly the same thing and the only thing that prevented her from suggesting it was the look on Michelle's face. They couldn't leave her with him.

"We could get someone." Tessa was insistent.

Karen shook her head. She wanted to get help, but the look on Michelle's face stopped her. They couldn't leave her—where would they go? They were in the middle of nowhere. There'd hardly been any cars on the road in broad daylight, never mind in the dead of night. There was simply no way that she was going to leave Michelle with Stefan. No way.

Karen moved her head mechanically toward Dane. She could feel his body shivering beside her. What a mess. This was all her fault. Her head snapped back up toward the tent as Michelle called out.

"Kaz!" The gurgling and spluttering told Tessa and Karen all they needed to know. Tessa stood up, swapping Karen's hand for Dane's. They both knew what was happening and what would happen next. They ran toward the forest as fast as they could. Dane's tiny feet hardly touched the ground.

CHAPTER NINETEEN

Elise got to work earlier than usual on the day of Stefan's release, her last day at work. She had booked the afternoon off so she could head into the city and catch the train to Grenholme prison to meet and accompany Stefan on his journey home. She more often than not arrived to work fifteen minutes or so earlier than her appointed time, but today she had a deep sense of unease. She hadn't slept a wink—that scrawny, ugly hand of doubt had reached out and gripped her. What if she couldn't go through with it all, was she strong enough? Was she ready? What if she were attacked? Everything felt so real all of a sudden. Of course, she had known what she was letting herself in for up till now, but today felt different. She stirred her coffee absentmindedly. Carol the receptionist stepped quietly and carefully toward her, placing her hand on Elise's shoulder. Elise was startled and spun round.

"Are you okay, Elise? You don't look yourself." Carol had children of her own and often mothered her co-workers. She found Elise to be a very confident, sure of herself type; she'd never really gotten to know her, not properly, and today the young woman seemed spooked: she was pale and visibly shaken.

"I— I'm good. Thanks for asking". Elise continued stirring and headed toward her office.

Carol was not convinced. "If you need anything, I..."

Elise closed her office door on Carol's sentence. Carol was a lovely lady, but Elise wasn't about to let anyone in on her secret. Nobody would understand and most would have only tried to dissuade her from getting involved with Stefan in the first place. Elise knew it and she didn't want to hear it. She didn't have time to listen to protestations and judgments. She knew exactly what she was doing, and she didn't need to explain a damn thing.

She sat down at her desk and began sipping her coffee. She was trying to understand where all these doubts had come flooding in from. She had planned everything down to the last minuscule detail, so to get cold feet at this stage had truly thrown her off balance. Was it a sign?

She knew she was going to go ahead; she knew that was the only way forward. Stefan was all hers now, and she was not about to mess up. She knew what she was doing; she gave herself a good talking to.

Elise checked her diary knowingly. She had deliberately left the morning free to catch up on paperwork and leave everything ship-shape for the next person who would take her seat. She hated leaving things unfinished and undone. She didn't like the idea that someone else could come and take her seat and not understand how everything worked. She believed that anyone should be able to log onto their system and see what required attention and what was completed. It should be a smooth transition.

Elise checked her handbag for her train ticket. This was actually happening today, and instead of feeling elated she was full of worry and doubt. She took a long swig of coffee and sat up straighter in her chair, attempting to regain control of the situation and her emotions.

The corner of the envelope containing her letter of resignation and apology for giving such short notice peeped out of her handbag. She eyed it, and thoughts of what Mike, her boss, might think or say, irritated her. She crossed her fingers automatically hoping that he would not try to contact her or call her to try to convince her not to leave and the worst-case scenario, turn up at her flat looking for an explanation. The thought made her queasy. He wouldn't be so stupid, surely? She hadn't thought of that before today and therefore did not have a plan. Every other base was covered; why had she not thought of this before? She slipped her hand into her trouser pocket and pulled out a small plastic container. Glancing up, she scanned the office to check no one was watching her, she flipped open the container and tipped out the small blue tablet. She placed it onto her tongue, tipped her head back and took another sip of her coffee.

Mike liked her a lot. He was always praising her efforts and had recommended her for both of her promotions. She knew he saw her as a friend as well as a colleague and at times more. She had over the years deliberately kept him at a distance. There had been the odd awkward silence between them, which she had always filled, times where he had stepped into her personal space and she had stepped away. Times when he had enquired about her personal life and she had shut him down with one-word answers and blank expressions. She could tell that he was intrigued by her myste-riousness and had even described her as elusive when he had once tried to contact her to locate the keys for a property and she had been unreachable.

He'd rung her phone seven times in total, leaving messages on the sixth and seventh. He had genuinely sounded worried and Elise remem-bered feeling tremendously guilty. She had, in fact, been visiting Stefan. She had thrown Mike some lame excuse about her battery being dead and get-ting stuck in traffic. The lie sat heavily between them. He had come knock-ing on her front door and left a note saying that he was worried about her and that she should call him as soon as she read the note. What if he worried about her resigning at such short notice and just turned up? She couldn't believe that she had been so stupid and careless in not having a plan, and she questioned whether she was self-sabotaging.

Elise looked out of the window of her office to the open plan space. Her colleagues were arriving, making tea, gossiping, laughing. Elise wondered what they would all think if they knew the truth about her. They would all know sooner or later but that didn't bother her. Once she had Stefan all to herself, she didn't care what the world thought. In spite of herself she pictured their reactions and suppressed an urge to giggle. That would give them something worthy to gossip about over their morning coffee.

Arrangements had been made for her to meet Stefan inside the prison. Due to the nature of his crimes, he was to be driven by his parole officer to her home and Stefan had insisted that she accompany him on that drive. He was nervous and she wanted to be supportive and show him that every-thing was okay once they had each other.

CHAPTER TWENTY

MAY 7, 2005

Aaron Mason, Stefan's parole officer, arrived at two o'clock. He had sat in his car waiting until exactly three minutes before and took his time strolling up to the reception. He was a regular at the prison and knew exactly how long it would take to run through all the safety and security procedures. He didn't want to spend one minute extra in Stefan's presence; the man sickened him. He had dealt with prisoners like him in the past, but Stefan made his stomach turn; he didn't like him one bit and had even gone so far as to request that Stefan be removed from his list. The problem was there was not one parole officer who was willing to swap. No one wanted this man on their list. Aaron was stuck with him.

"Ready?" Aaron tried to sound friendly. He sounded official and cold.

"Elise is coming. She should be here." Stefan noted Aaron's abruptness and met it with a cool assertive response, but he was much more concerned with the fact that Elise had specifically stated she would arrive early and here she was late. She was never ever late for anything. The panic gripped his throat, constricting his speech and breath. If Elise had changed her mind, would he end up in one of those hostels with no one? He hadn't prepared for that, he started to feel agitated and angry. If it weren't for her, he would have prepared, he could have requested to live in a completely different location. He could have got used to the idea. All along he had relied on the fact that he would have Elise as his best friend, lover, and confidant. Where was she?

CHAPTER TWENTY-ONE

Elise sat at her desk, checking her watch every minute or so. She watched as the little hands of her silver Rotary ticked mechanically round. Carol had been in to check on her several times. Elise began to worry whether she knew something. Did she know something? Carol had never really paid her any mind before; why today? It was two fifteen. Elise closed her eyes and inhaled deeply. It's now or never, she reprimanded herself. All those years of planning and preparation. Now, now!

The realization hit her, eyes wide, alert. She shot out of her seat snatching up her handbag and coat. She dropped her letter of resignation addressed to Mike Sweeney on her computer keyboard, swung open her office door and strode from the building without a backward glance or word.

CHAPTER TWENTY-TWO

"We have to get going." Aaron's words hung in the air. Stefan glanced up at the plain black and white clock on the wall. Two fifty-five. "Look, we can take you to the address on your parole papers, and if Elise isn't there, I have to bring you back so that other arrangements can be made." Stefan noted Aaron's matter of fact tone, not at all apologetic or empathetic.

Stefan sat motionless. He knew something must be amiss. Elise was not the kind of woman to be late let alone let him down. Not after all they had been through together. All the visits, telephone conversations and letters. Five years of companionship, friendship, and love. There was just no way she would just change her mind like that. The thought was unconceivable. Stefan stood slowly shaking out his legs to wake them up; they felt weak. He felt weak, his stomach was churning, his throat dry, his heart ached. She wouldn't let him down: he had resigned himself to the fact that something was seriously wrong.

He clasped hold of his little carryall, which Elise had sent him especially for this day. Everything in the bag had been a gift from Elise. The clothes he was wearing, all of it, everything in his life right now was because of Elise. He pulled the black Nike baseball cap onto his head resignedly as an overwhelming feeling of vulnerability washed over him.

Elise was his rock, she was the problem solver, and she had cared for him, cared about him, but for the first time he understood that she held all the power, and his heart sank. Had this all been some kind of game to her? Had he really been that desperate to allow her to lead him on? She was everything to him. They had made plans together, plans that would allow him to slot back into society undetected. Without her, he didn't really stand a chance. She had promised to marry him; she had told him over and over again how much she loved him. Elise had made him feel human again where everyone else had either distanced themselves or shown complete and utter contempt. He was and would always be, eternally grateful, but if she let him down today of all days, he would hunt her down and make her pay. He would not be made a fool of.

"Each child belongs to all of us
and they will bring us a tomorrow
in direct relation to the responsibility
we have shown to them."

—Maya Angelou

CHAPTER TWENTY-THREE

MAY 7, 2005

Shauna arrived home hungry, shivering, vexed, and irritated. She sloped upstairs, knowing that Kent was home, knowing and not caring. She knew she had no right to be angry with him, but there was no one else to take it out on, so he would just have to do.

Shauna and Kent had met at a university football match. He played center forward and she had been working part time as a receptionist at the leisure center. There had been plenty of eye contact and glances across the pitch, yet they hadn't really spoken until his best friend Nigel had recognized her as a fellow student from college. They had both studied criminology at A level. For Kent and Shauna, there had been an immediate physical attraction and for both an underlying sense that they had somehow met before or knew each other, perhaps from a past life, he had joked.

In all that time, they had stuck together through thick and thin: when his mother had passed away from thyroid cancer, when her brother had been sectioned, when her sister had emigrated to Australia, when his father had been arrested for several armed robberies and consequently sentenced to fifty-two years without parole. Neither of their lives had been a walk in the park, and they both appreciated and respected each other.

When Kent had proposed, she had accepted immediately because she had felt it was the right thing to do. She loved and respected him and could envision a future with him but, ultimately, she simply did not want to hurt him. If she had said no and explained her true feelings, that she never wanted to marry or have children, she knew that he would have been devastated. She convinced herself that she loved him and needed him and was happy to live with him for the rest of her life. He made her feel safe. She would make a great wife, do her best as a mother, and promised herself to never give up on their bond. Their love had grown out of necessity, a need for someone in their lives who understood them and accepted them, warts and all. The only wish that had been granted to them thus far. Shauna had saved Kent but had not allowed him to return the favor.

It had been Shauna's idea that they both seek out individual counselling to deal with their ups and downs and he had thrown himself wholeheartedly into the process. His therapist had had a great impact on his life, and he was learning how to deal with the day-to-day stresses and equally dealing with his past, his childhood. She had been seeing a therapist way longer than she cared to admit and it worked for her. She wanted him to find his own ways of coping with some of the traumas that he had encountered, rather than leaning on her.

Shauna had answers to everything, or so Kent thought. A good suggestion, a way through, impartial advice. She never buttered him up or sugar-coated anything. She said it how it was, and he loved her for it. For Kent though, there seemed to be an extra door that was locked to him, another layer that she would not peel back. Even though Shauna was sincere and trustworthy, there had always been an underlying feeling for him that there was more going on beneath the surface and sometimes this frightened him, though he never probed or broached the subject. He believed, hoped, that when she was ready, she would open up fully to him. This invisible but almost tangible veil draped over their relationship.

As she placed her weary foot on the top step, she mimed the words, "Shauna, are you okay?" As she padded along the landing, sure enough Kent was as the foot of the stairs.

"Shauna. Are you okay?" His concern was genuine.

"Got caught in the rain." Her response monotone, she continued across to their bedroom, dropping her bag, her coat, and lethargically removed her clothes. She daren't look in the mirror; she avoided it. She could hear Kent's hesitant footsteps on the stairs and made a dash for the en suite, slamming the shower on and hopping into the spacious glass cubicle. She tensed her body, allowing the flourish of icy water to flow down over her, turning the temperature gauge to max, waiting for the water to sting a little before turning the temperature gauge back to half way.

She stood under the torrent of water and relaxed, almost, one ear waiting for Kent to enter and ask her if she needed anything.

Kent entered; she felt him hesitating at the door, observing her. She stood still, not daring to turn around.

"Shall I bring you coffee?" He couldn't disguise the sadness in his voice. He knew that she didn't feel the same way about him as he did her. He knew she could have any man she chose. He knew that he was perhaps a tad predictable. He knew all this, but he still wanted Shauna to want him as he did her.

Shauna turned to see him peeping in at her, and her heart skipped a beat. He was so handsome, caring, strong, and determined, and he was desperately in love with her. What was wrong with her? Why couldn't she give of herself? There had been more than one occasion where she'd felt that she should just open up, reveal all, give it to him full on but where would she start? How could she find the words?

Shauna was fully aware that Kent had always wanted to know every detail of her life, mainly because he had spilled his guts about his. It was like some unspoken rule, he shared all, she should share all, but she didn't believe that. She believed a person should share what they felt comfortable with and that should be satisfactory. There was no point going over things that had happened way in the past. Who would benefit from that?

No one.

Shauna smiled and threw him a cheeky wink. Kent stepped into the en suite, the grin of a Cheshire cat, granted permission to enter. He wasn't sure what mood she was in and welcomed what appeared to be playful Shauna. She opened the shower cubicle door.

"I'd love a coffee. Afterwards." She draped her arms around his neck. Kent loosened his jeans and allowed them to fall the floor, he slipped his boxers down and responded to Shauna's kisses. She pulled him into the shower as he eagerly pulled his t-shirt up over his head, closing the door behind him.

Kent usually initiated their lovemaking and was overjoyed at Shauna showing initiative. Her moans loud and pleasurable as she pushed him up against the wall, pulling him down to her height, she pulled her legs up, wrapping them around his waist, never once allowing her lips to leave his. She slowly pushed herself on him, feeling him ready and alert for her, her body responding to him, taking him deeply, closing her eyes to her worries and fixations. The warm water streamed down over their bodies. Kent wanted that moment to last forever.

Stefan Mademan's image flashed up in her mind, big, strong, and vivid. She closed her eyes tighter, her kisses became harder, trying to erase his face from her memory. Kent enveloped her enthusiasm. Determined to make the most of this occasion, he felt her body tensing and held her tighter, pulling her hair back. Shauna's eyes flashed open and she glared at Kent in his moment of exquisite pleasure; she felt the need to hurt him, really hurt him.

"You like that?" she questioned, a hardened tone to her voice disguised in her whisper.

"Hmmm, yeah, I love that." Kent nuzzled into her neck.

Shauna grabbed a clump of his hair and pulled it back violently. She nuzzled his neck and bit him just below his ear. Kent enjoyed the pleasure and pain for a moment, but she wasn't letting go. He felt her teeth sinking deeper and tried to gently pull her away. She held on fast, her breath hard and steady.

"Shauna." He tried pulling her off again, firmer this time. Her teeth sunk in a millimeter more.

He grabbed her by her shoulders and yanked her away with all his strength. He stared down at her incredulously. She smiled up at him a sly smile, revealing small speckles of blood on her teeth.

Kent pushed her aside, wrenched open the cubicle door and stood in front of the mirror, turning his face to see the four puncture marks on his neck.

"What the fuck?!" Kent could feel his heart rate ramping up. Shauna grinned as she switched the shower off, pulling a towel from the hook and wrapping herself up in the soft fluffy toweling. She could taste his blood and ran her tongue over her teeth.

"Thought I'd spice things up a little for you. What? Don't you like it?"

Kent eyed her suspiciously. "No, Shauna. No, I don't." He snatched his jeans from the floor and pulled them on. She watched on amused. As he fastened his belt, he could feel her watching him. He was afraid: something about her just didn't feel right.

"Have you been drinking?" That could be the only explanation.

"What's the matter, baby?" she said, reaching out to touch his cheek. She never called him baby or any terms of endearment in that way. Something was definitely amiss. She swiftly reached up and wrapped her arms around his neck again, forcefully pushing her body against him. She swayed from side to side, the darkness emanating through her sickly smile. He sensed her sheer and utter wickedness. He attempted to pull her away from him but this time she interlocked her fingers behind his head.

He was trying not to exert too much strength, but she held on too tightly. He knew that her intention was to inflict as much pain as possible.

He grabbed her, pulling her arms down to her side and pushed his face into hers.

"Sort yourself out."

She snarled back. "And what if I don't? What are you going to do, eh?"

Kent immediately let go of her and walked out of the bedroom, turning to make sure she wasn't following him. He closed the door behind him, confused and concerned. What the hell was that all about? His calm, caring, adorable fiancée was not in that room, and he didn't know who that was but he also knew there was something seriously wrong. Wrong with their relationship, wrong with them.

Kent made his way down stairs, listening out for any sound that she might follow. Not a peep.

Shauna stood in her towel, and her tears fell in huge, fat dollops rolling down her cheeks; she didn't wipe them. She simply stood there, allowing her anger to subside, ashamed at what Kent had just witnessed, questioning her own actions. She truly had no idea what had come over her. She felt guilt and a deep sense of hatred that held her, glued to the spot. She felt a chill: she hadn't dried herself off. She turned to see herself in the mirror. Who was she? What was she doing?

Shauna loved Kent but didn't want to marry him let alone bear his children. She hated her job and all the people she worked with, colleagues and criminals alike. She loathed this home that they shared—it was all Kent's taste: modern, chic and showy. She often window shopped at small independent stores where the furniture would suit a small cottage, lots of wood and textures, and instead she stood in what felt a like a showroom. Everything in her life was fake. The realization hit her like a heavyweight's knockout punch. She slumped down on the bed clasping hold of the towel around her chest. She looked toward her mirrored dressing table, opulent, tasteful but not her taste, adorned with expensive perfumes and cosmetics. She reached out and swiped the contents of the dressing table to the floor.

One by one, she pulled out the drawers and allowed them to crash onto the parquet. A small Lalique vase held its place on her dressing table, and she glared at it. Kent had bought it for her twenty-fourth birthday, opalescent blue-stained glass which held a single white rose. She had admonished Kent for his extravagance. Snatching it up, she hurled it at the mirrored wardrobes with such strength that she smashed both the vase and the wardrobe, and tiny splinters of glass ricocheted back into her face.

Sitting at the bottom of the stairs, holding his head in his hands, listening to Shauna destroying their home, Kent was distraught. He couldn't understand what was happening. Had he put too much pressure on her? Was he forcing her into a marriage that she didn't want? Or, was she having a break down? He decided right there and then that he was going to help her like just as she had helped him and together: they could work things out.

CHAPTER TWENTY-FOUR

Stefan's temper had risen way past boiling point as Aaron pulled up outside a block of maisonnettes. Stefan knew that his anger was born out of extreme fear but that didn't alleviate his concerns one bit. He was seething and had brooded quietly in the back of the car for the whole hour-long journey. Elise and her betrayal rolled around in his mind. If she had been held up, why hadn't she called the prison and left a message? They would have passed it on to him; she must know that. Today was an extremely important day for him and she knew it, it was she who had hammered the importance of the day into him. The first day of the rest of his life. It symbolized a fresh start for them both. So why, if the day was so fucking important, hadn't she prepared for every eventuality. This was difficult for him without her messing things up. What was she thinking?

"Are you coming?" Stefan realized that Aaron had opened the door and was waiting for him to alight.

"What about my bags?" Stefan wanted any excuse to delay the inevitable.

"Let's just see if she's here first, shall we?" Aaron secretly hoped that Elise had come to her bloody senses. What on earth was a beautiful young woman like her doing giving this piece of scum the time of day? It made no sense to him at all. He beckoned for Stefan to get out of the car again.

Stefan slowly placed one foot on the ground and pulled the baseball cap down further over his face, nervously looking around to see if anybody was watching. He felt sick to his stomach. He had made up his mind that Elise had abandoned him; he felt like a fool. He didn't want the humiliation of getting to the front door with this wanker enjoying every moment of his discomfort when she didn't answer.

"You go. I'll wait here," he snapped. Stefan quickly pulled his leg back in the car, snatched the door shut, slamming the lock down, and turned to face the driver's seat, flinging his arms tightly around his chest and burying his chin into his jacket. He felt childish and stubborn and truly wanted to punch Aaron in his smug face.

Aaron smirked, whistling a cheery tune as he headed up the pathway leading to the maisonnettes. Before he had chance to locate the buzzer for number seven, Elise came flying out of the entrance, running across the grass toward the car. Stefan only noticed her when she was banging rapidly on the car window.

Stefan felt all the anger seep away through his every pore. Her beautiful face and sunny smile beaming down upon him. He was elated and shocked. She wasn't a fake or a fraud, she had meant every word she had spoken and now, and here she was in all her splendor.

"Open up, then!" Her voice reminded him of a bird singing. He carefully opened the door and before he could step out, she leant in and wrapped her arms tightly around his neck.

"I'm so, so sorry Stefan. I'm so sorry. I got held up at work and of course I couldn't say where I needed to be, so by the time they let me go, there was no way I was going to make it, so I headed straight home. I called Trenholme, but they said you had already left." Elise's ramblings were sweet music to his ears.

Stefan loosened her grip and clambered out of the car. He was surprised to find that his voice failed him and the lump in his throat felt as if it were going to explode. He held her gently by her shoulders, taking in her radiant beauty. He still couldn't believe that she wanted him. It had been much easier to believe that this had all been a setup. She wanted him, she was here for him, she was going to marry him, and at that moment nothing else in the world mattered.

"Are you okay?" Her concern touched him; if only she knew how he had been cursing her. He couldn't tell her that he actually thought she had been conning him and didn't expect her to be home or that the address was somehow fake.

He nodded and bent down to squeeze her tightly. She seemed so much smaller than she did in the visiting room. Everything about her seemed smaller: her hands, her frame; she was tiny and fragile-looking. He had never been allowed to embrace her or even touch her before. Overwhelmed, he inhaled deeply taking in the smell of expensive shampoo and hint of light perfume. He felt himself harden and pulled away from her, embarrassed that he could not control himself.

Elise gently stepped back and took in his huge frame. "Come on, the neighbors will be having a field day." Stefan untangled himself and tapped the boot for Aaron to open it. Elise and Stefan stood there on the pavement grinning at each other.

Aaron watched the display, horrified that this Elise woman was genuine. She was stunning—what on earth did she see in this monster? He marched toward the boot of the car. Stefan pulled out his carryall and slammed the boot shut triumphantly.

He knew that Aaron had no faith at all in Elise and had enjoyed his turmoil for the whole journey. Stefan noted that Aaron was green with envy and shocked that Elise had in fact got held up. Stefan was elated. All his worries and doubts simply drifted away. It still slighted him that she had not turned up when she had promised and part of him believed that she'd had a wobble, changed her mind, and then changed it back again. But she was here now and the life that they had planned together had started in that very moment. This was the first day of the rest of his life and he intended it to continue as it had started. Stefan and Elise strolled up the pathway together, hand in hand.

Aaron climbed back into his car and watched until they were inside. Officially, he was supposed to make sure Stefan stepped across the threshold of his nominated address, but he couldn't be bothered to enforce this detail. He was finished for the day and simply wanted to get home.

CHAPTER TWENTY-FIVE

Kent had sat outside their bedroom door and waited. Waited for silence. He knew she would have to stop at some stage. Her rampage had gone on for sixteen minutes. He didn't care about the damage to the room, he cared about the damage that she might have done to herself. He could hear her crying as she smashed her way around the room, sobbing her heart out, sounding more like a wounded animal the whole time. It had been difficult to hear, Shauna in such pain and him unable to help in any way because she wouldn't allow him into her world.

Finally she had stopped, and he could only hear her muffled sobs. He waited till he was sure she had calmed down or better still, fallen asleep before slowly opening the door. Carefully he scraped the door open, the weight of the debris behind the door surprised him. He was prepared to find their room obliterated and he was not at all wrong in his estimation. Every single mirrored door of their wardrobe was scattered into a million pieces on the floor, a colossal, sparkling mosaic. Everything in the room that could be broken was broken. Only their clothes and shoes were untouched though he assumed they would be full of glass splinters. He noticed Shauna's feet on the bed, and he inched the door open a little more to see her fast asleep, her towel wrapped tightly around her beautiful body, her face peaceful, only tiny freckles of blood spotted her face. He witnessed her vulnerability in its fullness for the very first time, surrounded by destruction. Her destruction, in the middle of the glass ocean she had created. Kent watched her sleep.

He couldn't enter the room. He was barefooted and he really did not want to disturb her from her sleep. Worried in case she had injured herself more seriously, he focused on her chest, ensuring he could see it rising and falling.

He crept back down stairs and headed out into the back garden to unlock the large shed. He located his wellington boots, pushing his feet in quickly then searched around until he found the garden refuse sacks and a heavy shovel. Making his way back to the destruction and damaged room, he wondered for the hundredth time, what had happened to Shauna.

She lay there, still and snoozing lightly. He crept into the room placing his Wellington boots as strategically as he could, every foot step crunched and crinkled. He leant over her.

"Shauna," he whispered. She stirred a little, but he could see she was in her deep sleep mode. They had often joked that a herd of elephants couldn't wake her once she hit deep sleep. He scooped her up from the bed and made his way downstairs, placing her on the enormous corner couch. He covered her with the fur throw which was draped over the back of the couch, tucking her in, taking great care not to wake her. He knelt before her, taking in her beauty, wondering what trauma had befallen her and what could possibly be so bad that she could not speak of it.

Shauna sensed his presence, awakening as if she had heard his thoughts. They simply gazed questioningly into each other's eyes.

"I'm so sorry, Kent." Shauna meant it. She had never been so embarrassed in her entire life. She felt as if she had stepped out of her body and taken on a whole new being, a terrifying being.

Kent reached out and pushed her hair back from her face. Her eyes were puffy, her skin blotchy and blood-stained, her lips dry and cracked and still he saw her beauty. Nothing more, nothing less.

"No Shauna, we're going to sort this out together." He kissed her lightly on her cheek as her eyes lids drooped closed.

CHAPTER TWENTY-SIX

Kent waded through the ocean of broken glass. He had thought about calling their cleaner in to sort the room but thought better of it. He didn't want
anyone to know what had happened, how would it look to an outsider? He
considered taking ownership of smashing their bedroom to smithereens but
of course that would have stirred up more questions. What kind of man
would do that? He simply did not have the energy to concoct a story that
sounded reasonable. Looking at Shauna's handiwork, he knew that there
simply were no reasonable explanations.

He packed shovel after shovel of heaped shards of glass into the
garden waste bag, all the time trying to makes sense of Shauna's outburst.
He ran his mind over the past week, searching for any changes in her, any
upset. As he swept, pulling the heavy broom, he knew that the parquet
would be damaged, feeling shards of glass sticking into the highly polished
floor, admonishing himself for thinking about the damage to the floor when
he should be thinking about how badly damaged Shauna was. He noticed
a rather large piece of the Lalique vase, and he slumped down on the bed,
turning the stunning piece of glass around, unable to believe what had
just happened.

His heart heavy, he had thought that together they were both doing
the right thing for them. Getting married wasn't supposed to be a chore
or one of those things you had to get through. Now when he looked back
remembering the night he had proposed to Shauna, she hadn't exactly been
overjoyed at the prospect, rather she had taken it all in her stride. There were
no tears of joy, exclamations of her undying love, or even a slight giggle of
excitement. Shauna had simply accepted, and it was he that had thrown his
arms around her, thanking her. He had actually thanked her as if he were
some sort of ogre that was grateful to be accepted into her life.

Kent began to feel his own temper rising. She always made him feel
as if he should be grateful to even exist in her presence.

In her defense, though, she just had that air about her, he had witnessed her aloofness with others too. Kent knew then that if this relationship was going to go any further, they were going to have to talk through absolutely everything. He didn't want to lose her, but neither did he want to make her so unhappy that she had to smash their home up. He placed the piece of Lalique vase on the dressing table. He didn't know why: it wasn't as if he could get it repaired. As he did so, he noticed a brown manila A4 envelope taped to the inside of what was left of the Shauna's dressing table. He leant forward to make sure it wasn't just the light's reflection playing tricks on him. He hunkered down and ran his fingers around the taped edges. The envelope stuck out considerably as if packed with something. He turned toward the bedroom door and listened out for any sounds. Not a peep. Carefully, he pulled the dressing table away from the wall and used a large sherd of glass to wedge between the wood of the back of the dressing table enough to slip his hand in; he edged the top of the envelope that was taped down and slowly pulled the contents out of the envelope.

Sitting on the bed, he sifted through the papers. Documents from The Farmhouse children's home and social services. Kent couldn't make head nor tale of what he was reading. Karen and Dane Woods were handed over to social services by their parents, Stephen and Melissa Woods. Letters between social services and the children's home stating that Dane Woods was a danger to himself and others and recommending that he be sectioned due to self-harm and extreme violence. None of it was making sense, yet all of it was making sense. If, as he thought, Shauna had changed her identity, everything seemed to slot into place, but there were still so many questions.

There were police reports with some of the numbered pages missing but they suggested that police had been called several times to their home with regards to neglect. Shauna never spoke of her parents. Very early on in their relationship, Shauna had simply stated that her parents weren't the nurturing kind; she had never mentioned being taken into care, and every time he tried to broach the subject of meeting them, Shauna had shut him down.

Kent felt the pieces of the puzzle slotting together, but there were still pieces missing. He knew that this was not the time to probe Shauna, especially after the night's events, but he had to know. He wanted to help

Shauna as she had so easily helped him. He loved the bones of her and if their relationship was to survive, he had to know.

Kent slid his mobile phone out of his pocket and googled The Farmhouse. The results showed a young offenders facility, no mention of a children's home. Nothing showed in the results that made any sense to Kent.

Kent's anger subsided and was replaced with a wave of sadness. How could he have been so inconsiderate? He should've known that whatever Shauna was unable to talk about must have been pretty serious and damaging. He thought about how Shauna and Lee must have been bundled off, unwanted and unloved and how Shauna, still to this day, looked out for Lee—she was always saying, "I'm all he's got." Guilt rained down on Kent: all along he had believed that Shauna was simply holding back a part of herself for reasons which he didn't understand, and a part of him had actually started to believe that she was heartbroken for some lost love. He was annoyed with himself. How could he have been so selfish and self-centered? Now he knew that there was much more to her than he realized. Today's events didn't answer all of his questions but to him the picture became a little clearer.

He slid the documents back into the envelope and pushed the back of the dressing table back together. Pushing the dressing table back in place, and quietly closing the bedroom door, Kent made up his mind to do his best to get to the bottom of this and help Shauna. He made a phone call to Nigel, listed in his mobile as Nigel P, his best friend.

"Nigel."

"Baxter. You and Shauna good?"

"Yeah, yeah, we're good, yeah. How's things your end?"

"Good. Relaxing with a beer for once. Can't tell you the last time I was just able to put my feet up."

"Still working on that promotion?"

"Absolutely. There are a few changes happening and I'm not even sure if that's a good or bad thing right about now, but I can only do my best."

"You worry too much. You'll get through."

"Thanks for that vote of confidence. You should come down and put a good word in for me." They both laughed. Nigel sensed that Kent's call wasn't his usual how-you-doing—there was more.

"You sure you're good?"

Kent hesitated. "Listen, I need to ask you a big favor and don't feel bad if it's something you can't do. I'm clutching at straws here, but if I were to give you the name of a children's home and a couple of police report numbers, could you find out the details? Anything at all?"

"What's up?"

"I can't really talk right now but anything.... There's a connection with social services, too, but... Look, I don't even know if I should be digging myself and.... ?"

"I'll see what I can do. Give us these police report numbers."

"We're talking the eighties here."

"Shouldn't be a problem. A lot of cases were never changed over to digital, but it's no issue, just might take a while. I'll see what I can find out."

Kent relayed the information tersely, giving the basic details, aware that once Nigel looked into this, he would work out the connection to Shauna. He trusted Nigel. Nigel, who had always as far as he could remember, had his back. "I think its Shauna." Kent knew he could trust him; there was no doubt in his mind.

Kent continued "Date of birth for Shauna is the second of March, nineteen seventy-four."

"Shauna doesn't know you're looking into this." It was a statement rather than a question. Kent sighed.

"I need to know."

Kent heard Nigel keying the information into his phone.

"I'll see what I can find. Sure you're okay, mate?" Nigel was concerned. This was so out of character for Kent.

"Yeah, yeah, all good." Kent did not sound at all convincing.

"Catch you later." Nigel was intrigued. He'd always found Shauna a bit odd, a nice enough girl but he doubted their relationship on more than one occasion, though he had never spoken his thoughts out loud to Kent. Kent worshipped the ground she walked on.

"Later." Kent ended the call and dropped his phone onto the bed.

CHAPTER TWENTY-SEVEN

MAY 7, 2005

Glancing down at her mobile phone, "Mike Boss" flashed up at her urgently. Elise considered not answering and ran through the scenario in lightning speed. If she didn't answer, Mike would perhaps believe that something was wrong and continue to pester her, or, worst-case scenario, turn up at her flat. Bad idea. Answering and not being able to answer his questions in a timely fashion or sounding in anyway unsure could lead him again to think something was wrong and come and check on her. Another bad idea. Elise made up her mind, answer, put him straight, tell him to fuck off if needs be, end of story. Elise locked herself in the bathroom and answered.

"Hello."

"Elise, I just received your letter of resignation."

"Yes, I'm sorry I couldn't give more notice. I have personal issues that I really need to deal with."

"Is there anything I can do, help with, just name it. You know you can always talk to me."

"I know, Mike, and I do appreciate it, but I just feel it's best all round to move on."

"Look I'm not going to accept your resignation. Just take your time, sort out whatever it is that you need to sort out, and come back. Call it a sabbatical."

"I don't think that's a good idea, Mike, really I..."

"Elise, you are a credit to us, and we want you back." Elise made the decision, putting him straight was the only way forward.

"I'm not fucking coming back. Don't you get it? I've given you my resignation, accept it, it's final. I'm a grown woman, I can take care of myself. I've resigned, that's it."

Elise hesitated, Mike's shock and hurt at her outburst hung between them, he unsure of what to say, horrified, she waiting for some come back and hoping that she did not have to hammer the facts home any more than she already had done.

Silence.

Elise ended the call.

Another task ticked off the to-do list. Elise was satisfied she would not be hearing from him again.

Her thoughts stayed with the interaction, and she felt guilty as hell, Mike was a nice guy who had always had her back and now he'd made her speak to him like that. Elise became more and more annoyed, her thoughts a mass of uncertainty, but instead of calling back and apologizing, a thought which fleeted through her mind, she had to justify her actions to herself. Why do people have to make things so difficult? Her letter should have been enough. Why did men, especially, always feel as if she needed saving from herself? She was annoyed: just the tone in Mike's voice had set her teeth on edge. How dare he. Wasn't she capable of making a simple decision, didn't she know her own mind? She knew that she could run that business ten times more efficiently than he could, and she knew he knew it, too. No matter how hard she tried to remain annoyed with him, she couldn't, she wasn't. What was done was done, and she had a new chapter to look forward too and Mike wasn't a part of her new life. Even if she wanted him to be, it was impossible. If she was going to make a success of the next phase of her life, this job couldn't be a part of it. Mike would simply not understand.

She tried to hammer the cold hard facts out in her mind. Mike didn't give two damns about her, and he only cared that he would have to get up of his measly ass and do some work. She had never been a slave to her work, she worked because she enjoyed it and there were perks. No one could hold her to ransom over a job, she made sure of that. She saw that illness all around her, every single day. Sitting in traffic, observing the commuters, some travelling an hour or more to get to a job or career that was using up all their best years, their creativity, their vibrancy, and when their employers were ready, they would just spit them out. Not needed and unwanted, it was a total lack of respect as far as she was concerned and because she was not locked into her job, she could simply waltz away, and Mike had no power to tempt her back in to his clutches.

If things were different, if she were just a normal woman working her way up the ladder, she knew that the job was everything she would have wanted and more. She wasn't a normal woman. She had plans, bigger things ahead of her, different dreams and goals. The job had been a means to an end.

She was financially comfortable through shrewd investments and managing her money extremely carefully. She needed for nothing and had always worked toward that independence; she was never going to allow herself to be tied to a job or a man, or anything else for that matter, over money.

Mike would just have to shove it in his pipe and smoke it. Visions of him announcing her resignation and her ex-colleagues reaction—they'll be shitting themselves, she giggled to herself.

She pictured the office staff in a flurry, some eager to get their hands on the deals she had sourced and be more than happy to collect her commissions, others at a loss, searching for ways to blame her for their shortcomings. It would be chaos for a day or two, then everything would settle down. They didn't need her. Stefan needed her, more than even he knew.

To Elise there was simply no choice. Stefan would always come first: her life and future was her one and only priority and everything else paled in importance. Keeping her job was not an option; now that Stefan was here with her there was the risk that her identity would be compromised and she was not ready to have those judgmental colleagues all up in her business, selling their stories or any sort of intrusion into her private life. She was doing them a favor, saving them the trouble and the chaos that was bound to ensue. They would all soon see and be grateful that she moved on before the proverbial well and truly hit the fan.

She hadn't yet told Stefan, not that he'd mind, and financially they'd be just fine. She wanted to spend every second of his life outside those prison walls with him. Just the two of them. She wanted to ease him back into society and she couldn't do that popping off to the office every single morning. No, it was out of the question: she had made the right decision, and it was best all round for everyone.

Elise's sense of pride swelled in her chest. She was taking charge, making choices and decisions which were bringing about change, lasting change. That job had never been a long-term plan. She was bound for better things. She wanted to take center stage in Stefan's life. That was where she belonged and if Stefan didn't already know it, he would soon enough.

"We worry about what a child will become tomorrow, yet we forget that he is someone today."

—Stacia Tauscher

CHAPTER TWENTY-EIGHT

The dense forest made it difficult to navigate in the darkness. Karen and Tessa could hear Stefan's footsteps following them for several minutes, but then there was nothing. Tessa and Dane cried in silence all the way; none of them spoke: fear had captured their voices, and there was only enough room in their minds to process the act of running for their lives in the deepest dark that any of them had experienced.

Karen didn't know where they were going; she just knew that getting away was the aim and if Stefan caught up with them, they'd hurt him like they had Will and even that she was unsure of, since they had no weapons, nothing they could hit him with.

"Psst!"

Karen and Tessa stopped in their tracks. They looked to each other, wanting to know if the other had heard the same thing.

"Oi! Over here." Without considering their options or discussing the matter, the three children looked to where the loud stage whisper had come from. Jason, one of the teenage boys who'd run off earlier, was peeking out from behind a tree. Another head popped out, further away—Luke. Karen hesitated. Relief rushed over her, but she was cautious. Both of them knew Stefan, and he could have sent them. Karen reasoned with herself: she had seen them run away, but what were they doing here now?

"What?" Karen couldn't think of what else to say.

"Come on, this way. We'll get you home." Not waiting for objections and discussion, Jason turned and dodged through the trees, expertly bobbing and weaving between the trees, and clearly the darkness was no hindrance. He knew the forest like the back of his hand. Luke followed; they didn't run together but close enough for the three to follow.

Dane's feet and legs were tired, he wanted to throw himself on the ground and sleep but he knew that he didn't want the bad man to get him again so he kept up the best he could, with no word of complaint.

Within minutes, they all stood at the road side. They were near the bottom of the hill, the curve of the road, wrapping around the hillside, where the sun had begun to rise, awakening them from their nightmare.

Out of breath, Karen spluttered, "He's got our friend Michelle." Karen wasn't sure what she wanted them to say or do; she knew there was no going back. Speaking words, saying Michelle's name gripped at her heart, and she clenched her eyes tightly shut for a moment, making a wish hoping against hope that saying her name would somehow bring her back to them, that she would appear magically and the four of them could get away together. Karen and Tessa knew in their hearts that they would never see Michelle again. They knew that the sound of her being crushed and damaged would forever reverberate in their ears.

Jason shrugged his shoulders helplessly. "We can't go back now." His voice tense and sad.

Tessa looked to Karen reassuringly. "We'll tell the police." Jason and Luke shifted uneasily at the mention of police.

"We'll get you home, then you're on your own." Jason headed a little further down the road and disappeared round the bend.

"Come on." Luke beckoned for them to keep moving. They followed the bend in the road to a little clapped-out white Austin Maestro. Jason opened the rear seat door and they all climbed in.

The danger was behind them, and they instinctively knew that Jason and Luke wouldn't hurt them, that this wasn't a trick, that they were real-life savers. Dane snuggled into Karen, sniffling and shivering, his tiny feet scratched and dirty, but he was safe in Karen's arms.

No one spoke on that car journey. Occasionally, Jason would nod toward Luke knowingly. This appeared to be their own way of communication. The girls' thoughts were a mixture of tremendous sadness, fear, and the reality of what had happened.

Neither of the girls wanted to be taken home. Tessa could only imagine what her father was going to say: first of all the fact that she had lied and said that the camping trip had been organized by the school, secondly that she had left her school bag containing all his precious Tupperware. Her father wasn't going to be buying another school bag. She could hear him then: "Do you think money grows on trees?" What he would have to say about her going camping with her friends didn't bear thinking about, let alone what had happened to Michelle. Her father would find a way of blaming her. When things were good it was all his doing, when things went wrong or he was unhappy about a situation, it was all her fault and she would have to listen to him reel off the story of her mother's absence and how she had been the reason her mother had left. She questioned herself. Had tonight been her fault too? Had they all done something wrong? She felt confused, frightened, and believed the only people who would at least listen to them and perhaps believe them, would be the police.

Karen, too, knew what would be awaiting her, and she was tired. She didn't want to have to try to explain to her parents what had happened: they'd be angry with her, she knew they would. She and Dane were inconveniences, troublesome and bothersome; Karen had heard these words on many occasions. This night's horrors would be no exception. Their parents were more likely to show indifference to what had happened, and Karen feared that more. She simply wanted to lie down somewhere safe so she could fall asleep and never wake again.

CHAPTER TWENTY-NINE

Julia Robinson, the young female police officer on duty that morning had been visibly shaken when Karen, Tessa, and Dane had turned up at the police station reeling off the events of the past seventeen hours.

The three children had all been talking at once, startled, bewildered, and clearly traumatized. The two girls were caked in blood, the little boy with no pants. She was new to the job and had completed her training only two months prior. Nothing had prepared her for anything remotely like this. She had offered them a hot drink, which they had all refused, found something for Dane to wear, and immediately contacted her superior. She knew instinctively that that this case was going to take precedence over everything. The man they had described, Stefan—they didn't know his surname—and this old couple, Mr. and Mrs. Rosehill, what kind of people were they? Was she really cut out for this kind of work? She wanted to remove the scum from the streets: that had been her intention when she had applied to join the force. She wanted the bad people to pay for their crimes and believed she had something about her that could get the job done. She cared a great deal and wanted to live in a good, decent, and safe society. A society where people looked out for each other, where the bad people were put away to allow those civilized members of the community to get on with their lives, without fear of what might be around the corner.

After hearing the children's account of what they had experienced she just wasn't so sure anymore. It was just too much. She realized then that her job wasn't just about burglaries, robberies, drunken brawls, drug dealers and soliciting; this was the real grit, this was the society she was part of and wanted to clean up. She just didn't know if she could. Seeing those children's faces, hearing their voices explaining in their clear and simple language, the horror that they had faced, their bravery and determination to run for their lives. She held back her tears as they cried over and over that their friend Michelle was still with this monster and the man that they believed they had killed. It was a real-life nightmare come to life, one which would live with her for the rest of her days.

CHAPTER THIRTY

Stefan Mademan was apprehended within four hours of the children reporting their ordeal. The police had found Stefan, deep in the woods, digging a hole, Michelle's tiny broken body laid out next to Will's. He had been planning to bury them together. Arresting police had later described Stefan as arrogant and dismissive of their questions, showing not one modicum of remorse. Every officer involved in the investigation was repulsed and sickened by Stefan. He admitted to the crimes after the duty solicitor advised him that there was simply no way around it for him. It all seemed a little too easy: he held up his hands and even took the blame for taking Will's life. He wanted it all to be over quickly and cleanly, no digging further into his life.

Mr. and Mrs. Rosehill were also arrested and their shop closed down when it was discovered through their admittance that they had been sending children between the ages of nine and fifteen to Stefan for over nine months. Mr. and Mrs. Rosehill groomed the children, got to know them, gained the trust of the children and parents alike, and would then pass them on to Stefan and his cronies.

The investigation didn't end with Stefan's incarceration. Stefan's poisonous tentacles spread wide and far across the land. He actively sought out areas of poverty and would insert people like Mr. and Mrs. Rosehill right in the heart of the community. His network of groomers included shopkeepers, community center workers, park attendants, or leisure center staff, the only criteria being a community where children were mostly left to their own devices, with low income, high crime, and unemployment. Stefan was clever in that the police were unable to find a list. The only clues came from those who came forward with information, and whilst the police were able to secure a hefty sentence for Stefan, they were left with a feeling of great concern that even with Stefan behind bars, his crime syndicate would continue and thrive.

The story made front-page news of all the papers: a child abuser who had raped and killed a ten-year-old little girl would always make front-page news, but what made this case different was the sophistication of Stefan's operation. People all over the country questioned the people they knew, who their children spent time with. Who were their neighbors? Were the schools safe? The police force that carried out the investigation were all left with a sense of failure: yes, they had gotten, Stefan Mademan but they knew this particular incident was merely the tip of the iceberg.

Stefan never went to trial. Advised by his solicitor to plead guilty, he was sentenced to thirty years with parole after twenty. The media echoed the feelings of the country: anger, resentment, and fear.

Whilst the case had been running, the media had clambered all over Stefan's life and those of his associates' uncovering hundreds of his victims. The country was in agreement that Stefan should receive the maximum sentence, and some demanded the death sentence.

One week into Stefan's sentence, a national newspaper received an anonymous letter warning that the three children involved in the Stefan Mademan case were not safe. They were being watched and the letter specifically stated that the children should be given anonymity.

Everybody on the Bournbrook estate already knew who the victims were and word had gotten to the press, who had revealed their names and even the estate where they lived.

CHAPTER THIRTY-ONE

Karen and Dane, after much scrutiny and on the insistence of their parents, were sent to a children's home. Karen had admitted to throttling Will and received therapy alongside Dane. Karen had insisted and kicked up a fuss when the suggestion was made that they be separated. It had taken some doing, with many hours of persistence from their social worker, but they were allowed to remain together.

Tessa's father had, as Tessa knew he would, blamed her. For many years he had held on to the hope that his wife would return, and now with new identities and new addresses he felt that all hope was lost. Their relationship was never the same, and he believed Tessa was tainted and broken, that no one would want her as a wife or even as an employee, that she was good for nothing. There was no point keeping her; his wife would never return now because of the shame of it all. He couldn't look her in the eye. He sent her away; he wanted nothing to do with her.

Michelle's parents dismayed and heartbroken, veered further down into a pit of despair. Having already lost their eldest child to the system, she had been removed from their home due to her violent and destructive behavior. Now their youngest was never coming home. They held themselves responsible. Her mother, Lorna, hardworking, grafting all the hours she could handle, stopped. She was exhausted, and for what? She no longer had the strength or a reason to carry on as she had been doing. Her husband, Gregg, suffered from debilitating depression since the eldest had been placed in care. He drank and slept; that was his life. Failing as a husband and a father, and now this. He had no control over his circumstances, could not improve them or change them, so he believed, and he felt he was dragging his family down with him. There was only one thing left for him to do.

Gregg Muller was found hanging in a disused garage at the back of the estate. Children from the estate had found him, pale and blue lipped.

Lorna simply carried on where he had left off, reclusive with only the bottle for company and sympathy.

Stefan Mademan had destroyed a community in one fell swoop.

CHAPTER THIRTY-TWO

Stefan stood awkwardly in the center of Elise's sparsely decorated lounge. Elise forced a smile. The whole thing felt forced. After all those years of writing and getting to know the man, seeing him standing there, unsure of whether to sit or stand, she realized she did not know him at all. She was aware of his crimes, and knew there was a real man behind all the hype and media reports: that's who she wanted, that's who she had focused all her attentions on. She wanted to get under his skin, wanted him to need her, rely on her, trust in her beyond all else and everyone else. She recounted his letters of appreciation, but she did not really know him.

"Sit down, and put your feet up." Elise puffed up a couple of stiff grey cushions indicating where she wanted him to sit. Stefan noticed a glint of silver around Elise's wrist, a delicate charm bracelet with miniscule links and only two charms. One a tiny horse shoe, the other a butterfly. Stefan froze for a moment, confused somewhat. He stepped toward her, lifting her wrist to get a closer look. He'd never seen her wearing it before, yet it appeared familiar.

"Who got you that? An ex?" Elise stared down at the bracket, thinking of the best answer to give.

Stefan felt her discomfort, chuckled uneasily, and took a seat.

"No. My mother gave it to me. Said it would always bring me luck, right when I needed it."

Stefan nodded slowly.

"You must be hungry?" Elise enquired. In his letters he'd stated that his favorite meal was lasagna and chips. He had a passion for pizza with any meat topping. His favorite sweet, apple pie and custard. Drink, lemonade. Alcohol, a pint of bitter. Snack, cheese and pickle on doorstep sliced white bread. He didn't do chocolate, hated chicken and vegetables except potatoes, and loved a good strong cup of Builder's tea with digestives. Elise had made a list and stocked up on everything. She scuttled into the kitchen and filled the kettle.

"How was the journey?" she called through from the kitchen.

"I know you said your parents wouldn't approve of us, but do you have any contact with them at all?"

"No." Elise locked off the conversation. That was all that she had to say. She had told him that she was fine with cutting off her family in order to be with him and that was an end to it as far as she was concerned.

Stefan took in his surroundings. After twenty years locked away, he was used to staring at four plain walls, but he hadn't expected to find the same in Elise's home. He had spent many an endless night visualizing Elise's home. Large ornamental bookcases filled with interesting books of all sorts, abstract paintings on the walls, photographs of her family, he had expected to find a home that was warm and welcoming, but it felt bland.

"Awful, to tell the truth." He was too tired to sugarcoat it.

"The whole time I was worried, you know, in case you changed your mind about... about us."

Elise appeared at the doorway. "Really? Did you really think that I would go back on my word?" Elise sat carefully beside him, taking his hand, placing it in hers, and resting it on her knee.

"I could see why you might: this whole thing is difficult, and it made sense, but I couldn't get my head around it." Stefan needed to let her know that he had been feeling vulnerable, make her understand that she was all he had in the world, all the cards were in her hands and that felt uncomfortable.

"But I...." Elise needed to set the record straight.

Stefan placed a finger gently on her lips. "Sh, sh, sh. I need to tell you. The past five years, you have made all the difference in my life. Before you, there was nothing. Nothing to look forward to. Nothing good to think about and then you came along and brightened up everything. And today, I had a taste of that emptiness again." Stefan lowered his head.

"Stefan, all you need to know is that I'm here now, real, in the flesh and you're not going to get rid of me any time soon." She smiled, Stefan lifted his head, their eyes met, and he leant in to kiss her. He felt her stiffen: instead of giving her the kiss that he had longed for and dreamt of so often, he pecked her on the cheek. This was the strangest situation he had ever been in and he knew it would take some time to adjust. He'd been away for so long and wanted to take his time with her, but he also wanted proof, consummation of her devotion to him. She too was vulnerable and so delicate he had to gain her trust, and he truly needed that.

The sound of the kettle bubbling to the boil alerted Elise.

"Let me get that tea." Elise disappeared into the kitchen. Stefan stood and went to the window, the blank street view which looked out over the perfectly cut, neat communal lawn and the quiet road. This was exactly what he needed.

Stefan was a city man. He'd grown up in a big city, had always gravitated toward noise, dirt, crowds of people, the hustle and bustle. He had wanted to blend in. He didn't want to stand out to others mainly so that he could go about his business and not have too many people notice his comings and goings, asking questions, poking their noses in. Here everything stood out. He wasn't sure he liked that, but it was definitely what he needed right now, peace and quiet.

Space to think and plan out his next move. He felt love for Elise, but he knew that that love would only continue if she was willing to become a part of his world. He knew that sooner or later her feminine charms would not be enough for him, he would have to return to form—the thought excited him. He only hoped that Elise could find a way to stick by him; she was good for him, he knew that much, and she was the perfect decoy. The world would surely have to believe he was a changed man with a little wife in tow. More than anything, he knew she could help him get things back to the way they had been before. His customer base was huge and open to new

potential: people were using the internet now to satisfy their urges. He had big plans and he wanted Elise to be a part of it all. He just hoped that she loved him enough.

Stefan had known early on who he was and what he wanted. Even as a teenager, he had always preferred the company of younger people. He could be in charge, they looked up to him, and he loved to manipulate and lead. He wanted to feel that he was needed and respected and in doing so could get people to do exactly as he had wanted them to, he wanted control and needed to be surrounded by vulnerable people, people who didn't know their own minds, wanted to be guided, and be told what to do. People hurt people all the time, especially children. Parents discarded, used, and abused their children, leaving them open to influence. Cults, religious groups, gangs, Stefan knew his niche, his corner of the market. Those who lacked attention and care were always on the lookout for the soft touch and he had made it his business to be that warm arm draped around their shoulders, the safe place to rest their heads, the one who had to be pleased and satisfied. Without him these rejects would soon find another who would not be as attentive and kind as him. He thrived on the look of fear in a child's eyes, that's what really did for him.

He knew that he still had the urge, and he didn't deny this to himself. To him the urge was instinctive and natural. Why should he hold back? He knew he wasn't the only one, he had built a whole network and business based on the urges of others. Kings and the like before him had had the same needs, why should he be punished. He was sorry for the deaths that had occurred, he had been caught with Michelle but there had been others. Murder had never been his intention.

He wanted to open up to Elise about his life and crimes, gauge her reaction, but strangely she had never broached the subject, he wasn't sure why, but he would soon find out. It was a discussion that could not be avoided for much longer.

Elise returned with a small wooden white tray, holding two mugs of tea and a plate of digestives; she placed the tray down on the bare coffee table.

Elise sat down opposite Stefan. He glanced at the empty space beside him. Was she afraid of him? He took his mug of tea, smiling into the cup. Fear was a very good start.

"There are things we really need to talk about, Elise. I know that we've not had this conversation before, but I do think I need to explain stuff to you."

"No need." Elise held her mug to her lips but didn't drink. The mug shielded the curl of her lips. She eyed Stefan, staring right through him. She shut down the conversation with her words and tone. Stefan felt an icy coldness spreading throughout the room.

"I was thinking we could pop down to Lorenzo's for dinner tonight, as a special welcome home for you." Her shoulders dropped and she placed her cup on the tray, relaxing a little.

Stefan was thrown. She had shut him down and dismissed him. Here he was trying to have a heart to heart, and she was talking about some restaurant.

"Lorenzo's?"

"An amazing pizza place. You are going to love it." Elise's eyes brightened, excited at the prospect and searching Stefan's eyes for approval. There was something behind her smile that Stefan couldn't read, and it sent a shiver down his spine. Stefan thought he was a really good judge of character. He could smell fear and rejection, taste desperation and suffering, and see sacrifice in the eyes of even the youngest of souls. She wasn't ready to hear what he had to say. He thought better of pushing the conversation, and, after all, they had plenty of time to talk. He decided that he should enjoy his first evening of freedom and they could talk another day.

"Sounds good," Stefan nodded in agreement. He drank his tea. "You make the perfect cuppa."

"Great. Drink up then. I'll go and unpack your bags and run you a lovely bath. How's that?" Elise was on her feet, snatching up his bag before he had chance to respond.

"Thank you." Stefan sipped his tea and strolled around the lounge, then into the kitchen. The whole flat had an empty feel to it. If he hadn't received five years' worth of letters from this exact address, he would have believed Elise had just moved in, but even then there should be a box or two. The kitchen was spotless: everything you would expect a kitchen to have was visible, but there was something missing.

Stefan shook his head, trying to clear these irrational thoughts from his mind. Elise had been his rock and she would continue to be so. She had given up so much for him: her family, she had made it clear they would not contend with this situation; her falling in love with a convicted criminal was not what they had in mind for their precious daughter. She had told him that she was an only child, her parents had kept her at a distance, she had been schooled privately, kept separate from other children, not a typical childhood. Stefan saw their similarities, and they were each clinging on to the other for dear life. He had no right to expect her to jump at his beck and call, yet she did, and he didn't even have to call. She was there, providing what he needed when he needed it, as if reading his mind, cowing to his expectations. He loved her because she had been there for him and sacrificed any sort of normality that she could have hoped for, all for him. He made a mental note to relax and enjoy his freedom and just with that thought he sat down, spread out on the sofa and felt his whole body relax. It had only just occurred to him how tired he was.

CHAPTER THIRTY-THREE

Lorenzo's wasn't quite what Stefan had envisioned for a pizzeria. It stood on the main street that ran through the village. A butcher, greengrocer, post office, charity shop, and a selection of designer boutiques surrounded it. A little pub stood right on the corner. Lorenzo's place was upmarket, with a mahogany frontage, the name in a sliver of gold handwritten-styled lettering. Elise handed her car keys to the valet and Stefan realized that Elise had made a reservation when she gave her name to the hostess who swiftly showed them to a table for two.

Stefan's stomach flipped and somersaulted as the aromas that wafted in from the kitchen, every time a waiter passed in or out, were simply exquisite. He had never been one for eating out. He felt on top of the world. He wore soft navy corduroy trousers, a white shirt with thin navy stripes, a pair of black dress shoes, and a navy three-quarter-length real wool overcoat. Elise had concealed and powdered his birthmark and had helped him insert the dark-brown contact lenses. He looked and felt like a new man. He was confident that no one could possibly recognize him and, as the waiter took their drinks order, he reached out and took Elise's hand across the table.

"This is something else. I didn't know fancy pizza places existed."

"They've only been here a year or so. I've never eaten in before, but I ordered a takeout and it's become my secret addiction. The pizzas are to die for. They do lasagna, too."

"No, pizza will do me."

Elise nodded, pleased that she'd made the right selection for him. The sound of a grand orchestra weaved its notes from under the table. Elise bought her mobile phone level to the table, not quite hiding it from Stefan, but shielding the phone screen. She read the message, her cheeks flushed slightly as she pushed the phone back into her small handbag. Stefan waited expectantly for her to explain who had been interrupting their precious time together and what they wanted. He wasn't sure whether the music was a ring tone and she had declined the call or a message. There was no explanation.

Stefan made a mental note that there would be no secrets between them. Elise had given him a smart mobile phone, but it hadn't been set up and he had no one to give his number to, not yet. He was itching to ask who had called or sent a message, but if she was not offering up the information, he was not going to beg. There were, he could see, a few little creases to iron out between them—nothing major, but they had to come to an understanding. Stefan wanted his rightful place in the relationship, the lead, and Elise would just have to get used to it.

"A grown child is a
dangerous thing."

—Alice Walker

CHAPTER THIRTY-FOUR

Slightly tipsy, red-cheeked, and in high spirits, Stefan and Elise stood outside Lorenzo's waiting for the valet to arrive with the car. Not a drop of alcohol had touched Stefan's lips for over twenty years. Alcohol and all the narcotics known to man had been freely and widely available in prison, but Stefan hadn't trusted any of the dealers. He had been warned that the other inmates were always on the lookout for an opportunity to catch him off guard. Stefan didn't trust the inmates, the guards, the cleaners: no one, as far as he was concerned, gave a damn about him and his welfare, so he had taken great care to be extra vigilant. Tonight, the brandy had gone straight to his head.

Stefan had always a lived in an extremely frugal manner; his tastes were very simple, and his one and only pleasure in life was strictly taboo. He knew nothing of fine clothes, wines, restaurants, but he sensed that Elise would be educating him on how to really spoil himself. The brandy had been exceptional, and if he had not been mistaken cost almost forty pounds per shot. He had held his tongue and watched as Elise had taken great pleasure in introducing him to this new life. She had had enjoyed a couple of large glasses of red wine, and the two of them were totally relaxed and at ease. Elise had hinted in more than one of her letters that she was a virgin. Stefan hadn't been sure at the time whether or not she had been telling the truth, but he saw it now, perhaps why she was a little reserved and coy when he had shown her affection or been tactile, and she appeared overly shy. The thought of taking her virginity danced around in his fuzzy mind: he would own her, she would be pliable and want to please him. He planned to take her and show her who was really in charge.

The street was quiet, and only the muffled sounds of pub conversations and music could be heard, and Elise's tinkling laughter overlay the background sounds. He loved it when she laughed; she made him feel as if he were in a soppy rom-com. Stefan heard voices and raucous laughter in the distance. Glancing up the street, he noticed a group of teenagers approaching on the other side, their movements animated and exaggerated.

Stefan knew he had overdone it with the brandy. As the hooded teenagers passed, they fell into silence, each one of them, six in total, glared over at them. Stefan narrowed his eyes, feeling the need to see their faces. Were they looking at them? There was no one else on the street. Perhaps they were more interested in the restaurant. Stefan couldn't be sure. He wanted to be sure. His heartbeat ramped up, his palms became clammy and moist. He looked down at Elise, happily chattering away, her arm linked tightly with his; she appeared not to notice the sudden change in climate.

The group crossed the road toward them, and everything slowed down, Stefan felt they should return inside to the safety of the restaurant, yet he was frozen to the spot.

Too late, the group were upon them. A fist connected with his chin, the world around him seemed to express into fast forward as he hit the ground. A dark cloud of hoods above him, the sound of kicking and punching yet Stefan couldn't feel a thing. He tried to turn his head to find Elise, but he couldn't see her, he didn't hear her. Darkness enveloped him.

CHAPTER THIRTY-FIVE

"I thought you said he was going to be fine?" The sound of Elise's worried voice bought Stefan round. He could feel her small soft hands gently placed on top of his. Wincing as he attempted to open his eyes, the pain was excruciating, and he let out a small grunt of pain.

"Stefan, Stefan, it's me. Elise." He couldn't see her, but her voice sounded different, as if she were having difficulty speaking. He tried again to open his eyes.

"Okay, Mr. Mademan, try to relax. Don't try to open your eyes. They're badly swollen." Stefan felt the gentle weight of a hand on his shoulder. A male doctor.

"Stefan, everything's going to be okay. The doctors are looking after you. Can you hear me, Stefan? Can he hear me?" Elise turned to the doctor, sounding impatient and desperate.

"Yes, he should be able to hear you." The doctor answered. Stefan read the little note of annoyance in his voice.

Stefan felt Elise's breath close to his ear. "Squeeze my hand a little if you can hear me." Stefan gave her hand a slight squeeze. Footsteps, departing, those of the doctor, he thought.

"Do you remember what happened?" Elise's constant questions gave Stefan a sense of foreboding. Stefan squeezed again, this time firmer, wanting to give her strength when all he truly felt was fear.

Stefan remembered everything. This was it, what he had been waiting for, what he had expected. He knew it would come: he hadn't envisioned it would happen so quickly perhaps, but he knew it would come and expected more. This was his life now, Elise's life too; he wasn't sure whether she had been ready and prepared for all of this. Writing letters, visiting, it was all quite anonymous, but they had both known that once he was free, things would change. Stefan doubted whether Elise would be able to stand beside him for any length of time. Stefan felt bile rising in his throat, he was going to die, he didn't want it to be some painful random beating from thugs in the street, if he had to die and he would try his best to survive, then he wanted to be in control of that, he would take his own life. He'd survived twenty years in prison with some of the most violent prisoners in the country, to come out to this treatment only served to anger him more. How dare they.

Elise had done a marvelous job disguising him. He hadn't recognized himself, so how those kids knew who he was, was beyond him. He threw his mind back to the restaurant: he could see a clear picture of everyone dining, no one paying any particular attention to him; he remembered stepping outside; the hooded group, vicious in their attack and their words. After the first blow, he had only heard a loud buzzing but now he remembered, grunting and chanting, "Nonce, paedo, fucking freak."

At the beginning of his sentence, he'd experienced recurring dreams, faceless assassins coming for him in the night. The only difference was he was still alive and he wasn't sure that he was one hundred percent grateful for it. The dreams had stopped after the first few months, and he hadn't remembered them till now.

Stefan lifted his hand trying to find Elise's face, but he withdrew quickly. Her face was bandaged.

"I'm okay—just a little cut, that's all," Elise reassured him. He could hear her holding back. There was more, he could feel it; she was protecting him. He had put her in danger, and all along he knew that being involved with her could only end in catastrophe. Only one quiet night out and he had been spotted and now people would know what Elise looked like too. He should never have agreed to this relationship; he knew it was selfish. He wanted to believe that there was someone in the world who could look past his crimes and take the time to get to know the whole man and she had come along and shaken up his whole world. How could he let go now? He knew he should, but he didn't want to. And why should he? She was an adult. She must have realized at some stage what she was getting herself into. She wouldn't leave him now, surely not. He squeezed her hand tighter, willing his eyes to open so he could see her, allow her to see just how much he needed her.

"Ms. Miles, Mr. Mademan." SIO Octavia Middleton stepped into the room, followed by DCI Mark West.

"I'm SIO Middleton, senior investigating officer and this is my colleague, DCI West."

Stefan gasped and wheezed. He had plenty to say but he was out of breath, as if a tremendous weight sat in the middle of his chest. Elise felt his grip loosen, and she squeezed his hand reassuringly.

"Yes." Elise was cautious. Stefan noted her immediate defensiveness.

"We've spoken to witnesses at the scene, so we have a very detailed explanation of what happened tonight, but we do need your account of the evening's events, if you feel up to it?"

"We were attacked by thugs in hoods. I didn't see their faces. They were all dressed in dark clothes, all male as far as I know, by their voices."

"Do you have any idea, why they...."

"Yes, and I know that you know why they attacked us, so let's not play games and waste any time here. We all know. That doesn't make this right."

"I'm sorry, Elise. Can I call you Elise?"

"That's my name, SIO Middleton. Have you caught them?"

"Not yet, but we are going to need statements from both of you as soon as you feel up to it."

"As you can see, we're not."

"That's fine. When you're ready." SIO Middleton handed her card to Elise. Stefan heard the two sets of footsteps leaving then stop.

"Oh, one thing, Elise. Did you tell anyone that you were dining at Lorenzo's this evening?" DCI West enquired. Middleton frowned, she hadn't told him to ask any questions. She had bought him along on a whim, and he wasn't even on her team.

"No. I didn't tell a soul. Stefan didn't even know where we were going until we got there."

"Did you make a reservation?" DCI West pushed.

"No, we just turned up." Stefan squeezed Elise's hand, which didn't go unnoticed by either of the officers.

"So no one knew, no family members, friends?" Both Elise and Stefan knew that the police must already know that Elise had reserved the table.

"I just told you, not one person knew." Elise stuck to her guns. West was agitating her. Middleton gestured for him to follow her.

"No problem. Give us a call when you're ready." SOI Middleton led the way and they left.

Stefan could feel the atmosphere thick around him. The only reassurance he had that Elise had not left him alone was her hand holding his. He didn't understand why she had lied; there was no reason at all for her to lie. She began stroking his hand with a firmness that did not feel gentle and soothing, but more hostile and aggressive.

"Wankers." Elise hissed.

"Trying to make out this was my fault. No one knows about us. I made the reservation in my name, a table for two under Ms. Miles. How could anyone deduce that I would be accompanied by you?" Elise spat, her face contorted and twisted.

Elise sounded bitter and angry. Stefan couldn't imagine Elise's face in his mind's eye. He had never heard her sounding so defiant and he was surprised at the level of venom entwined in her words. Stefan enjoyed her disgust of the police; he hated them, the way they had treated him, their embellishments of the truth, and they hated him, and he hated them and here was his little miss goody two shoes hating them too.

"We should go." Elise whispered into his ear, followed by a delicate kiss on his cheek.

"If we stay, they're only going to draw more attention to us. We'll become prisoners in our own home. I can't bear the idea of them snooping around and trying to tell us what to do."

Stefan couldn't have agreed more: the further away from the prying eyes of the law, the better, as far as he was concerned. He so wanted to speak but even breathing was painful. He had many questions but right now getting back to the flat was the most appealing.

"I'm going to go and get the car, pack some things, and we're out of here." Stefan squeezed her hand, again trying to open his eyes and speak at the same time. When she said leave, he had hoped that she meant leave the hospital, not the flat. He had to let his probation officer know where they were going. He had expected him to come to the hospital, though he wasn't surprised at his lack of interest. He'd hadn't been out of prison for twenty-four hours and he was already fearing for his life.

Stefan felt a sharp plastic tube pushing roughly against his lips.

"Try and drink some water. The doctor said that you should keep hydrated." Elise persisted and Stefan was able to moisten his dry, cracked lips a little. He cleared his throat.

"My uncle has a cottage in Buxton, the Peak District. We can stay there for as long as we like." Elise was thinking out loud, paying little attention to the fear rising in Stefan. He squeezed her hand intermittently, but it was if she was totally unaware of his presence.

"I'll discharge you, and we can be on the motorway in a couple of hours." Stefan squeezed her hand as hard as he could. They couldn't just leave—why should they run away? Part of him wanted to just disappear, to another country perhaps: he'd always fancied Thailand, or Brazil, even. Their problems would only follow them down to the Peak District. If a group of thugs recognized him on a simple and innocent night out, they stood no chance. There was nowhere safe, and they would have to inform his probation officer. He felt weak, lifeless; the energy had been drained out of him, his thoughts cloudy, and he felt confused. He had butterflies and not the fluttering, pleasant kind; these butterflies were dense, murky, and churned around his stomach, leaving a trail of menace in their wake.

CHAPTER THIRTY-SIX

Elise guided Stefan out of the hospital lift to the basement car park. It was well lit, and people were coming and going. Seeing two bandaged and injured individuals was no surprising scene, and no one paid them any mind. Stefan had six broken ribs, a broken nose, and both his eyes blackened. Elise had a small but wide gash beneath her left eye and a broken arm. The hospital and police had advised that they should both stay put, at least overnight, but Elise had made her mind up. The thought of the papers arriving and camping outside awaiting their discharge was more than she could cope with right now. They had to get out of there immediately; they had to get away. Stefan felt Elise's steps slowing as they approached the car.

"The little cowards gave us a spray job. Nothing I can't sort out with a few paint strokes. I'll get a few coats over it, and we can hop straight on the motorway."

Stefan was glad he couldn't see what was sprayed onto the car. He could imagine, "Die, paedo." Elise guided him to the passenger side and opened the door. Stefan stopped and leaned his hand against the roof of the car. Elise looked up at him. Elise could see that Stefan was feeling overwhelmed, almost as if he wanted to give up, but there was no way she was giving up, not after having invested so much of her time and dreams into him. She had plans for her life. She had thought that Stefan was made of stronger stuff, but twenty years in prison had clearly not made a hard man out of him. She gave him a nudge.

"The sooner we leave, the better." Her word was final.

Elise opened the car door, and Stefan eased himself inside. The little bastards had really wanted to make their mark and had succeeded. Elise was right: they couldn't stay.

CHAPTER THIRTY-SEVEN

They hit the motorway at around three o'clock in the morning. Elise had packed the bare minimum, stating that the cottage was fully furnished and they'd need for nothing. She had crudely sloshed red gloss paint up and down both wings and doors of the car, covering the vile vandalism. Stefan sat helplessly until she guided him from the flat and back to the car. He wanted to ask what injuries she had; it couldn't have been all that bad because she seemed to be coping just fine. She was a tough cookie. Stefan was truly only now seeing how tough.

Stefan had shown great concern for Elise driving with only one good arm, but Elise had just got on with it. Stefan saw Elise's determination and true strength, and he admired her. Nothing fazed her: she saw what needed to be done and got on with it.

Elise had filled two large flasks, one with warm water and the other with strong black coffee. She encouraged him to take small sips of the warm water. The hospital had advised to keep him hydrated. The coffee was her beverage of choice, as there was a long night's drive ahead.

"Not what we planned, eh?" Her voice high-pitched and bordering hysteria. Child-like and agitated, Stefan knew she was freaking out.

Stefan sighed loudly and reached out, finding her thigh, and he rested his hand. She tensed, jamming hard onto the clutch, and the car stalled, flinging them both forward. Stefan reached forward and held onto the dashboard, grateful that he couldn't see at that moment. Elise gave more gas.

"The cottage is lovely. Two bedrooms, both en suite, two living rooms; there's a den and a basement. Plenty of room, and the back garden is half an acre, apple and pear trees: it's really something to see. No one has to know we're there. The village is about five minutes by car, twenty if you're walking, but we can get groceries delivered and we'll want for nothing. It's safe and secluded."

Stefan relaxed back in his seat. The cottage sounded perfect. They could both get themselves back to full health and work out their next steps. Stefan didn't like the idea of being totally secluded, since if anyone found out where they were, they were sitting ducks. For now it would do; with Elise by his side he felt safe. She took care of everything and he was looking forward to the time where he could take his rightful place in the relationship. The more he thought about it, the more he realized that she would follow him to the end of the world and back. She wasn't going to just let go and walk away because of his desires and needs; of course she would stand by him. She was prepared to pack up her whole life to be with him and anyway, so she wouldn't have much choice.

We're coming off the motorway now, not far to go."

Stefan floated in and out of a disturbed sleep, assured that Elise had everything under control.

CHAPTER THIRTY-EIGHT

MAY 8, 2005

The sun rose high and early as Elise pulled up to the little cottage, following the driveway off the road which led around to the rear of the cottage. Beyond the cottage's expanse of garden, they were surrounded by lush green fields. The road they had taken could be viewed in the distance, making it easy to see any cars or people approaching from either direction.

Elise watched Stefan as he snored lightly, his seat reclined, his breath even and calm. Elise was satisfied. No one was going to find them here, not if she had anything to do with it.

She left Stefan to sleep, gathering their belongings from the boot of the car and entered the cottage. Elise hurried around, placing fresh sheets on the bed, closing the curtains of the bedroom, and filling the kettle. They were totally alone in the middle of nowhere.

Making her way back out to the car, she found Stefan still sound asleep. She wanted to wake him, but watched. Stefan stirred, sensing her presence automatically; he forced his eyes open, and it took some doing but they cracked open. He winced and shut them immediately. The sun bright and searing, Elise appeared as a silhouette, bigger, broader, sinister. Stefan flinched noticeably: the pain killers were having a very strange effect on him. He held up his heavy arm to shield him from the sun, while nausea rose in his throat, apprehensive to re-open his eyes.

Elise opened the car door, leaned in and pecked him on the cheek. "Wakey, wakey sleepy head. We're here." Elise gently took his hand and helped him from the car. Stefan's body ached all over, his legs stiff and sore, his head throbbed, and his throat dry as sandpaper. This was not how he had planned on spending their first forty-eight hours. He noticed the car was different. He was sure that they had started their journey in Elise's red VW, but now they were in a black Ford KA. He was confused, and he turned to Elise to ask what happened to the car, but he whispered incoherently. His tongue felt heavy in his mouth, and he needed to lie down, take the weight off his feet, and rest.

CHAPTER THIRTY-NINE

MAY 8, 2005

Stefan slept soundly for thirteen hours, awakening only to the sound of Elise's mobile. Now able to open his eyes a crack, he saw Elise sitting in a chair beside his bed. Her mobile rang constantly.

"Don't you want to answer that?" Stefan croaked surprised at the sound of his own voice.

"No, no. They'll leave a message if it's important. You must be hungry." Elise spoke over the persistent trill of her phone.

"Who is it?"

"No one important." Elise rose from her chair, and Stefan saw that all was not well.

"Answer the phone." Stefan tried to sit up in bed. Elise rushed to his side.

"Okay, you rest. I'll answer."

Elise answered the phone whilst tapping Stefan's shoulder.

"Elise? Elise Miles, this is SIO Middleton."

"What do you want?"

"I'd like to know how you and Mr. Mademan are doing? You discharged yourselves from the hospital and…"

"We're just fine."

"You haven't returned home?"

"No."

"Are you safe? You know, Mr. Mademan has been paroled to your address in…."

Elise hung up the phone.

"The police, they want to know where we are."

"We have to call my probation officer."

"No we don't. We don't have to do anything."

"Elise, if we don't return to the flat or let him know where we are, they'll come looking for me."

Elise shook her head in response and walked over to the bedroom door, turning to face him.

"I have a delicious lasagna in the oven." She left the room, closing the door behind her.

Stefan didn't want to go back to prison and Elise was overthinking the whole thing. All they had to do was let his probation officer know what had happened and where they were, and everything would be fine.

Stefan tried to swing his legs out of the bed, but he felt lethargic and sluggish. He was in a lot of pain, his feet heavy to lift from the ground. He heard Elise's phone ringing and she was answering; he just had to let the police know where he was, and all would be well. Stefan staggered across to the bedroom door. His legs gave way beneath him, and he fell to his knees gripping the door handle. He pulled it downwards. The door was locked.

"Elise. Elise!" He croaked, knowing there was no way she would be able to hear him.

"What do you want?" Elise spoke in a harsh whisper.

"Those kids filmed the beating last night. Your image is clear and is circulating all over social media as we speak. Just tell us where you are and we'll make sure you're protected. That's all you need to do. Elise?"

"Stefan is mine, and the best thing you can do is leave us alone."

"You are in danger. Forget about Stefan for a minute. *You* are in danger, Elise."

Elise hung up.

CHAPTER FORTY

Elise pulled the lasagna out of the oven, inhaling deeply, taking in the fresh aroma. "Perfect."

She cut into the lasagna, a generous piece for Stefan and just a sliver for herself.

Stefan was sitting on the floor besides the door when she entered.

"Here we go. It's delicious."

"The door was locked." Stefan was frustrated. Had she even noticed that he was sitting there on the floor?

Elise placed the tray down on the table and tried to help Stefan into a chair.

"The damn door was locked, Elise." His voice rose an octave.

"I'm keeping you safe. I'm looking after you." Stefan frowned. She sounded mechanical, robot-like. He recognized, though, that she had no sleep at all. He didn't know how she was still standing. Everything she did, she did for him, and he was getting used to being taken care of. She made him feel secure, the cottage was picturesque and solid, and there was really nothing to worry about.

"You said we were safe here. No one knows we're here. Do they?"

"Let's get you back into bed."

Stefan allowed Elise to help him back to the bed. She lifted his legs one by one, propping up his pillows and gently pushing him back.

"You need to eat. It's your favorite." Elise placed the tray in front of him, handing him the knife and fork.

Stefan was hungry and the dish smelled delicious. He slowly cut into the lasagna and took a mouthful.

"Wow. You made this?" Stefan tucked in. Elise watched on, ecstatic that he was enjoying her cooking and eating heartily. She couldn't keep her eyes off him.

"We need to call my probation officer. They won't stop calling until we do."

"I'll call them first thing. I promise."

Stefan nodded and continued eating.

CHAPTER FORTY-ONE

8 MAY 2005

There was nothing Nigel Pemberton wanted more than to get the promotion he had worked so hard to achieve. Nothing else in the world mattered and it wasn't about the money. He wanted to make his mark, and to him this was the job and the role that would showcase his talents to the world, the world which he occupied: the West Midlands Metropolitan Police. He didn't care about the notoriety outside the region; he wanted to be a big fish in a medium-sized pond.

Thirty years of age, unmarried, no baggage or ties. All was his for the taking, and he wasn't going to allow anything to stand in his way. Often, he looked for cases that he believed would bring him notoriety, let the bigwigs at the top see his progress and true potential, allowing him to rise. He didn't want the role that required sitting behind a desk giving orders, or meetings that lasted all day, traveling around the country, addressing politicians and the like. He was the man on the ground, desperate to be seen as intelligent and smart, a man who would get the job done, right in the thick of things, taking action, risking his life. He actively sought the most difficult situations and put himself smack bang in the middle, most of the time not really having a clue what he was doing but always finding a way out, a way out that made him the hero. It was the rush that he chased after. He was addicted. He'd had a few scrapes over the years, putting himself in the wrong place at the wrong time with some of the most dangerous people in the country but he always came out unscathed. This is how he wanted to live. Solving crimes, catching the bad guys, making the impossible, possible, living on the edge. This was his calling and he took his calling seriously.

The role he coveted so desperately was SIO, Senior Investigating Officer, the role of his superstar superior Octavia Middleton. She had bought down one of the most dangerous and elusive crime leaders in the United Kingdom and was now circling his associates. Her hard work, wit, and relentless drive had bought about changes in the way the police force dealt with cases such as these. Receiving the Police Bravery award and Investigation of the Year awards, she was like an express train, with one destination, no stops, she was going all the way, and the best part about it all, she was humble. Nigel not only respected Octavia he also found her devastatingly beautiful. She had recently moved to the region, had made her mark and was now looking to make a huge leap forward again. Nothing stopped this woman. Nigel had tried his best to get her attention through his work, but she never seemed to notice him. The first day she had arrived, his colleagues had nicknamed her Campbell, as in Naomi. She was a sight for sore eyes, tall, slender, a true firecracker with an abundant afro that framed her ebony fine features with the smoothest dark chocolate skin. She was like an Amazonian princess: gleaming teeth and sparkling determined eyes.

He'd heard through the rumor mill that she was heading off to pastures new, being promoted again and moving to Scotland Yard. He thought that getting to know her could perhaps help him move forward. Simply being associated with her, being able to say he'd worked with her held sway.

Kent had asked him to dig into the Farmhouse children's home and that was exactly what he would do. Kent never asked him for anything. It was Nigel's absolute pleasure to be able to do Kent a favor, be of assistance. Kent had been Nigel's wingman for their entire lives. Two sides of the same coin. Kent had known that Shauna was the girl for him right from day one and Nigel was in no position to influence or change that, neither did he want to. Nigel had had many girlfriends but had never connected with a girl the way that Kent had with Shauna. He like Shauna, aloof at times but no one could question her feelings toward Kent, always putting him first, right by his side and Kent was a happier man for it. She didn't seem bothered by the glitz and glamour of Kent's business, had never been. If Kent thought she was a winner, then so did he.

Nigel was in no way jealous, and he wanted Kent to be happy. Up until Kent had met Shauna, they were on the same track, dating girls, playing the field, and enjoying their teenage years. As soon as Kent met Shauna, Nigel saw the change immediately. Kent wanted to plan his future, he was looking ahead, whereas the two of them usually didn't have a plan for the day ahead, let alone years.

Shauna grabbed Kent's attention and everything else slotted into second place. So long as Kent got what he wanted, Nigel was happy, in fact Kent and Shauna's relationship only cemented his determination to get what he wanted out of life. He didn't care about the big house, marriage, and kids. He cared about living every single day as an adventure, and his adventure did not include getting hitched and finding the woman of his dreams, though he had admitted to himself that Octavia was the first woman to really capture his imagination. Instead of daydreaming about settling down with her, he dreamt of the two of them as a team on the same track, with the same goals in mind and, of course, amazing sex.

Nigel had never let Kent down in his life and this being the first time he had chance to get down to the archives, he grabbed a coffee and headed down to Liza the archives administrator.

"Hey you." Liza was a bubbly and cheerful soul whom Nigel had slept with twice, once at the Christmas party a year ago and the second after working his most recent case pulling an all-nighter. He had flirted lightly to see where the land lay, and she had accepted his charms. She too was not looking for anything serious as a recent divorcee she wanted to live a little, let her hair down and the bonus being able to boast to the other fitter, more attractive, in her eyes, female officers. Nigel received plenty of attention, though he was choosy. He could sense the ladies that wanted to settle down and those that were happy for an evening of pure lust. He was open, letting every potential conquest know he had no intention or desire to start a relationship or explore those parameters, it was all good fun, if they were up for it.

Many had simply appreciated his truthfulness and declined his advances or more often than not, tried to prove to him that he just needed a good woman and he would be ready to settle, the latter always had him headed in the opposite direction. Honesty was the best policy when it came to the opposite sex though, at times, he almost felt as if some women wanted him to lie to them. Tell them he was searching for the right woman. He found it absurd. No, no, he could do without the drama, if they were like-minded, it was win, win.

Straight up and open was the name of the game and this had gained him more fans. Some believed he'd had some major heartbreak and that he didn't want to get hurt again, which only made him more endearing. Nigel, a strong, muscular six foot two, twinkly topaz blue eyes, and dark wavy hair which he spent little to no time on. His apparent disregard for his appearance only served to add to his allure. Women saw him as a diamond in the rough. He needed a woman's touch, but the thing most women found irresistible about Nigel was the fact that he didn't know how handsome he really was.

"Hey, happy lady. I've got a couple of report numbers here I need the files on." Nigel lent over the counter giving Liza a wink and a cheeky grin; he handed the piece of paper with the numbers written on.

Liza gave her best smile and took the piece of paper. "Erm, these will be way back. Can you give me a couple of hours?"

"Sure, I can't come and help you. I mean, if it's way down in the back."

"You're such a gent, but you know I can't let you do my job." Liza raised an eyebrow as if tempting him to persuade her.

"You're busy, right?"

"Uh huh."

"So let me take a little weight off." Nigel raised his eyebrows as if this was the most reasonable and gallant offer she was going to get all day.

Liza needed little persuasion: she unlocked and lifted the hatch, stepping back to allow Nigel access.

He pecked her on the cheek and took the piece of paper from her hand as he passed.

"Angel."

"I know this." She countered.

Nigel disappeared around the corner.

"I'm on lunch in forty," she called after him.

"Back in ten." He strode down the corridor, lifting his arm in the air and giving a thumbs up.

Nigel made his way along a corridor of mud brown-painted doors, beside each door, was a board listing the file numbers stored in each room, he scanned each briefly as he flitted past.

Finally, coming across the correct list, he pushed the door open, the compact room filled from floor to ceiling with old metal shelves holding decrepit archive boxes. He began scouring the labels of each box, finding the relevant one almost immediately. He dragged it toward him; taking the weight into his stomach, he slid the box down from the shelf, removed the lid, and began sifting through the folders inside.

"Yep." He pulled out a weathered buff-colored folder. Checking the short list of police numbers he had scrawled down on the piece of paper, he located the police report numbers that Kent had given him. Crouching down he sped read through the report. Kent had clearly stated that his enquiry was about Shauna. But he couldn't see any link with Shauna. The children named in the report were Karen and Dane, who had been admitted to a secure facility for children, but it was no ordinary children's home. The Farmhouse was a home for children who had committed serious crimes.

Nigel sank back onto the floor. He hadn't really known what to expect when Kent had asked him to look in to this but he couldn't find the link to Shauna? It didn't fit together at all. There were reports from a child psychologist documenting three years of therapy sessions. Most of which described the named children as having suffered some sort of terrible tragedy. Nigel couldn't focus. There was some link, there had to be. What exactly was Kent looking for? Why did he have these random police numbers and what did Shauna have to do with this lot?

Nigel continued scanning through the official papers of Karen and Dane Woods. Why would Shauna be keeping documents on some random kids? On further inspection, something struck him, there were two children and their dates of birth. The date of birth for Karen Woods stood out on the page, illuminated. Nigel's heart skipped a beat. Karen Woods had the same date of birth as Shauna. He couldn't be sure of Dane's exact date of birth, but the year seemed about right. Nigel doubted himself. It didn't fit. Shauna had a brother but no sister. The best thing he could do was report back to Kent and find out what the hell was going on.

Nigel thought for a moment, "Shauna and Lee had their names changed?" The more he read, the more he thought that there had been some mix-up and there seemed to be a whole batch of information missing. Nigel turned to the back of the file noticing where a sheet of paper had been glued and indicated that this file was connected to others, a list of files which would, Nigel hoped, give further answers.

One thing he knew for sure was that Shauna or Karen had been involved in something a lot bigger than petty crime. Nigel wasn't sure that he should dig deeper; he wanted to know for his own benefit, but he didn't know how he was supposed to repeat this all back to Kent and more importantly whether he should. Telling Kent what he had found was all well and good but of course Kent too would ask the very same questions that he had.

Digging further would give Kent the answers but were they answers that he'd want to hear and worse still, Nigel just couldn't start reeling out details of past cases to his mate just because he'd asked. Other people were involved and that wasn't what he was about. Yes, he'd bent a few rules and regulations in the past, but they had always been in the best interest of his cases. Nigel wasn't sure whose best interests were at stake here.

Nigel looked up at the empty space from where he'd taken the box, and he looked back down to the list. The file numbers were mostly in order, and the next three boxes along from the empty space were the boxes listed. Nigel stared at the boxes; he'd never been in a predicament such as this before. On the one hand, he really wanted to give Kent peace of mind, and whatever Kent thought this was all about, he wanted to be the one to allay his worries. On the other hand, what if Shauna had been involved in some-thing that Kent should know about? It would then be on his shoulders to divulge the information. Was he ready for that?

The door swung open startling Nigel, and Octavia stood in the door-way. She cocked her head to the side as if sizing him up. Nigel jumped to his feet dropping the file to the floor. Both their eyes went down to the scattered papers. She slowly raised her eyes up the full length of Nigel's body, taking in every detail appreciatively. Nigel was knocked off-kilter for a moment, was she checking him out?

"Hey, I'm sergeant...." Nigel held out his hand.

"Nigel Pemberton. I know." Octavia took his hand in hers and gave it a firm shake. Nigel noticed the softness of her hands, her elegant fingers and inhaled a waft of her intoxicating perfume.

"Oh, erm, nice to meet you sup...."

"Octavia."

There was a long pause, their hands still clasped together. Octavia gently eased her hand from Nigel's.

"Busy?" She gestured toward the files on the floor.

"Yes. I mean well, to be honest with you, I'm just...." Nigel paused he wasn't sure whether to tell her exactly what he was doing. Octavia had never even looked in his direction before; this was his opportunity to impress her not show her that he was acting unprofessionally.

Octavia crouched down and began collecting the scattered paperwork from the floor and slipped them back into the file, Nigel joined her.

"Look I'm going to be honest with you."

Octavia nodded, amused. "Good start." She smiled, and his heart pounded in his chest.

"A friend of mine asked me to check out a couple of crime report numbers and I just thought..."

"You'd have a little dig?" Octavia clasped the file to her chest, raising her eyebrows.

"I don't usually do this sort of thing but he's a good friend and I didn't think for one second that..."

Octavia rose and held out her hand. Nigel took her hand, not for support but he saw this as a gesture of friendship and wanted to touch her again.

"Look, we've all done it, stop panicking. If this is really your first time trying to get some information unrelated to your work, then you're a finer officer than me. Perks of the job."

Nigel breathed easy. She made him feel totally relaxed. A tiny part of him felt she was making a mental and it would inevitably catch up with him at a later date but for now she seemed genuine. And so beautiful.

"Find what you were looking for?" Octavia enquired as she slotted the files back into the box.

"Not really. The notes here suggest I look into the next three boxes but I'm worried about what I might find."

Octavia nodded sympathetically.

"Interesting, though."

"What is?" Nigel queried.

"I'm looking into the Stefan Mademan case. The next three boxes."

Nigel swallowed slowly, trying to not to look shocked. He knew exactly who Stefan Mademan was and if there was a connection between Shauna, Lee, and Mademan, he could only guess that this was not the type of information he wanted to relay back to Kent.

"Don't look so worried. Help me back to my office with these and let's see what we come up with."

Nigel's heart beat a little faster. He could not believe his luck.

CHAPTER FORTY-TWO

Octavia directed Nigel to place the boxes on the floor near to her desk. He noted that Octavia was not at all organized. There were files piled on every conceivable space.

"Coffee?" Octavia asked as she placed two of the boxes on top of the boxes Nigel had put on the floor. Nigel didn't want yet another coffee but didn't want to refuse.

"Yeah, two sugars and a little milk."

Octavia left the office, leaving the door open. Octavia's awards and accolades took pride of place on a filing cabinet closest to her desk. There were several pictures of her receiving her awards. Nigel knew that she wasn't married and was pleased to see there were no pictures of children. He removed files from a seat in front of her desk. Nigel felt nervous, he'd dreamt of getting Octavia's attention and now here he was, in her office. He wanted desperately to impress her and prove himself to her. He tried to think of a strategy to keep her company after this little tête-à-tête, how he could perhaps worm his way into her team but he couldn't think straight, visions of her kissing him pushed all professional thoughts to one side.

Octavia returned, tipping the door behind her with her foot.

"So, Nigel, what's it all about, eh?" She pushed aside a pile of files on her desk and rested a mug in front of him, taking a seat up close and personal, she sipped her coffee and waited for the down low.

"Look. My friend, he's about to get married to this, I mean she's a great woman, she's got everything going for her, but about a week ago, he called me up and asked if I could find out the details on a couple of crime numbers."

"Which is the file you were looking through?"

"Yes."

"No harm, but you know that Mademan is missing right now, don't you?"

"Yeah, but what's Mademan got to do with Shauna? I probably need to take a look through these." Nigel stood and went to flip the lid off the top box.

"Is he a very good friend?" Octavia placed her hand over the lid, preventing him from opening the box.

"The only friend." Nigel held onto the box.

"In my experience, sometimes, most of the time, people think they want to know it all, especially when it comes to a potential life partner but the truth of it is, we don't truly want to know everything."

Nigel hesitated, he knew she was right, once he read through these files, he couldn't unread what he found and he didn't want to hide anything from Kent.

"My advice to you is, tell your good friend as little as possible. If his wife to be is a good woman, he won't need to know more than that."

Nigel nodded, unsure of what to say next, slowly dropping his hand from the box, he drank his coffee.

"As you perhaps know, Mademan is on the missing list. He and his fiancée were attacked last night, hasn't contacted his probation officer, and as of this morning, isn't at his probation address."

"I heard the attackers were baying for blood." Nigel couldn't help it: he wondered how on earth Shauna could be mixed up with the likes of Mademan. He could take an educated guess but decided on omitting the connection to Mademan to Kent. He did not want to be the bearer of crazy news, and it may be better to speak to Shauna and tell her to tell Kent straight herself. That proposition didn't sit well with him either, he wasn't supposed to be digging, the fewer people who knew about this the better. Maybe he should just keep his nose of Kent's business—full stop. He felt better now that he had a plan.

"Yes and plenty of it. Wherever they're hiding out, is probably the best place for them."

"And the cases are definitely linked?" Nigel already knew the answer; the thought of one of the most prolific child abusers in the country with his hands on Shauna sent a shiver down his spine.

Octavia nodded. Nigel's heart sank. I

f Shauna was one of Mademan's victims he could only imagine what she may have been through and how Kent would feel with that knowledge.

He knew Kent well enough to know he'd only want to protect her. It might even make them stronger if that was at all possible but that would be down to Kent. On the other hand, if Kent knowing was all too much for Shauna, which was perhaps why she hadn't opened up to Kent in the first place, this could end their relationship and Nigel was not about to cause his best friend heartache, there was just no way. Nigel was grateful to Octavia for preventing a catastrophe.

"Children are the living message we send to a time we will not see."

—John F. Kennedy

CHAPTER FORTY-THREE

Shauna had exactly an hour and a half before she would have to be back in her office and she was never late. She was punctual to a fault and felt that everyone should have the same ethics. It was simple, if she said she would be somewhere at a particular time, then she would be. There were no excuses or reasons to veer from her word except of course in exceptional circumstances, which in Shauna's life there were none, not so far.

Shauna visited her brother every other day. She had fought for many years for him to come and live with her and Kent, but the hospital had recommended numerous times that he would be safer with twenty-four-hour care, something that she was simply not able to give. There was no reason for her to feel guilty yet every time she had to leave him, her sense of abandonment gripped her heart like a vice. They had each other, there was no family to speak of. Lee stayed with them for a week at Christmas and went on holidays with them, he had never been a problem.

Lee had been diagnosed with Asperger's at the age of thirteen, though Shauna did not at all agree with the diagnosis. Lee was capable of interacting in social situations. People loved him. He was a bundle of laughs, had a terrific sense of humor, and he could look after himself to a certain extent.

At the age of twelve he had been knocked down by a car, and he had got up and walked away with a fractured arm. When Shauna had asked him what had happened, he simply said that he was crossing the road.

"Yes, but did you see the car coming?" Shauna had persisted.

Lee had rolled his eyes in exasperation. "Of course I saw the car coming. There were lots of cars coming. I told them to wait."

"What do you mean?" Shauna was almost fearful of what his response might be.

"I put my hand up and crossed. The cars are supposed to stop." Lee was very matter of fact.

"No, you are supposed to go to the crossroads and wait for the cars to stop: you know that."

He had pondered a while on Shauna's words then answered.

"If I was driving and I saw me crossing the road, I would stop."

It made sense to Shauna, in a way, but they were simply not the rules of the road. Not only had he hurt himself, but the outcome could have involved others.

On another occasion, he had become extremely upset and violent with a classmate who had shot a Magpie with a pellet gun for fun. Lee had wrestled the pellet gun from the boy and shot him in chest with it. When asked, he had explained that he wanted to show the boy what it felt like.

Lee had his own rules, his own way of dealing with situations, and this had often ended with someone including himself getting hurt. To Shauna, it was as if he believed that he was invincible. He had on more than one occasion jumped out of windows, stating that it was quicker than the stairs.

Shauna had taken him to myriad doctors and specialists, some suggesting there was nothing wrong with him and others concluding that he was high up on the Autistic spectrum. He had been sectioned at age fourteen after watching a documentary on YouTube about the war in Iraq. He had flown into a rage, running out on to the streets, screaming incoherently. It had taken six police men to hold him down. Shauna had been contacted at college and had immediately made her way to the hospital. He was inconsolable, he couldn't understand why people hurt other people, it was as simple as that and Shauna's explanations only tipped him over the edge. It had been a difficult time for Shauna. Lee knew he was right and believed he could change the world, all by himself. Shauna's heart was broken. She had so many hopes for him, to live a happy life, especially after their childhood had ended so early and abruptly.

The hospital looked after him well, Shauna made sure of that. He had his own room, a TV, a DVD player, he loved movies and his first love, painting. He only painted landscapes and nature. Shauna recognized many of his paintings to be from their childhood—the parks, the fields, the open spaces where they had played. He had always adored the outdoors, and this showed in his art, he was particularly gifted. Shauna, upon Kent's advice, had set up a Facebook page and Lee's work sold extremely well. She was so proud of him. Lee didn't really understand the concept of money; he'd never had to worry about it, or spend it, and it meant nothing to him. All of Lee's concerns centered around his art, his room, and Shauna.

Shauna knocked on the door whilst peeping through the wired glass pane. Lee, sat at his little stool, paint brush in hand, in front of his easel; he spun around and grinned. Shauna stepped inside the room and embraced him.

"How are you, soldier?"

"Painting."

"Yes, this is beautiful. Really stunning."

Lee stood back proudly, allowing Shauna room to explore his latest work. The bright hues of the yellows leapt from the canvas and warmed the whole room. This was perhaps one of the largest canvases Lee had painted and it was impressive.

"Buttercups," Lee uttered.

"Hmmm. It's really, really lovely," Shauna whispered as she gazed in closer and took steps around the painting, taking in its glory from all angles. He had never drawn buttercups before.

Lee was always excited to see Shauna's reaction to his work. The staff at the hospital constantly sung his praises and told him how amazing he was, his doctors too. Lee had painted for them all, giving them his art as gifts but the only person he wanted to impress was Shauna.

Shauna knew nothing about art, it had been Kent's idea to put Lee's work up for sale online. Kent had priced the artwork and had many pieces in his restaurant Sloan's which was where Lee's work had become some-what famous.

"They're buttercups." Lee needed more of a response and Shauna knew it.

"Yes, they're absolutely beautiful buttercups." Shauna held back. Lee's memories and fixations could at times throw him into terrible and destructive fits of anger. Shauna was always careful to gauge his mood and temperament, but even she sometimes got it wrong.

"Buttercups from the fields?" Shauna chose her words carefully.

Lee, still with paint brush in hand slammed the heel of his hand against his forehead.

"No, no. Yes, from the fields but here, too." He raced to the other side of the room, to his bedside cabinet, and grabbed a small envelope which had typed in small font "Shauna Kelly." Shana took the envelope and opened it, inside were a small cluster of wilting buttercups.

"Where did you get these from?" Shauna spluttered her words, not quite believing what she was seeing. Lee was unimpressed, annoyed. She was pretending again. He hated when she pretended. He plonked himself down at his easel, turning his back to her, and continued with his work.

Shauna stood in front of the easel, waiting for him to make eye contact. He ignored her.

"Who gave you this envelope?" Her voice rose slightly, unable to disguise her fear and alarm.

Lee dipped his brush into a small circle of yellow of which there were many shades, each different and unique on his palette and mixed two together, adding dabs of deep, dark blue.

"Lee?" He questioned, whilst continuing to mix his paints, focused.

"Did the nurse bring this to you? Have you had any visitors?" Shauna was shaken.

"You're pretending."

"No Lee, I'm not pretending. I...."

"Where is he?" Lee tilted his head, inspecting his last brushstrokes.

"Wh-where's who?"

"Lee." Lee smiled as he continued.

Lee was the only person on the planet who had the skill to render Shauna speechless. She allowed him to take the upper hand as and when he pleased. Away from her work, she saw a reflection of herself in him: he asked the questions she could not ask of herself. He stated the obvious when she skirted around it. He admitted openly to all of his faults and prejudices and those of others, where she beat around the bush, skirted around conversations, avoided confrontation where possible and both of their lives were a testament to each of their decisions and choices. To Shauna it was painfully obvious that Lee was brave and she was a coward. Lee cared nothing of what others thought of him, Shauna thrived on the approval of others. Lee hid nothing about himself, Shauna hid everything.

Shauna stared down into the small envelope, she raised her hand ready to touch them, she hesitated. She knew what those buttercups meant. Her whole life she had anxiously awaited their delivery, and here they were.

"I need to speak to the nurse." Shauna explained as she left Lee to his painting. She had told the nurses over and over again, there shouldn't be any other visitors except for her and Kent. How dare they allow someone else to visit without her prior knowledge and acceptance.

Shauna pressed the bell at the reception, noticing the time, she'd have to leave in a short while. She pressed the bell a second and third time before Carol appeared from the back office.

"Hello, Shauna. How's things?"

"Has Lee had any visitors?"

Carol noticed Shauna's irritation, which she found very unusual. Shauna had always been very pleasant and polite. Carol was inspired by Shauna's care and love for Lee.

"Not that I'm aware of but just let me check the signing in book." Carol pulled the signing-in book toward herself and flicked through a couple of pages, shaking her head, she looked up at Shauna.

"No visitors in the last two days, apart from you." Shauna handed Carol the envelope.

"Someone gave this to Lee." Shauna tried her utmost to keep her hand from trembling.

Carol shook her head again. "I've no idea. It has your name on it."

"I know, but I didn't give it to him."

"Oh, we went out into the woods yesterday for a picnic, seven patients including Lee, but if someone had approached him, we'd know about it. It's not as if we let them roam around on their own."

Shauna held out her hand. Carol handed the envelope back.

"Everyone here knows that they should contact me, no matter the time, if anybody comes here asking for him or wants to visit, don't they?"

"Yes, everybody knows. It's in Lee's notes and all the new nurses are made aware of any special instructions right from the start. We haven't had any new staff in a while though."

"It doesn't matter, forget it." She was frustrated, she knew this wasn't Carol's fault. She had only herself to blame.

"I'm sorry, Shauna. I'll ask around for you." Carol spoke to Shauna's retreating back.

Lee had painted a cluster of tiny buttercups that were much darker than all of the rest. It stood out as if it was being shaded by something or someone.

Shauna caught her breath.

"I have to go now." Shauna stood behind Lee and rubbed his shoulder. No response.

"I'm sorry, Lee. I just worry about you that's all."

"Why would you worry about me? We're all safe now."

She nodded, bent down, and kissed him lightly on the cheek, squeezing him into her.

"Bye. I'll see you the day after tomorrow." Shauna opened the door.

"That'll be Thursday then. I love you." Lee called out to her, as if everything was well with his world, which of course it was.

"Love you more." She responded.

Lee continued on with his painting.

Shauna left the room, the feeling of abandonment a shadow in her every step. She knew that the buttercups were a signal, a sign. Shauna couldn't believe that, after all these years, the day she had dreaded and equally hoped for was upon them. A mixture of relief, sadness, and fear entwined around her every thought. She was not a bystander, she was an instigator and part of that role included fear and doubts. She continuously reminded herself that ultimately she was a good person and sometimes good people had to do bad things for good reason. It was too late to have a change of heart, and it wasn't possible to turn back the clock. She and she alone had started the fire, now she had to watch it burn. She could have stopped it at any stage, but she had gone ahead. Up until this point, she had believed she would get some sort of enjoyment out of it all but now that everything was real, she wasn't so sure. If anything happened to her, who would take care of Lee? She questioned her own feelings. She was a part of this; there was nothing she could do to change things now. All she could do was sit and wait for the inevitable.

CHAPTER FORTY-FOUR

Sloane's, the most exclusive restaurant in the city, Kent's second love, was always busy; they had bookings for the next four months and still people would turn up at the door requesting a table. Kent usually dealt with the disappointments, he enjoyed giving people hope. He'd turn on his charm telling them that there was no possible way they could find a table. He would hand them his personal business card, which wasn't personal at all, the number went straight through to a voicemail telling them that they should email or call the main switchboard to make a reservation, but for that moment, as Kent the sole proprietor, a celebrity in his own right, handed them that embossed glossy card, they felt important. They felt that Kent was now a friend; they could only hear the part of the conversation that suited them.

Kent could see their eyes glimmer, and they stood a whole foot taller because he had made them feel special and to Kent that meant everything. He loved to make people feel special and he knew he was good at it. Kent also wanted to be made to feel special but only by one person, Shauna, his wife-to-be. She either made him feel on top of the world with a wink or a smile or smaller than a measly ant when she dismissed his opinions or ignored his requests. Shauna kept him on his toes, they both knew it and up till now it had worked, that was how they had operated right from day one, now Kent wanted more.

He wanted to give her his all, if only she would allow him to be that man. He craved her attention, her praise, her love, and if she wasn't in the mood, she would scoot him aside and he would have to wait until she was ready to give her winning smile. Kent saw their relationship clearly now for the first time. He felt ashamed for taking the scraps, never demanding more of her and all the time she had been hurting inside, something so deep and so bad she had erased a big chunk of her life.

Kent surveyed the road outside, trying to spot Nigel in the throng of the crowds out on the town. Kent envied them, they were carefree, enjoying life. He particularly focused on the couples, simply enjoying each other's company. To Kent, everyone else's relationship seemed easy and natural; his was the only relationship that required guts and balls of steel.

Whatever Nigel was about to report back to him, he was ready, he could take it, and he was prepared to give Shauna all the time and support that was required to get things on track between them. They had their whole lives ahead of them and Kent was not about to give up on their future together, right at the first hurdle.

Nigel sat down across from Kent.

"You good?" Nigel's voice was quieter than intended. Octavia had given him the best advice, he could see that now: it was the best way. No lies, or skirting around the truth.

Kent nodded, calling the waiter over.

"Scotch and coke." Nigel ordered.

"Double." Kent spoke as the waiter left the table.

"No, I'm back on in a couple hours." Nigel wanted to make this quick and straightforward.

Kent lent forward. "Not good?" His nerves had got the better of him, and he didn't know what to expect but had prepared himself for the worst, though he wasn't sure what the worst could possibly be.

"Not bad. The crime numbers relate to two incidents of GBH (grievous body harm) for which it seems her parents gave her and Lee up for adoption. No takers there, so they were sent to the Farmhouse, which at the time was a children's home but they also dealt with kids who committed crimes. A good place by all accounts."

Kent allowed the information to sink in. Nigel felt he needed to talk; the more he spoke, the less Kent would ask.

"The GBH was always in defense of others, her brother, friends, never something that she started, and from what I can make out, her parents weren't that great to start with. Shauna and Lee were pretty much left to their own devices. Shauna was the mother."

Kent nodded.

"GBH? Who?"

"Couldn't go that far. Most of the details have been obscured, which means they were in connection with other crimes. I have to request permission to access those files, which I'm afraid is a no-go."

Kent nodded.

"And the change of names?"

"Now I can't be sure, but it seems that was Shauna's decision, to make it difficult for her parents to track her down, if they tried." Nigel surprised himself with how easily he could tell a lie to his best friend. He had allowed himself just one lie and it was in Kent's best interests. Nigel hadn't looked in the corresponding boxes so when he told his friend that was all he knew, that was all he knew.

"Thanks Nigel. I really appreciate it, you know."

"Look mate, why don't you try and get the details from Shauna? You're about to get married, you should be ironing all this out. This is the time to get it all cleared up."

Kent nodded. Nigel's heart sank: he could see the painful answer etched into Kent's brow. If Shauna was open to talking, there was no way he would have come to him in the first place.

"Maybe none of this stuff matters anyway? You know the past is just our stuff that gets in the way of now, sometimes, it's just better left where it is, and you just work on now and the future."

"You're right, but I cannot help but think, if Shauna has left this all in the past, why is she holding onto the paperwork, hiding this stuff in our home? I don't know, I suppose I feel that I was meant to find it."

Nigel nodded and downed his drink in one.

"Sure you don't want to eat?" Kent didn't want him to leave.

"No, got a big night ahead, and I don't do good on a full stomach."

"Promotion all set?"

"Not long now, I hope. Gotta give it a little more time, but I'm on it. You know me, always on it."

"Twenty-four seven, you're the hardest working man that I know."

Nigel gestured for a handshake, and he clasped Kent's hand in his and looked him in the eye.

"What else is there, eh? Listen, try not to worry. Shauna loves you, you love her, and that's all that matters. You're getting married." Nigel's grasping attempt to sound upbeat did not go un-missed by Kent.

WHAT LITTLE GIRLS ARE MADE OF

Kent broke into a smile, a real warm and genuine smile.

"That's better. It'll sort itself out, trust me." Nigel stood.

"Hope you're right."

"I'm always right." Nigel patted Kent on the shoulder. "Catch you later." Nigel left.

Kent knew what he had to do.

"Children begin by loving their parents; after a time they judge them; rarely, if ever, do they forgive them."

—Oscar Wilde

CHAPTER FORTY-FIVE

"Hello. Hellooo." The two college students were trying to get the old woman's attention. Godiva was slumped on the bench in the bus stop, resting her eyes, as she described it. A bus was approaching, and the two young girls wanted to make sure that she wouldn't miss it.

One of them reached out and tapped her on the knee.

"Hello, lady, the bus is coming." She withdrew quickly, she knew how cantankerous Godiva could be.

Godiva stirred, opening her eyes wide and looking about her.

"The bus." The girl repeated.

"Not today, love." Godiva saw the familiar kind face and smiled.

"Have you got money for lunch?" The girl dug her hand into her backpack and pulled out her purse.

"What you giving her money for? She'll only throw it away on drink." The plumper of the two screwed up her face and scowled.

Godiva sat upright, "I'm no drinker, you cheeky bleeder."

The girl handed her two-pound coins. "Get yourself a sandwich or something."

"Thank you, darlin'. And you get yourself a nice friend—she's full of it."

Godiva threw daggers in the direction of the other girl.

The two girls hopped on the bus. Godiva clasped hold of the two coins, considering where the nearest burger joint was. As the bus pulled away, her eyes lit up. She had a thirst on and just her luck, an oasis in the midst of the desert, the Grapevine, an upmarket wine bar.

Godiva stood, stretched, and marched across the street. She deserved a small glass of wine; she'd show that cheeky little wretch. Godiva pushed open the doors and headed straight for the bar.

"A small glass of house red please." She placed the two coins on the counter.

The man behind the bar reached for a large wine glass and an open bottle of red wine.

"How you doing, me lady?" The barman poured a full glass of wine.

"Very well, thank you. Sun's shining and I thought I'd treat m'self today."

"And you deserve it." The barman pushed the glass toward Godiva. She pushed the two coins toward him.

"This one's on me." He smiled and pushed the coins back toward her.

Godiva grinned, snatched up the coins, and took a dainty sip of the wine.

"Mmmm. Lovely." She noticed a group of three suited-and-booted twenty somethings, watching her, whispering, and laughing. She stuck her middle finger up, scooped her glass from the bar, and found herself a spot tucked up in the corner. The perfect spot to catch a bit of news. What was happening in the world today? She made herself comfortable and sipped her wine. There was no sound, but the headlines scrolled along the bottom of the screen.

A man falling from a high rise. "Poor bleeder."

A young mother with child recovering from meningitis. "Bless."

An A-list celebrity couple divorcing after three months. "Nice problems to have."

Stefan Mademan, after being granted parole, had been attacked outside a restaurant. Godiva choked on her wine.

"Turn it up can't ya?" Godiva hollered, a few heads turned, the barman heard her request, and turned the sound up. The news report caught everyone's attention.

Stefan Mademan had been released, serving only two thirds of his sentence. The report also mentioned a fiancée, a young woman who he'd been in contact with for five years, who'd also been attacked. The two were taken to hospital, wounding thought to be superficial. The report showed a blurry image from the restaurant's CCTV. Godiva leaned forward, squinting at the screen. It couldn't be. Surely not. "Jesus Christ, no."

Godiva made a dash for the exit, leaving her wine behind. As she raced from the Grapevine, she already knew the answer to her question, which beggared further questions. Why? How was this possible? Did she know? She couldn't possibly.

CHAPTER FORTY-SIX

The last thing Stefan recalled was scraping his plate clean. The lasagna had been hearty and delicious. He did not however remember going down into the basement which was where he found himself. Naked and strapped down to a cold metal table in silent darkness. He could make out the ceiling, the wooden rafters, and cracks of daylight leaked through, and smell the musty dampness. He could feel the cold steel against the back of his body. He was shivering, a cool draft whispered over his skin. His body ached all over, feeling as if he'd taken another beating; he groaned as he tried to lift his head but was unable.

Afraid. Afraid of where he was and who might be hovering in the darkness. No strength to pull himself up. His head swam with images of the hooded youths, teeth bared, long and sharp like vampires, Elise's bare flat, empty and soulless, driving on the motorway, and all along he was in the center of every event. Attempting to lift his hand, he found he was stuck, his legs too felt heavy. Weak and dizzy, he couldn't make sense of it all. He called out "Hello. Elise. Elise!"

A low lightbulb clicked on, a dim spotlight right above his head, he squeezed his eyes shut. A presence beside him.

"I, I can't move. Help me." Stefan tried to reach out pulling against the restraints that bound him to his cold metal bed. Elise stood beside him, lowered her lips and kissed him on the forehead.

"I'm here."

"I can't move." Stefan whined.

"You don't need to move. You need to rest and I've made sure of that." Elise smoothed her hand over his forehead.

"Did you call my probation officer?"

"Stefan, don't worry. Everything is in hand. Relax now: you worry too much."

The panic rose in Stefan's chest. She wasn't listening again. Her smile unnerved him, and the shadows of her movements danced around him in the dark basement; his breath became more labored and hoarse. "Please, help me."

"I am the help? I've been waiting to help you for such a long time now."

"Please."

"Begging?" Elis was mocking.

"What do you mean?"

"Michelle begged you, didn't she? Did you help her? I think not."

Stefan froze. She had never mentioned Michelle before. She had not mentioned his crimes. What was happening? His mind was blurry, nothing seemed clear, and he couldn't understand why he was naked.

"It was an accident. I didn't plan it that way."

"What was your plan, rape?"

"Elise, I can explain, just untie me. Please?" Stefan was confused and light-headed.

She disappeared from his eye shot, and he could hear her light footsteps. She returned carrying a plastic tumbler with a bright red straw. She pushed the straw into his mouth.

"Drink up. You have to stay hydrated."

Stefan jerked his head away from the straw.

"You, you've poisoned me?" Stefan wanted to push her away, but his arms were fixed by his side, no wiggle room. He could only recount Elise feeding him. From the moment he had stepped inside her flat, she had continuously been feeding him. All the time he had put his nausea down to being overwhelmed but, really, she had been slowly drugging him, with what he had no clue.

He pursed his lips together and wiggled his head from side to side.

Elise pinched his nostrils tightly. Stefan gasped for breath, and in the same moment Elise wedged the tumbler into his mouth and emptied the cup down his throat. Spluttering, choking, the panic in his eyes pleased Elise.

"Relax, the more you struggle, the more painful it's going to get."

Since the day that Stefan had been sentenced, he had lived in constant fear. Fear of other inmates, the wardens, the cooks, the cleaners, the outside world. The psychologist had said it was normal and that he shouldn't let his paranoia take over him and the chance of having a normal life. Wrong. He knew now that he had every reason to feel afraid, though the one person he had not feared was Elise. She had been so kind, considerate, patient, and loving. Was she having some sort of episode? Stefan didn't know who she was; he had thought that he had gotten to know her over the years, but he didn't know a damn thing about her.

Elise stared down at him. His eyes flickered closed, and he was having difficulty keeping them open. His tongue heavy in his mouth. He had so many questions but couldn't pronounce the words.

"You know I love you. I love you to death."

CHAPTER FORTY-SEVEN

Godiva rubbed her hands together vigorously. The tiny spurt of foamy soap that splatted against her palm didn't seem enough, so she pumped over and over again until she had a handful. That was more like it. The sink half-filled with water, she scrubbed her hands and her face as quickly as possible. She'd been thrown out of the library before and she didn't want to give them any excuses, not today. If her hands were clean and she looked presentable they couldn't stop her from using the computers. She had rights: the library was a public service.

Stooping down to dry her face under the powerful jet of the hand dryer, she sighed blissfully: the heated blast on her face felt so good. She pulled the front of her filthy sweater forward and allowed the hot gust to shoot down her body.

Standing to observe herself in the mirror, she was under no illusions. She knew how she looked, but what kind of world was this? So she didn't have any money, she had nowhere to live, but that didn't mean she wasn't a person, or someone to be bullied, run out, disrespected. She was a live, kicking, breathing human being; why should she shuffle away into obscurity to make people feel better? She would not. She was going out there to use the computers and woe betide anyone who tried to stop her this day.

She made her way to an empty seat right in the corner. She ignored the stares, people turning their backs, holding on to their back packs.

Fuck 'em!

As she sat at the table, she inhaled deeply. She memorized her passcode, a special day, zero, nine, zero, five. She knew her eyes had not deceived her, knew that in her worst nightmare this could not occur. She needed details.

The woman who was planning on marrying him, living with him, standing by his side. It couldn't be true, simply could not be true, but she had to find out for herself and if it was fact, then she knew what she had to do. Her hands trembled as she entered his name. She gulped back the pain and forced the dark memories to the back of her mind.

Godiva saw herself as a very lucky person. She didn't have to worry about rent, bills, or keeping up appearances. She did what she wanted, when she wanted, she was as free as a bird. Winter was really tough; the cold was unbearable, but she always found a way to manage and pull through. But the summers, they were blissfully perfect; everything seemed just right in the summer. The flowers, the green trees, the smiling faces. She'd had the best conversations with complete strangers in the summer. This was certainly not how she had planned her life, but taking into account her younger years, she saw these years, her wiser years, her autumn, as a blessing every single day.

She was so grateful for every meal, every glass of water, shelter for the night, and knowing that there was nothing to worry about. It appeared however, that her youth had come back to haunt her. Her blood pumped through her veins at an astronomical speed, and she took deep breaths to control her overwhelming anxiety.

Stefan Mademan's picture popped up on the screen. Balling her fists, she stared into his soulless eyes. The guilt, the hatred, the stench of him, his touch, all sent shivers down her spine. Jesus Christ! How could this be happening? She'd known the day would come when he would be released and she had prepared herself, but so early? His early release was greatly disturbing to her to say the least, but hearing of this woman who had been writing to him, in love with him, and planning on marriage. Marriage! It wasn't possible.

Godiva rolled the mouse wheel slowly. There it was: not just a photograph, but a video of Stefan with his fiancée being attacked outside a restaurant. Godiva's world came crashing down around her.

"Fucking 'ell! Fucking 'ell!" Godiva screeched. Covering her mouth she propelled herself back in the chair, losing her balance. The chair toppled over and she landed in a heap.

Scrambling to her knees, "You have to help her," Godiva screamed at the top of her voice. "She doesn't know, she doesn't know!" She wailed uncontrollably as two security guards rushed to see what all the commotion was about. Lifting her by her elbows, they carried her toward the exit. "No, no!" Godiva screamed and struggled wildly, her strength taking them by surprise. She punched and kicked until they finally dropped her on the floor.

"You need to find them, now." She wagged an accusing finger at them. The head librarian had called the police and watched on in horror as the poor woman who she had seen roaming the street for years went into meltdown.

"All of our dreams can come true."

—**Walt Disney**

CHAPTER FORTY-EIGHT

Stefan drifted in and out of consciousness, muttering incoherently, disturbed by the shadows, the images that rampaged through his mind.

"I'm sorry, I'm so sorry."

"For what?"

"Everything."

"You're sorry now because you're afraid but you weren't sorry then. You haven't been sorry for the past twenty years."

"It's not true."

"Oh, but it is."

"Why are you doing this?"

"I'm doing this for you, This has all been for you, can't you see that?" Elise ran her hand over his forehead gently. "I'm the one who's been looking out for you, the one who's kept you company for the past five years. Now it's payback."

"I did my time, and they released me. I've paid...."

Elise leaned right over him, and he felt her eyes boring holes into his. Stefan could bear it no longer and turned his head, and there he saw it, the glint of the axe she held in her left hand. He inhaled sharply and tensed his whole body.

"Don't be so stupid Stefan. Don't disappoint me. I arranged for you to be released. Me. Do you really think your little time away is payment for my sister's life? Really? The countless children you've hurt, their families? You are a destroyer of children."

"Sister?" Stefan's voice was but a whisper. The word reverberated over in his eardrums.

"My beautiful little sister. Did you think you could just take her away from me without consequence?"

"No, you've made a mistake. There has to be...."

Elise raised the axe up to his eye level and pushed it up against his cheek.

"You are the mistake."

"Your mother, L-Lorna, is that her name?" Elise took a step back, horrified at the mention of her mother's name.

"A-and your father, Gregg. We was friends, back in the day. We were all friends and Michelle was an accident. I didn't know till after, who she was."

Elise lurched forward "What do you mean friends?"

"Me and Gregg, Gregg used to work for me and Lorna, well I…"

Elise raised the axe.

"No! I'm your dad. Please, it's the truth. I'm your Dad. Me and Lorna kind of got together, but Gregg didn't know. It was just a one-off. She didn't tell me about you until you were born." Stefan rambled, words toppling over each other, hopeful that this could be his only chance for a modicum of redemption.

Elise's hands trembled as she grasped the axe. She could hear the bells ringing faintly as if at a distance. She stepped slowly away from Stefan, stepping backwards into the darkness until her feet found a crate. She paused before slumping down onto it, axe held loosely in hand.

She needed sleep, but this wasn't the time. This was not the time. Her sister was dead; this man had taken her sister's life. Her father was dead. Stefan thought he could con her, lead her down a winding path, and then who knew.

She needed sleep. Stefan wasn't going anywhere. She could just sit back and take a breath. No harm. No one knew where they were, no one was going to find them. The whole world knew her as Stefan's fiancée, his guardian, his lover, and best friend. Just a couple of minutes and she'd be as right as rain.

Elise rested her head against the wall and allowed her eyes to close.

"Elise, Elise. It's the truth, please believe me. I'm sorry, okay. Elise!"

Truth, lies, love, hate—it was all the same to her. A lifetime of planning, had it all been worth it? She was right where she wanted to be, doing what she had always wanted to do. Everything she had ever wanted culminated at this moment. What did she want? She wanted to feel safe and protected, yet her life had been devoid of comfort.

She felt the bile rise in her throat. Her Dad? Her father had been a weak and helpless man, full of his own self-pity. What a choice, the dead beat or the rapist murderer. In that moment Elise realized what she had really wanted, what she had been searching for in all the wrong places. Love.

"I loved you, Elise. I believed in you." Stefan stated adamantly. Elise could barely open her eyes. She whispered.

"Do you know? I've never felt true love. Apparently that's one of life's big questions. What is love? I used to believe that it was clear and people who said it was a subjective question were stupid, but I get it now. To love a child is to put that child before everything and everyone, nothing else matters apart from protecting that child and ensuring that child stays safe and feels loved. Hugs, kisses, rules, and explanations, and as that child grows you let go just a little, guiding them as best you can, allowing them to make their own mistakes but always being there for them to fall back on. Gradually letting go until they are able to live in the world independently and hope against all hope they make a contribution to the world. Always there never failing. I've never met a parent who does this so maybe my idea of love for a child it too idealistic. Maybe. Being a parent isn't just providing a warm and safe roof over a child's head, a hot meal, education, and structure. Children aren't an inconvenience, just popping them out as a result of a sexual interaction, oh the surprise when you're left with something weak and unpredictable. You have a responsibility. But if you haven't ever received love, how can you know how to give it?"

"I didn't know."

"Would that have made a difference? Would you have been a good daddy?" Elise giggled.

"I-I just want to explain."

"There is no love in you, Stefan, and people like you. You've never been shown pure unconditional love, therefore how can you know how to love? I've learned to love and I love you, Stefan Mademan. When you love someone with a pure and unconditional love, you can let go because you look at the big picture and see all the answers. It becomes easy to work out your path, it hits you right between the eyes. I was the bad sister, I was the one who got into big trouble all the time. I knew I wasn't loved, I knew Michelle and I weren't loved. Our mother couldn't get passed the idea that her mother treated her like an outsider, worth nothing, useless. When she met our father, she thought she didn't deserve better. Our father was a weak, selfish man who could only see his failings and instead of seeing us as blessings, focused on himself, what he didn't have. Instead of going out into the world and getting what he wanted, he sat back and wept over the injustice of his life. Michelle and I didn't stand a chance."

"I'm sorry."

"I was eight years old when I cut my teacher Mr. Francis, with scissors. He tried to get me to sit on his lap, he tried to touch me. I didn't want to. Nobody listened to me, they took his word over mine. I was labeled a violent troublemaker with a screw loose. I have no regrets, I wouldn't change a thing apart from not being there when you and that pervert took Michelle and her friends into the woods."

"Please let me go."

"They sent me away, those people who see what they want to see and hear what they want to hear. They sent me away and he kept teaching. Funny that. I waited and planned I made Mr. Francis pay. That was easy. He was easy. Following him home, telling him a sob story, he was so desperate to believe that I needed his help. I could see the greed in his eyes, he actually thought I was going to allow him to violate me. Mr. Francis no longer has balls."

Stefan flinched and held his breath.

"I fended for myself. I couldn't stand it, watching my Mom slaving away and my father drowning in his own self-pity. I should have known that Michelle would need my help and I wasn't there. I was living on the streets, doing what I had to, to survive. Doing what I already knew, my talent, my only worth. Planning to make something of myself so I could come back to save her. I really believed I could save her and that we would live happily ever after. Tessa and Karen needed my help, too, but I let them all down. I promised myself that I would make it up to them. It was too late for Michelle, but Tessa and Karen, I could help them feel better. We all know what it feels like to be treated as less than human.

"I told them, you don't have to be dictated a life of someone else's choosing, you can make choices and decisions that can change things. That's all I'm trying to do—make change. I am not going to campaign, protest, and march, that's not taking action, that's spouting crap for all those who are ready and receptive to hear it. I take action, I will continue to take action."

Elise was shouting now, Stefan lay quite still, hoping against hope that she had somehow forgotten about him. He heard her shuffling to her feet, he pressed his eyes tightly shut.

"I will not be pushed around, I will not be told what to do, I will not lay down and beg for my freedom. I've taken my freedom. People are always trying to push me around, tell me what to do, even if it's bad but I know the difference between wrong and right, they don't. They were always trying to cover up their mistakes and make me pay. Make me pay for their mistakes and wrongdoing. That isn't right but who listens? No one hears, they pretend to hear, they pretend to care but really, throwing a man in prison for murdering and raping a ten-year-old is not listening. They call it justice. If that's justice, then screw justice. I need to show them, I'll show you, you perpetrators. No one else loves you, you do realize that, don't you?"

Stefan kept his eyes closed, the cold was becoming unbearable, he clamped his mouth shut to prevent his teeth from chattering, not wanting to make a sound.

"I want you to understand the error of your ways. My love is all-encompassing, you trusted me, you loved me back, and now I'm going to end it for you. No more pain. If you love someone, you don't want to see them in pain, right?"

Stefan's mind ran rampantly over all the various scenarios. Someone must know that he was in trouble, in danger. No, they didn't, the world believed he was with the love of his life and she was protecting him. His probation officer would recognize that something was wrong but no one in the world knew where they were and more importantly, no one cared.

"If my childhood had been pink ribbons, bows, sugar, spice and all things nice then I wouldn't be here now and all those children who have suffered would still be suffering and would go on to suffer, growing into damaged adults who go on to inflict more pain in the world. It's a vicious cycle and I have to end the cycle. You do understand that, don't you?"

Elise was by his side now, Stefan restricted his breath, he knew that this was the end, he knew that he had not one chance of seeing the morning sun rise. This is how it is all going to end, in a dusty basement at the hand of his own flesh and blood.

"Please Elise."

"Oh it's not just me, there's a whole network of us. People whose lives you destroyed. Remember Luke and Jason, the boys you used to lure other children on your little camping trips?

Stefan slowly opened his eyes.

"Yes, and they remember you too. Not boys anymore. They were only too happy to give you the kicking of your life. You see we're all fighting to survive, none of us want any other kids to go what we went through. We're all fighting. That's what life is, war. We, each of us, are at war. The great war, the war against ourselves. Denying ourselves and resenting it, indulging ourselves, and carrying guilt. It's war. A crazy, dirty war. We're in war with those that are nearest and dearest to us, our neighbors, colleagues, the man at the checkout in the supermarket. Our siblings, parents and children. Our communities are at war with each other, the rich versus the poor, black versus white, Christians versus Catholics, male versus female. We're at war with our governments; they do what they please and we oppose them. We're at war with other countries, for oil, gold, wealth, power. We're at war! And the children are the produce of these wars, but I can change that. Heal the children."

"You're a crazy, fucked-up bitch!" Stefan spat.

"I'm the realest person you have ever met."

"What are you going to do?"

"Show you mercy, love you."

"Elise, please, can't we just work something out?" The low light high-lighted Elise's delight and glee.

"Victoria."

"What?"

"My name."

"Okay, okay. Victoria, what can I do? What do you want?"

"I have everything I want. For now."

Elise carefully lifted his flaccid penis.

Stefan blacked out. He knew what was coming next. Elise took to her bloody work.

"Yes mother. I can see you are flawed. You have not hidden it. That is your greatest gift to me."

—Alice Walker

CHAPTER FORTY-NINE

Godiva slumped in the corner of the police cell, wringing her hands and crying, "My angel, my little baby. Oh God help her!"

She crawled over to the door.

"Just listen to me, won't ya! I'm not mad, you need to help my angel!"

Godiva hesitated, closing her eyes, she listened out for footsteps, any sound of life behind the door.

She banged the door, weakly. "I know what you think of me. This ain't about me! He'll hurt her and youse lot'll 'av to pay. Do you hear me?"

Her attempts at catching someone's attention were futile. She'd been in the cell for two hours and no one was listening. No one cared. She was spent, her throat was dry, her fists red raw, the energy was draining from her. All her life she'd felt helpless, unable to stand up and fend for herself, why would today be any different. This was turning out to be the worst day of her life.

She hated God, or so she told herself but there was nothing else to do but pray.

She rolled over onto her knees, clasped her hands together, and rasped, "Dear God, I know you ain't heard from me in years, but this is a fucking emergency. If you're real, you'll fucking sort this shit out won't ya? I ain't asking for me, I'm asking for my angel, you know she's a good'un, hasn't she suffered enough?" A heavy tear rolled down her grimy cheek. "I ain't joking, help her won't ya."

Godiva's will was weakening. All along she had thought that Elise was strong, upstanding, and would be A-okay without the likes of her hampering her chances at a good life. She kicked herself. She should have told Elise the truth, the whole truth. She didn't think she'd need to. How could she tell her the truth, the truth had seemed like a cruel thing to do all those years ago.

Godiva still couldn't believe this was all happening: there had to be a reasonable explanation. Her angel with the devil himself, in love, due to marry. There was nothing reasonable or rational about any of it.

She resigned herself, even if she wasn't banged up, she wouldn't have a clue what to do. She didn't know where to go, no one seemed to want to help. What use was she? She knew Stefan, she knew what he was capable of, her angel didn't. All she wanted to do was warn her; she wouldn't stick around for a second if she knew.

CHAPTER FIFTY

MAY 8, 2005

Stefan was woken with a bucket of ice-cold water. Spluttering and struggling against the restraints, the excruciating pain spreading from his groin throughout his body.

"There's no point you being asleep. You need to feel it."

Stefan shrieked and wailed, unable to believe his fate.

"Get it over with, kill me!"

Elise did not wait for a second plea. She raised the axe high, landing it with a thud, a clean cut through his left wrist. His screams reverberated in his own ears. No one could hear him. Elise grinned, visibly chuffed with her work. She hummed a light and breezy melody, as if she was preparing Sunday dinner. Every effort was made to make each cut a clean one. She wasn't at all bothered by the amount of blood or his cries.

"There we go," she whispered, conversing with his body. "Now, then, not as bad or as difficult as I thought it'd be."

Stefan howled, as she rose the axe again and slammed it down on his right wrist.

"How's that. Dad?" She scanned his face, not wanting to miss one expression of pain. The release of years of frustration, anger, bitterness, and resentment in every single blow.

Stefan eyes fell shut, he finally accepted his fate. The release of tension in itself was a total relief. A kaleidoscope of colors swirled beneath his closed lids. He allowed the numbness to envelope his body, releasing himself into nothingness. The moment before his heart stopped, he entered a blissful state, peace, of which he had never experienced before in his entire life.

Elise felt his body relax. She gazed, bewildered as his chest rose for the final time and became still. She stood closer to his face now. She was pleased, but the anger remained, still there, churning through her veins, deep inside of her, gripping her heart and bodily organs. She still wanted to hurt him even though she knew he could no longer feel anything.

Snatching a pair of pruning shears from the table behind her and a small transparent sealable bag, she stood over him and plunged the shears deep into his left eye socket, gouging out his eye and placing it into the bag. She held the bag up toward the dim light, turning the bag, wanting to view his eyeball in its fullness. She did the same with his right eye. Sealing the bag, she sighed.

"Thank you, Elise. You're welcome, Stefan."

Elise washed her hands in the old cracked sink in the corner, removing all her clothes and leaving them where she stood. She climbed the stairs, carrying only the bag containing Stefan's eyes. Reaching the top of the stairs, she slipped into a pair of slippers and sloped into the kitchen. Exhausted and yet elated, she poured herself a glass of wine and sat down at the kitchen table. Gulping down her wine, she allowed a tear to fall.

"Pretty much all the honest truth telling there is in the world is done by children."

—Oliver Wendell Holmes

CHAPTER FIFTY-ONE

Nigel waited in Octavia's office. She'd been called, she'd told him to wait, but Nigel wasn't used to waiting and sitting still. He had to feel that he was doing something. Octavia had indicated that he could come along with her once they tracked down Mademan and his fiancée.

Twiddling his thumbs he ran over what he remembered from the history of the Mademan case. He'd been a kid when the news had broken, the rape and murder of little Michelle Muller. At the time the news had rocked the country, constantly on the TV, in the newspapers. He could even see an image of Stefan in his mind's eye.

Nigel ran his eyes over the case boxes, he wanted to read through to familiarize himself with the case, impress Octavia, he resisted because he knew that once he did, Shauna's name was bound to pop up and then he'd have to avoid Kent. He wasn't ready to change the dynamics of their relationship and he was truly wary of what he could discover about Shauna's past. His job though demanded that he take a look.

Opening one of the boxes, he slipped the first file of many out, opened it. All names apart from Stefan's had been omitted, blacked out with a thick black marker. He skimmed through the pages, every page had black lines through the text. Slotting the file back in its place, he randomly picked another file and another. He went through all three boxes to find the same. There was nothing to see, nothing to make sense of who was involved or a single clue as to where Stefan might go or with whom he may make contact. Nigel was flummoxed.

He flopped back down into the chair. Firstly, who had gone through the text with the black marker, why, and did Octavia realize they had nothing to go on? Had she seen the files?

Octavia popped her head around the door. "We've got Rob Carson right in the palm of our hands, coming with?"

Nigel sprang to his feet. "What about Mademan?"

Octavia shrugged her shoulders. "What about him? He's beat up, fled with his fiancée, the likelihood that they're winging their way to some far-flung corner of the earth is tantamount, and we've got real work to do."

She disappeared. Nigel followed her quick steps along the corridor. Was she simply going to drop Mademan, take her eye off the ball? Nigel was perplexed, he was a man that liked to finish what he started, leaving no stones unturned, and tying up a case before moving onto the next. The gritty truth of the matter was he knew that they should be ensuring that Mademan and his fiancée were located and kept an eye on. Absconding was not part of Mademan's parole and his job was to enforce it. They couldn't have a man like Mademan running around with no eyes on him, it was ridiculous. Octavia didn't seem bothered and what did she mean by "real" work, surely making sure that Mademan and his girlfriend were located and situated at a registered address was of the utmost importance right now.

From what he remembered, Mademan was not the kind of man who they should lose sight of, not with his past. Nigel wanted to make sure he was under careful watch as he should be. A big part of him was taking the Mademan situation personally; he hurt Shauna which in turn was affecting his best mate and if he could do anything to ensure the safety of children at large and prevent any other victims then he would, with one hundred per-cent heart. Octavia's lackadaisical approach was different and new to him. She clearly knew how to rise through the ranks so maybe he could learn something from her and pick up a tip or two along the way.

Octavia hurried down the three flights of stairs, avoiding using the lift, with Nigel in tow.

"He's at the Swallow hotel as we speak, meeting with his nearest and dearest. We've got uniform headed there now." She called behind her, encouraging him to keep up.

"Informant?"

"Informant, hard work, smarts, you know the score."

Nigel grinned. He had to admit, he liked her style.

Octavia beeped open her charcoal Z4, to Nigel's amazement. Trying not to look overly in awe, he joined her inside.

"This your weekend ride?"

Octavia smirked. She loved the reaction she got from men when they saw her car, especially when they witnessed her driving. If a man was comfortable with her driving, she knew they could handle her strength of character; if they took issue, criticized, or threw a strop, she nipped all contact or communication in the bud. Her Z4 for her was a good man radar. What all failed to realize was that she knew nothing about cars, only the bits that mattered, filling them up and driving them. She had inherited a few hundred thousand from her grandmother two years ago. The inheritance had come as a surprise as she'd never met her grandmother. She'd treated herself to the car. The remainder she stuck in the bank for a rainy day.

"This is my baby and she comes with me where ever I go. My lucky-charm." Starting the engine she gave Nigel a lazy smile. "Strap up."

"Yes sir." Nigel fastened his seatbelt. The thought of Mademan out there with no trace sat on his mind, squashing out all other clear thoughts, and even the fact that Octavia had clearly taken a shine to him wasn't enough to distract him. He had Octavia's full attention, wasn't that what he had wanted?

CHAPTER FIFTY-TWO

Shauna busied herself in the kitchen doing nothing in particular but doing a great job of seeming rushed off her feet, well aware that Kent was on his way home and she would have to start explaining. Conversation between them had been strained and she felt him tiptoeing around her which only made her feel worse. She had apologized over and over, but he still seemed to be on the verge of trying to get her to speak. She could speak all day about his work, the weather, or the state of the NHS, but there was only one conversation Kent was keen on, her past bought about by her smashing up the bedroom.

She desperately wanted to explain but how could she put it all into words, there were no words, how could she explain her behavior when she didn't understand it fully herself. Kent had hinted at couples' therapy, she swerved that suggestion successfully, though she was unsure for how long she could fend him off. Couples therapy would mean she would have to be wholly and fully open or else what was the point and there was no therapist on earth as far as she was concerned who could help her. Sure she could fake it, make Kent happy, keep him quiet but what about her? She would not be happy or satisfied, continually lying and hiding. Why couldn't they just abandon the past and move forward. Didn't everyone go off on a tangent sometimes? Wasn't that just human nature? Surely it didn't mean that one had to dig and delve in to the dark haunted recesses of their mind in order to move forward.

"Fancy dinner?" Kent crept up behind her, startling her for a second, she relaxed as she felt his thick strong arms weave their way around her waist.

"Mmm. Yes, please." She kissed him gently on the cheek. If she could keep strong in her resolve, she was sure they could act as if the past week hadn't happened and she made a promise to herself that from now on, when she was feeling frustrated, trapped, and angry that she would find herself in the gym in front of a punch bag.

Kent always offered suggestions from the menu. He loved his work, he was a qualified chef and a self-confessed foodie. His father had bought the building as a derelict heap and together they had bought about its original beauty, a tasteful merging of the old and new. Nine months later his father had been sent to prison. Kent designed and created the menus, and oversaw the running of the restaurant. He hired the best staff he could find, knowing that if he looked after them, the restaurant would look after itself. Relaxed in his classic grey, three-piece Tom Ford suit, navy shirt, and red silk tie. Tall, unassuming but sure of himself. No one would have guessed he carried the weight of the world upon his shoulders. He took a sip of his wine, then took Shauna's hand across the table.

"You look stunning." Tonight's meal was in preparation of the talk he had planned. He could think of nothing else. Shauna had frightened him, a fact he could not get his head around. He believed that if things were left as they were, swept under the carpet, ignored, that their relationship wouldn't survive. He couldn't bank on her not having another episode and hurting herself. It was as if she had had no self-awareness, unbothered by harming herself as if she no longer cared about her own well-being, mentally and physically.

Kent saw their relationship clearly and realized that Shauna was the master of disguise. All along showing him the tough, intelligent, no messing type of chick that she wanted to be perceived as, when really she was broken, detached, and worse still, woefully unhappy. He felt he should take at least some responsibility, he may not be responsible for her parents' actions, how could he be but he was responsible for not seeing the signs, not pushing her to open up and discuss things. At times he laid down the law and expected her to follow which she had done, at other times, he followed her lead. On the surface it was balanced but if deep down she held a rotting resentment for him, it would only grow and become so big that it would take over and ruin their relationship. He didn't want just half of the woman he was in love with, he wanted her whole, one hundred percent, the good, the bad, and the ugly just as she had accepted him.

"Well, you have to say that, don't you?"

"No, I really don't. I'm saying it because it's true, I know it and every-one here seems to know it." Kent's eyes surveyed the room, Shauna was receiving attentions from all angles. She wore a full-length powder blue figure-hugging dress with a plunging neckline, sheets of chiffon fell over her curves.

Shauna read the annoyance in Kent's voice and instead of counteract-ing on the defensive, she smiled demurely and accepted the compliment. Her intention from now was to just keep the peace, avoid any confronta-tions and difficult discussions, and look forward to the wedding.

"Thank you." She smiled. Kent nodded. She'd always had trouble accepting compliments, as if she thought the whole world were conspiring to tell her what they thought she wanted to hear, Kent regularly encouraged her to accept a compliment graciously and if that felt way too alien for her, then she should return one.

Over the main course, Kent took the plunge. It was now or never, as far as he was concerned. He figured his best tactic was to hit her with it, full on gauge her reaction and step inside her world, if she would finally let him. He braced himself.

"I found some documents in the bedroom." Kent kept his eyes on her, looking for indications of her perhaps wanting to change the subject or preventing him for moving too far in the wrong direction.

She ate slowly, chewing softly and returning his gaze, a slight smile on her lips, her eyes fixed on him. He could see that she wasn't sure where he was going with this.

"Some police reports and something about a children's home?" He actually thought he could hand over here and she would fill in the miss-ing pieces. Shauna continued eating, taking another mouthful, she chewed consistently, and looked to him to continue, as if he were telling her a little fairytale that was in no way connected to her, her eyes full of wonder. Kent shifted in his seat.

"Shauna, I want you to know, you can tell me anything you know, anything at all. I don't care what you did, I care about you, what happened to you, how you are, how you feel. I just want to be a full part of your life. Does that make sense?"

Shauna nodded still chewing. He pushed on. "Were you and Lee in a children's home?"

Shauna rested her knife and fork on the plate and dabbed at the corners of her mouth with her napkin.

"Lee and I were handed over to social services at a very young age and sent to a children's home, the Farmhouse. I got into some trouble, our parents saw us as a burden, they wanted to be free, live their lives without us two in tow. So the Farmhouse took us in, did an okay job and as soon as I was old enough, I got a job and looked after both of us."

"You were their responsibility; how could they just give up on the two of you like that?"

"I'm telling you what happened. I do not have the answers to my parents' frame of mind but I'm guessing they didn't give a fucking shit."

Kent cleared his throat. His eyes darted around to see if anyone of his patrons had overheard. The restaurant was full, but no one appeared to be taking much notice.

"I'm sorry. Thank you for telling me. You're right. I suppose the only people who know why would be your parents."

Shauna frowned, deep and furrowing eye brows, fire lit in her eyes. "I really, really hope that you are not thinking of asking them?"

"Shauna, my therapist says the way to clear the past is to make peace with it. Don't you want to find out why they treated you like that, what drove them to just let go, if they have regrets?"

"I've made peace with my past because it's in the past. I'm here today, living my life, with you, my job. We're getting married. I already know why they treated us that way because they were evil, sick bastards, who should never have had us in the first place." Shauna spoke through gritted teeth, her voice calm and low she didn't want to make a scene, she wanted to nip this in the bud and get on with what she had thought would be making up and papering over her problems. Kent had caught her off guard. How could she have been so stupid to keep those documents in the house, she kicked herself for not having destroyed them years ago. To her they were a reminder of where she'd been and where she needed to get to, a symbol of what she had achieved. Now they only served to expose her.

"Have you never thought about where they might be, finding them, getting answers?"

"No I have not." Shauna's voice rose an octave, incredulous, she leaned across the table. "I have no intention, never, ever, so let's just drop this now, please."

Kent's cheeks reddened. He could see that Shauna was not even going to consider his suggestion and in that moment decided to let it drop. It would hold for another time. The very fact that the mention of finding her parents had provoked such a reaction told him that her past was living with them in their relationship. This was the second time in as many weeks that he had seen that look of pure disgust and anger. In the whole time they had known each other, only twice had he felt that she was so angry that she could hurt someone, and he had been proved right in the first instance.

"I'm sorry."

"Good."

They ate in silence, far away in their own thoughts, only speaking when the waiter approached the table to clear their plates. Shauna was Sloane's desert menu's biggest fan. Kent had often asked her opinion on what to feature. She had a terrific sweet tooth. She refused the desert menu and asked for an Irish coffee instead.

"I'm sorry Shauna."

"It's okay—let's just drop it now." Shauna could feel her temper rising. Kent felt the icy cold temperature wrapping around him. He desperately wanted to save the evening, he loved her, couldn't she see that? He changed the subject trying to sound as cheery as possible. "When are you due back for your dress fitting?"

Shauna paused. Inside she was raging. How dare he try to sort out her life as if there was something wrong with her? How dare he assume that he knew best, snooping around in her private affairs?

The truth was no one had ever got close enough to want to know her fully, no one had noticed her pain, no one had ever tried to really help her in her entire life, and she felt ashamed. Ashamed of where she had come from, if her parents had so easily thrown her and Lee away, that must mean there was something wrong with them and now Kent knew. She was ashamed that she was living a lie in a house that she hated and didn't have the courage to speak up. She was ashamed that the persona she had created for herself was crumbling around her ears, she was a fraud and a fake but worse of all, she didn't know who she was, where she belonged, she was lost, and she could not afford to let anyone in on her deepest darkest secrets. She interpreted Kent's words as criticisms.

She rose slowly from the table, her eyes brimming with tears.

"Kent, I don't love you and I don't want to marry you. I'm sorry." She allowed sadness to take the place of her anger and shame. She didn't want to cause a scene. Her hands trembled, she desperately wanted to upturn the table and smash his face in with the wine bottle.

Instead, she swiftly moved from the table and out the front door. Kent caught up with her along the cobbled street.

"Shauna, please. Why can't we talk? That's what marriage is about. Talking, sharing, we can sort this out." Kent quickly grabbed at her arm, she pulled away violently, spinning around to face him.

"I'm going to the house to pack, don't follow me. Give me an hour and I'll be gone."

"How ridiculous, am I not allowed to ask questions, am I not allowed to enquire. Clearly there are issues, why can't we work them out together?"

"I am not a parrot, and I will not repeat myself over and over. You're a very special man and I'm not going to bore you with the 'It's me' speech but I think you can do better for yourself. You don't even know me, not one thing about me and I don't want to destroy your image of me further. So please, just let go."

Shauna nodded and walked away.

"I won't let go. What kind of man do you think I am? I won't walk away. You do what you need to do, I'll be waiting." Kent called after her.

"So long as little children are allowed to suffer, there is no true love in this world."

—**Isadora Duncan**

CHAPTER FIFTY-THREE

Nigel felt like a sidekick. Octavia's abrupt, no-nonsense approach to the job took him a little by surprise, though it really shouldn't have.

One minute one might think she was flirting, interested in who she was speaking to, she had a way of withdrawing information from people without them realizing, roundabout questions and enquiries. She presented herself as reasonable, caring and within a second she turned.

Rob Carson didn't stand a chance, he had absolutely no idea that she was a police officer let alone the fact that he was trapped, right up to the moment that Octavia made the arrest he believed it was his lucky night.

Nigel watched on as if viewing a movie screen. He could see why she had moved up the ranks so swiftly, she was charming, beautiful, alluring, the energy she projected wrapped people up so they felt warm and safe, as if she were the best friend that they had been missing all of their lives, extracting exactly what she needed, when she needed it. When she was in, she was deep within. She was a master at her game. Nigel was drawn in. It wasn't just seduction, she knew how to find people's weak points and impact them, with a look, a glance a touch, and once she started speaking, she knew how to make that person feel as if they were the smartest, most important person she had ever encountered. If Nigel knew nothing else, he knew it was an inherent part of human nature, everyone wants to feel smart, clever, knowledgeable and anyone who is able to do this, draws people in, instinctively. Nigel was drawn to her. He had never wanted a woman so much before in his life. Even though he knew her capture of Rob was all a ruse, he was still caught up in her web, he wanted Octavia to look at him the way she had looked at Rob, touched his shirt cuff, laughed at his jokes, brushed imaginary dust from his shoulder. Nigel wanted all that, but he wanted it to be real. He wanted her full attention, to be her focus and somehow, he knew that away from her work that would be an extremely difficult task. She was out of his reach and so he wanted her all the more.

He wanted to prove to her how smart and professional he really was, how attentive he could be, how she should accept him into her world.

It was Octavia's suggestion that he accompany her home for a night cap for the seriously good job done.

"I didn't do anything." Nigel protested, more a dig because he felt he should have had more of a role. He also knew there wasn't much more he could have done but he still felt as if had been a spectator rather than a valued member of the team.

"Never, ever put yourself down Nigel. You were there, you followed the plan, you had my back. I couldn't have gone in their alone or with uniform, could I?"

Nigel shrugged, he had to agree; he was just used to being the one taking action, the lead, not the backup. He so desperately wanted to show her what he could do.

"If you want my job, you have to big yourself up, not put yourself down mate."

He didn't want her to see him as a mate. He felt confused, he wanted to be her lover and her equal, but mate didn't really cover either.

Nigel checked the speedometer. She was within the forty mile per hour speed limit but the Z4 felt like it was shifting through sixty. The car was fast, she was fast, she missed nothing.

"Who said I wanted your job?" Nigel jested, Octavia recognized the truth when it was staring her in the face.

"You did." She giggled.

"When?" Nigel ran through every word and conversation that they had had and he remembered every word, every glance, every gesture. He knew he had not told her that he was desperately seeking promotion.

"Nigel. Sweet. You have to learn to read the words that aren't spoken. You work hard, you excel, you stand out amongst your colleagues, you're driven, you're not married, and you give that extra even when it's not required. You've never gone digging for your own personal gain, well only once. Of course you want my job, it's the next step up. The one that matters."

Nigel caught his breath was he that transparent. "I never stood out to you. You've been at the station for three months."

Octavia sighed. "I'm going to be honest now. I noticed you on my very first day. I didn't know your name, but you just walked through the office like you owned the place. It's in your stance, your aura. I asked around about you, you have an excellent reputation, everyone loves you."

"So why haven't we worked together before today?"

"Fate."

"Do you believe in all that crap?"

"Absolutely. Fate is what bought me to the force, what keeps me going, and of course what had us bump into each other yesterday. Now look at us. Best mates."

Nigel wished she would stop with the mates. He felt more, he was sure she did.

Nigel had no response, warmth spread throughout his body as he felt the first twinge of an erection. He couldn't speak, he was afraid of how his voice might sound, he had to use every ounce of his brain power to think unattractive thoughts. The homeless guy he had seen two weeks prior, chowing down on a discarded bag of chips, wet from the rain. That didn't work. The images of a brain dissection that he'd had to sit through in connection with a case. That was working, he just had to focus on the details.

"Any news on Mademan?" Nigel tested the water.

"Do I seem like the type to keep secrets from you?"

"No, I just thought..."

"No, you want to remind me that you haven't forgotten and you're very concerned that Mademan may well be out there offending with his fiancée as a possible accomplice." She turned and glanced at him quickly, wanting to know if she'd hit a nerve.

"Hopefully not offending, but we need to locate them."

"We should and we shall. Tomorrow." Octavia placed her hand on his thigh and gave it a good squeeze, she left her hand there.

Back to the brain dissection. Nigel turned his head, clenched his eyes shut and tried to focus on the details. She liked him, she must like him, no woman squeezes her mate's leg unless she's attracted to them. He didn't want to be an idiot, he had to get this right. It could be a friendly gesture coming from her. Any other woman and there wouldn't have been any confusion in his mind. Octavia was playful and sexy, but he would not like to be on the receiving end of reading the situation incorrectly. He sat rigid, trying not to appear awkward. Nigel was unaware of where she was headed, he didn't keep track, he focused on keeping his cool and staying soft.

"Fancy a stiff drink?" Octavia had parked up in an underground car park at the Tall Trees complex. An exclusive part of town, a mixture of apartments, three- and four-bed detached homes and a twenty-story block.

"This home?"

"Well I'm not going to break in to impress you, mate." She was out the car and opening his door, bowing and gesturing for him to step out. She made him smile, she understood him. He knew he would never understand her, even if she spelt it out. He followed.

"My grandmother passed away and I inherited." She was matter of fact.

"I'm sorry."

"Honestly? I didn't know her, never even met her. Only found out about her when she died. Of course I knew I must have grandparents somewhere, just never knew them."

"Must have been a surprise?"

"As unknown grandparents go, yep." Nigel took this as the end of that conversation.

The penthouse apartment was lush, comfortable, eclectic, well lived in and homely. Not what he had expected. She wasted no time, she slipped his jacket from his shoulders, up close, foreheads touched. She whisked off his jacket and slung it on the back of the huge circular sofa. She crossed the lounge to the open plan kitchen and reached into a large wine rack.

"Tequila?" Holding up a bottle of Don Julio.

"Erm, more of a brandy man."

She took two glasses from a glass shelf, displaying a multitude of drinks glasses, all in twos. None of the sets the same. She placed them on the counter and poured two shots.

"Every now and then, it's good to try something new and different. Explore the world." She swallowed her shot and waited for Nigel to follow suit.

She poured again.

"Because if you stick to the same things all the time, you never get to try anything new. You get comfortable, nothing exciting about comfortable, you have to get out of that comfort zone, Nigel."

Nigel downed his second shot and nodded in agreement. The liquor burned the back of his throat, and it felt good.

"What's your vice?" She slotted the empty glasses together, bottle under arm, took his hand and led him to the oversized couch.

"Work." His answer surprised him. He realized how lame he sounded, but it was the truth. There was literally nothing else in his life. Work, hanging out with Kent and Shauna on the odd occasion. There was nothing else.

"I don't believe that you want to be Jack. I believe you want to be Nigel."

"Jack?" Nigel felt the warmth of the tequila spreading throughout his body, he relaxed into the sofa, he was stirring but he didn't try to control it this time.

"All work and no play." She filled the glasses again and placed her glass on the huge wooden carved coffee table.

"You should have at least one vice. I can teach you. I have a few."

She crawled across the sofa and kissed him. Nigel accepted her kisses gratefully, relieved that he had been reading the right signs and hoped above all hope that this wasn't going to be a one off. Thoughts of locating Mademan drifted to the back of his mind. She was right: he needed to let go, unwind, really enjoy himself for once. No one was watching. Octavia was the woman of his dreams and she was here with him right now; he wanted to grab the moment and make the most of it: who knew when or if it would arise again.

Nigel took her by her waist and rolled her onto her back, undoing the buttons of her blouse. He looked down into her big doe brown eyes, soft, inviting, sexy with the distinct hint of danger and Nigel embraced and accepted every aspect of Octavia Middleton.

CHAPTER FIFTY-FOUR

The screaming, the calling, loud chanting, the other kids clawed at her naked skin. She plunged harder, deeper, panting for air, breathing restricted, where was the sun light? Over and over stabbing at his abdomen, covered in blood. He simply smiled up at her. Why wasn't he dying, why wasn't he dead? She clawed desperately at his face, sticking the knife in his throat. His smile deepened, and he slowly raised his hands toward her neck.

Elise sat jolted out of her sleep. Taking gulps of air, her life depended on it. She hauled the sheets from her and stood. Slapping her hand against her heart in the hope that it may somehow calm her heart rate.

Those damn tablets weren't working. Maybe she should stop taking them altogether. The only thing that she had noticed was that her urine smelled so much stronger, had a chemical stench to it. Other than that her dreams were becoming wilder and her hallucinations increasingly vivid.

The memory of Stefan and her earlier work bought a smirk to her face. "He is dead."

She opened the window into the early morning darkness and took in a deep breath of fresh country air. Nothing like it. Her plan and her next steps flooded her mind, she had a bounce in her step, and not a care in the world. Where there had been confusion, there was now clarity; where there had been doubts, there was now an unfaltering confidence; and where there had been fear, there was now roaring courage. Her whole life she had planned and waited and now she felt nothing could hold her back. There was nothing standing in her way. She knew her path and direction and she would follow it. Anything was now possible.

Bounding down the stairs, Elise had all the time in the world. She washed the dishes and cleaned each surface thoroughly, bleach, disinfectant, she wanted the place spick and span after all, there was nothing worse than buying a new place and not seeing it's true potential. Out of all the houses, apartments, bungalows and flats she had been shown, the ones that needed a simple clean always seemed to take that little bit longer to sell. People found it difficult to see beyond the filth of a place, renovation work was easier to envisage but grime and dirt stuck in peoples' minds. She wanted to leave the place nice and tidy apart from the basement of course, that would be down to the crime scene cleanup team, they would make fast work of it all and it'd be like brand new.

Elise made her way through the house, changing the sheets on the beds, dusting and vacuuming, spraying Febreze. This, she thought was how a home, a real home, should be kept. Ready for a real family to live happily ever after. She loved the little cottage, her favorite by far of all the places she had visited or stayed. The cottage belonged to Elise. She hadn't felt the need to tell Stefan about her own portfolio of property that she had acquired all over the world, nine in total.

Elise lived frugally and had made wise decisions in her first few house purchases, buying in regeneration areas, renovating and selling on, some were rented but she had kept three for herself empty, the cottage included. This was the type of cottage that Michelle would have loved, especially the gardens. The gardens were mature and the upkeep effortless, flowers bloomed every year, hedgerows, shrubs, apple and pear trees, there was even a strawberry patch to the rear, and buttercups sprang through the lawn but all of it was for Michelle; it was appropriate that Stefan should find love here, she thought. Elise had had the cottage's name plaque especially crafted when she had bought the place. Buttercup cottage.

Everything was exactly how she wanted it. She checked the time, with a couple spare hours and decided on a run. Four a.m. in the country-side, never was there a better time or place to run. She changed into her grey tracksuit, deciding to leave her ear pods, there was no need, the countryside was ultimately silent. The sound of birds were easily drowned out by her thoughts. Her plan had come together better than expected. So she had a few bruises, the broken arm had been a ruse, it was more than worth it to see the look on Stefan's face when she revealed that she had orchestrated the past five years of his life. She had been the controller, the puppeteer. She believed that by the end, he had come to terms with his fate, he had no other option. He had accepted her pure and unconditional love and he was free.

She didn't believe for one second his pathetic attempts, claiming he was her father. She couldn't really blame him, he would have done anything to survive. Wouldn't anyone? He was the lowest of the low and there was no way she would allow him to slither beneath her skin. Stefan was the past and she looked in earnest toward her exciting future.

She hadn't done anything wrong, she had simply allowed for his true destiny to be played out. She felt powerful, more alive than ever. Stefan had committed heinous crimes and the only real way to cure him of his evil illness was to eradicate him, wipe his stains from the face of the earth and this served society at large. No one would miss him; she hadn't taken away someone's beloved child, father, friend, or uncle. She had served the world and whether the law accepted her ways or not, it was done. Stefan's demise gave her strength. She knew that she had done the right thing and she was going to continue to right wrongs for as long as she lived. Stefan wasn't the only murderer and abuser of children. He had a whole network of ill men and women who could only be stopped, healed and loved by her, only she understood what was required, only she had the balls to carry out the dirty work, and only she would get away with it, allowing her to continue her good work. Elise was high on life, she smiled to herself satisfactorily. He could cause no more pain to anyone, Michelle could finally rest in peace, allowing Elise to continue, move forward with her life, she was exhilarated, positively glowing. She sprinted up along the narrow country road, thirty minutes each way and returned to the cottage. She knew she should rest, even though she was wide awake and buzzing, she'd only slept for an hour or so, she was well aware that her body and brain would need to slow down. She decided she could do that on the train.

Back at the cottage, she blended a bag of organic carrots and a small handful of coriander, her favorite soup. She poured a small bowl and filled a flask with the remainder. Two small pieces of unbuttered crusty bread accompanied her meal, she ate heartily, observing the time. Just a few hours before she would have to move on. She longed to stay, she loved the place, it reminded her of Michelle, even though Michelle had never stepped foot in the place. If things had been different, if their paths had been plotted differently, they would have shared this cottage.

In the bathroom, she took a pair of clippers to her hair, number eight. She was left with just over an inch of thick dirty blonde hair. Taking a tube of blue black Garnier hair color, she applied the dye carefully and expertly, she had changed her look on many occasions and was tired of the English rose look—the blonde hair had garnered far too much attention which was perfect for the task of catching Stefan. With blonde hair and lightened eyebrows it was easy for her to fall into her innocent and angel-faced facade; it had worked perfectly as she knew it would. Now, and she had never done black before, she needed to have her wits about her, look unapproachable. She wanted people to avoid exploring her face.

She hated false tan, but it was necessary. She applied a dark tanning mousse, massaging the sticky foam into her skin, ears, neck, top of her shoulders, chest, arms, and legs. She plucked her eyebrows into a thin strip, with sharp angled arches, dying them the same color as her hair. Her ears were pierced in five places—she had only used one as a blonde—three along the lobes and two on the upper cartilage, she slotted studs into every hole except for the bottom two on the lobe, there she inserted huge silver hoops. She had always wanted her nose pierced and hadn't got around to it; she used eyelash glue to stick a tiny Vajazzle jewel to her nostril.

She brushed her light-colored eyelashes with thick black mascara, filling them out and lengthening them. She observed herself in the full-length mirror in the bedroom, she thought the look would have pleased her more without the tan but she could always try that look another time, perhaps with a funky purple hair dye, a more gothic look, for now this would have to do.

She pulled on a pair of black, boy fit jeans, a bright pink short V-neck t-shirt, and red Converse All-star pumps. The finishing touches, bunches of silver bangles on each wrist, several silver and beaded long-neck chains and she was ready. The new Elise. Soon to be known as Ivy Cadeau. She smirked, remembering how she had chosen her new identity. Ivy as in poison and Cadeau, the French word for gift. She had pondered the name for a long time, was it too obvious? She had decided not and gone with it, requiring things to be finalized to purchase her new identity, bank account, driver's license, and passport in the said name. She loved it, knew that it suited her new look.

Having spent her life befriending and associating herself with people who could help her on her mission, most supported her ideas, she sifted through people to find those who needed to feel that their pain had not been in vain. Her network spread far and wide, she had international contacts, her intention had been to match Stefan's, yet she had exceeded his span and reach tenfold, a fact that she was proud of. This was her life's work and she had worked hard. No friends, having never had a real lover, her every waking moment had been about making them pay their true debt to society.

Prison as far as she was concerned didn't measure up. The only way to repay the debt of murdering a child was to die a slow and painful death. She had other punishments for those who abused and she had on many occasions meted out those punishments to those she found deserving. Stefan had been the pinnacle of her achievements, but she had a long way to go. Many more offenders for whom she had appointed herself judge and jury. The thought of moving on with her life excited her.

Elise packed her belongings, placing her memento of Stefan in her toiletries bag. She checked she had everything that she needed including her plastic expandable filing folder. She was ready to move on, one more stop before heading to the train station.

"Children's talent to endure
stems from their ignorance
of alternatives."

—Maya Angelou

CHAPTER FIFTY-FIVE

Elise checked every window lock and door, ensuring the cottage was secure. She decided to take took one last look at Stefan's remains. She made her way halfway down the basement steps, carefully avoiding her own bloody foot prints. She didn't want to trail blood through the rest of the cottage. She'd left the light on and stood on the stairs looking toward his body. She saw past his bloody torso and severed limbs, and she saw a vision, a symbol of his release from pain: to her he was at peace. She smiled, excited at the prospect of moving on, knowing that she could achieve anything that she set her mind to. Knowing that he could no longer hurt, abuse, or inflict pain on another living soul filled her with pride.

She imagined the scene when the police arrived, their horror at what she had done. She pictured the news as she knew it would be reported, that the most feared child murderer was now deceased by her hand. People could feel safe that he would never come back to haunt them; it was over for him and she had done that. She wanted the world to know.

CHAPTER FIFTY-SIX

Nigel rolled over in Octavia's king-sized bed, throwing the sheet back to allow the cool breeze entering through the floor to ceiling window to float over his body, refreshing. He lay for a moment considering how he should play it. Cool and act as if the night before was no big deal, as if they were still simply colleagues and shit happens, was his usual tack, ensuring there was no awkwardness, it usually worked but he didn't want that with Octavia. To him last night was a big deal; he wanted to be more than just a colleague or a mate. She hadn't given anything away as to what she felt or thought, and it was difficult for him to gauge and he certainly didn't want to make a complete fool of himself, he couldn't bear the idea that Octavia saw him as some kind of casual conquest. After all, he more than most could understand her need to keep her life baggage free.

The sound of the TV murmured from downstairs, cups and cutlery lightly clattered, the smell of salty bacon and nutty coffee wafted up his nostrils alerting his gut. Breakfast. Well that was a good sign, if she wanted him gone, surely she would have kicked him out of bed hours ago. He sat up and stretched, yawning loudly, he hadn't had such a good sleep in months, years in fact. He liked Octavia's bed, it was firm yet soft; he liked her home, which reflected her personality. An ornate reclaimed dressing table, holding a couple bottles of perfume, a few cosmetics, nothing too over the top, along with a photo of an old man, whom Nigel assumed to be her father, a head shot and the man was grinning into the camera. They had similar smiles and he wondered whether her father was still alive.

Her wardrobe, a huge old styled dark wood affair with intricate carvings, something she perhaps picked up at an antique shop. The whitewashed wooden floors covered with an expansive white and royal blue striped rope rug. He could only locate the shoes she had been wearing the day before, assuming she had them tucked away in the wardrobe, he tiptoed over to the wardrobe and took a peek. Her clothes and shoes were jumbled together.

He was hoping not to find everything color coordinated and assembled in an orderly fashion. She seemed to use her wardrobe to store her clothes and shoes not as some clothes store collection. He smiled to himself, warming to her all the more.

He sat on the bed and pulled on his socks; checking the time, he realized she was an earlier riser than him. It was just six thirty and she must have been up for at least a half hour. Dressed he made his way along the hallway, following the enticing aroma into the open plan kitchen.

"Morning." She was chirpy, sounded pleased to see him.

"Morning." He took a seat at the wide breakfast bar, clasped his hands together, and watched her flipping bacon. A large mug of coffee was slid across the counter toward him, followed by a small chrome sugar cup with a teaspoon and a carton of coconut milk.

"We've got a lot on today; we need to get a start on the boring stuff, the paperwork from last night, but more interestingly, we have a lead for a couple of Rob's cohorts who have conveniently come forward with information, hoping to vindicate themselves."

Nigel nodded running a hand through his tousled hair.

"Mademan and his girlfriend..."

Octavia picked up the remote control and raised the volume, and she nodded toward the fifty-inch flat screen hung on the wall.

Nigel followed her eye line, BBC news, the female newsreader announcing that their newsroom had received a telephone call from Elise Miles herself announcing that she had taken Mademan's life, she and she alone had wanted to make him pay for his crimes. She'd sent photographs to the newsroom's email which showed Mademan's dismembered body, these images were not of course shown but the newsreader stated that all information had been passed to the police and there was now a country-wide manhunt on for Elise Miles.

Nigel caught Octavia staring at him, waiting for his reaction. He was a little spooked by her calm, seemingly happy demeanor. Had she known what was going to happen? It wasn't possible. She didn't seem to care; she was nonchalant and dismissive of the biggest news of the day.

"DCI Shaw and his team are on the search, though from what the girlfriend is saying, I think she's going to give them the exact location."

"What makes you think that?" Nigel's defenses were up, uncomfortable with her relaxed attitude to the situation. A man was dead, and the murderer was controlling the investigation and the media: nothing about the whole scenario sat well with him.

"She called in to admit to a murder that no one knew had taken place. She's explaining her actions. No self-defense, no accusations, a simple revenge murder, and she wants the world to know. She's not going to sit around waiting for us to work it out; she's going to hand it to us on a plate."

Nigel nodded. She was making a lot of sense but it rankled him. Octavia was smart, determined, a powerhouse of action, yet for Mademan she hadn't taken any action. Why?

"Eat up. Can't work on an empty stomach." She leaned across the counter and kissed the tip of his nose.

Nigel grabbed her wrist and pulled her forward. "If I didn't know better, I'd say you're somewhat pleased that Mademan is out of the way." Nigel hadn't thought through his statement; he just allowed the words to spill from his mouth.

Octavia's brown eyes glinted and narrowed, more danger than sexy now, smiling as she kissed Nigel's lips.

"That, Mr. Pemberton, is why I am SIO and you are waiting with your hands out for crumbs." She kissed him again, this time on his forehead.

"Never wait for what you think you deserve; step up and take it, if you really believe in yourself and capabilities. No one is going to lift you up: you have to climb."

"I need to see the other files." He looked for any indication that she might try to deter him. Maybe he should re-read, see if he could find anything that might relate. He decided against mentioning the omitted text. He wasn't sure what he would find but he hoped there would be answers, he would make sure that he was on the team that was going to locate Mademan's body, knowing full well that did not include Octavia. He knew he was probably burying any chance of moving forward with her, more that he was isolating himself from her as a colleague.

Octavia pulled away slowly.

"You know where they are. Go see." Nigel watched her as she filled her mouth with a huge bite of her bacon sandwich, her eyes not leaving his.

WHAT LITTLE GIRLS ARE MADE OF

"Why don't you care?" He could feel resentment emanating from her toward him.

"Care about what?" She chewed precisely, unperturbed by Nigel's obvious discomfort.

"Mademan?" He answered incredulously.

"What's there to care about? A man who murdered and raped a little girl, a career abuser, has been wiped off the face of the earth. What am I going to do about that, eh? You think we're here to prevent crimes? No, Nigel, we are police. We sort out the mess after the fact. You know that, surely?"

Nigel was dumbfounded. That was not how he saw the job at all. "We should have looked into this as soon as we heard that they had gone missing."

"We? And done what exactly? Run out of here on some wild goose chase, not knowing where to look, where to start or what was going to happen? Is that how you see your job? Here's a question for you, why do you care so much?"

"It's my job." Nigel didn't skip a beat.

"Last night we took down the top man in organized crime in the United Kingdom. We took him out and got leads to others top rankers in his organization. That's our job. Not tracking down some pervert and his deluded girlfriend."

"She's a murderer."

"Rob Carson is a murderer. He and his crew have taken hundreds of lives and will continue to do so, even from inside prison. It is my job to reduce those mindless killings to the best of my ability. Who is this Elise Mademan, is she a mass murderer or did she take a life that should have been taken years ago? I How do we even know if she's the full ticket when we don't even know for sure if he is dead?"

Octavia dropped the remnants of her sandwich onto the plate and pushed it away.

"You make up your mind. You need to decide what side you're on and work toward that. I can't help you if you don't want to be helped." Octavia snatched the remote control up, switched the TV off, and grabbed her jacket from the back of the chair.

"You coming to work?" Octavia did not wait for a response, she headed toward the front door.

Nigel could have kicked himself. He had let the Mademan case get to him and he knew that was because of Kent and Shauna. Would Shauna feel the same way? Would she be glad that Mademan was dead? He was sure that he had made things really uncomfortable between himself and Octavia. She clearly didn't rate him. She was trying to get him on her team and he had royally messed that up.

CHAPTER FIFTY-SEVEN

Octavia and Nigel separated as they entered the police station. The drive had been a whole different experience from the drive the night before. Octavia didn't have much to say and he could tell that she thought that he was stupid, that he didn't see the bigger picture, wrapped up in the Mademan case. Was he blinkered, was he missing something?

Octavia headed to the Rob Carson meeting, throwing a "see you later" casually over her shoulder. Nigel decided it was the perfect time to go back through the box files from Octavia's office to see if there were any clues as to where Elise might be or why she had all of a sudden decided to take Mademan's life, if in fact she had.

The boxes weren't there. Octavia's office was exactly as they had left it except for the three box files. Perhaps Shaw's team now had them; if that was the case, he probably wouldn't get another chance to take a peek. Nigel ran down to the archives. The shutters were closed, Liza wouldn't be in for a couple of hours. He had to think. He was becoming more and more suspicious with every minute that passed.

The more he thought about it, the more he felt that Octavia had been guarding those files with her life, even before Mademan's murder. There was no possible way that she could have known what was going to happen, yet there was no mistaking the fact that she was quite happy to watch his murderer, Elise Miles, walk away. As far as he was concerned, a murderer was a murderer, and it didn't matter whose life had been taken, it was against the law. Why couldn't Octavia see it that way?

There had been plenty of criminals over the years who he had wanted to personally punish, take them into a back alley and beat the living daylights out of them, and, if he was being really honest with himself, there had been a few that he had wished were dead. The sad reality was that he could see a much better and safer world without the likes of Mademan in it. Judging another person was not down to him, it was down to a court of law. If he did his job right, then he could only then sit back and watch as the courts made the next decision. That is what he signed up for. It could be disheartening at times and he knew it well.

He recalled a case that had made him question his desire to work on the force after only eighteen months into the job. He had been called to a domestic; a woman with two small children had been beaten by her common-law husband. When he arrived, the woman, Zoe, in her early thirties, could barely stand, her pajamas were soaked with her own blood, and she clasped her two young children to her for dear life. He remembered he could barely look into her eyes, having to ask her questions about her relationship. Her hands constantly trembled and two of her teeth had been knocked out. Nigel had arranged for her to take her children into a hostel, a safe home for battered women. Initially he had thought she would go back to him, but she didn't, she stayed at the hostel and thrived. She was like a new woman. It had made Nigel feel as if she would be his pride case, the one where the actions and steps he had taken as a police officer, lead to a life change, peace, and harmony for all concerned.

Zoe had gone on to study at college, and she volunteered at the hostel, helping other battered men and women, get on with their lives. Nigel had often liaised with her on different cases. He remembered her bright smile; she was out there making a difference because he had cared enough. He believed that there was a connection, if he did the right thing, others did the right thing and so the world turns.

Twenty five months after his first visit with Zoe, he was horrified to discover that her ex had tracked her down, stalked her, and brought her and the children back to the family home. He had beaten her almost lifeless, but she was a fighter and stabbed the man to death whilst he slept. She had snapped, had had enough; she had seen a glimpse of a brighter future and lived it, and she couldn't bear the idea of going back to being his victim, so she ended his life. She was sentenced to life, her actions deemed as premeditated.

Nigel had struggled with the outcome, at times thinking he should have done more. Would it have made a difference if they had kept her ex under surveillance? They neither had the budget nor the man power for such a thing. His frustrations grew as he didn't have the answers and that case had haunted him for his whole career, but he had to keep doing his job to the best of his ability. Sometimes the bad guys got real justice, sometimes they got away. He didn't want to focus on the cases that irked him, he had to look at the whole picture. He was also acutely aware that he had been involved in cases where the wrong person was convicted. Innocent people locked up whilst the true perpetrators walked freed. In his line of work a real good sleep was hard to come by.

Sometimes none of it made sense, it sure as hell wasn't fair but he could not just sit back and ignore the law when it suited him. There'd be chaos. Everybody had a different opinion, everyone had something to say, whose version of punishment should they follow? That's why the court system was there, that's why as a society we follow the law, to keep order. Nigel reasoned with himself. This was one of those cases, he was struggling with what he was trained to do and the feeling in his heart. He knew the reason the Mademan case was getting to him was because he despised the man. Deep down he was glad that filth was dead and what hit hard was the fact he could see that Octavia felt the same, he was somehow wanting to punish her for feeling the same way he did. She'd never said as much but her lack of action told him everything he needed to know.

Whether they liked it or not, there was a woman out there running around freely after taking a man's life. She hadn't just shot him, or stabbed him, she had tortured the man. The question remained that it could be fake, a cover up or a diversion. As far as he was concerned it was planned, he felt it in his bones, she had taken him somewhere, tortured him, called the newspapers to announce what she had done and who knew what she planned to do next.

Nigel ran back up to lift and took it to the third floor. Maybe he could squeeze his way onto Andy Mason's team who were now looking for Elise. Octavia had simply passed the case on. He saw himself in Octavia, reaching for the stars, getting noticed, and getting that promotion; the Mademan case should surely be a case that she was all over, this was a case that could take her to where she wanted to be, with bells and whistles.

Nigel knocked the door assertively and entered. There were only a handful of officers assigned to the case. He stood by the door and glanced around the room hoping to see the box files, they weren't there. Andy Mason's whole demeanor was lackluster, and the room was devoid of any passion or urgency. Nigel realized that no one was making a real effort to locate Elise.

He raised his hand and asked whether they had heard from Elise since the initial confession call. There had been no more contact and the team seemed to agree that there was no way they were going to take a stab in the dark searching for her. They had spoken with Mademan's assigned probation officer Aaron Moor, who didn't believe for one second that Elise could have worked alone, she was too small, too delicate looking to be able to take a man like Mademan down. Aaron Moor was the only person that had seen them together as a couple, albeit for a couple of minutes, and he had described Mademan as the one in control and Elise had appeared subservient.

The team were following the case along the lines that Mademan had tried to overpower Elise or force her into something that she didn't want to do, perhaps sexual or maybe back to his old MO, predator, and Elise wouldn't go along with it. They were all finding it difficult to believe that the images that Elise had sent in were genuine even though there was no evidence that the images had been photo-shopped and edited. They also assumed that Mademan was weaker after the attack outside the restaurant. The one bit of hope they had was that Elise had in fact implied that she would notify the police of exactly where she had left the body. They simply didn't have much to go on.

The bottom line was, they didn't have Mademan's body, only Elise's word and those horrific images. Had Mademan put her up to it, staged the whole thing so he could move around undetected, preying on more children? Or did she have an accomplice? And why had she turned on him: apparently, they had been planning to get married. Nigel couldn't make sense of it all. They needed to locate Elise and find Mademan, dead or alive.

The team had been checking CCTV for Elise's red Golf which had last been seen at a service station headed north. After alerting the local station, they'd discovered Elise's red VW had been abandoned, the keys had been left in the ignition, the interior wiped down, no prints.

"Have we taken a look into Elise's background, who she is, where she's from, family members? Nigel enquired, trying not to sound too eager, he didn't want to offend or brush anybody up the wrong way.

Nigel wasn't surprised to discover they had nothing on her as yet. No known family connections at all, she had worked at "Locations Estate Agents" and had handed her notice in randomly without giving reason on the day of Mademan's release. That was it. That was all the team had come up with. No one was digging, searching; the whole team was disenchanted by the case. Nigel could taste it, smell it, and hear it in their nonchalant responses. No one gave a damn.

"I can go and speak to them, see if she spoke to anyone, had a close friend?" Nigel trod carefully.

Andy Mason nodded in agreement. "We have no idea why she contacted the press and we have to keep an open mind. If Mademan is dead, his body would be good. If this is a setup, a hoax, it can only spell trouble."

"In either case, why would she or they want to draw attention to themselves?" Nigel thought out loud for his own benefit.

"Maybe that's just it: pull our attention in one direction whilst she, or they, are free to do what they please. It's a decoy." Nigel was somewhat satisfied with his deductions.

"Been to her flat?" Nigel was on a roll, and he felt he was onto something. If no one else cared, he sure as hell did and he wanted to take action.

"We've been out there, found nothing of use." Andy sat down in his tatty brown leather seat with a sigh of boredom.

Nigel bit his tongue, doing everything in his power to remain calm. There was no point upsetting the man, he'd learned very early on to keep a calm head in order to get what he wanted. Losing his cool and accusing them of not giving a shit would not be helpful at this point.

"No harm in taking another look once I've been to see her employers." Nigel pushed gently.

Andy shuffled through some files on his desk and scribbled down the address.

"Knock yourself out." Andy was annoyed at being given the case. He held no hope that they would find either Elise or Mademan and knew that he had been given the crap that no one else wanted to deal with. If Mademan was dead and they found Elise, the case would define him, he'd be known to all as the man that took down Elise Miles after she'd done the world a big favor. If they didn't find the body or Elise he'd be seen as incompetent.

He was pissed off. Nigel's apparent interest in the case was exactly what he didn't need. Nigel meant business. Andy knew he would get results.

"Children are likely to live up to what you believe of them."

—Lady Bird Johnson

CHAPTER FIFTY-EIGHT

Nigel raced down the back stairs. The urge to do his job overtook all thoughts of Octavia, promotion, Kent, and Shauna. If Elise had taken Mademan's life, he wanted her, he wanted to be the one to capture her. He had to know either way because the alternative sent shivers down his spine, the thought of the two as partners in crime, out there laughing at the system infuriated him.

He skipped taking two steps at a time, and upon reaching the first floor PC Chris Beckworth interrupted his flow.

"You looking into Mademan?"

Nigel slowed right down, nodding as he continued. PC Beckworth followed.

"Someone you might want to speak to in custody."

Nigel stood still.

"Who?"

Beckworth checked his note pad. "A Lorna Muller. Says she's Elise's mother and that she's in danger if you don't find her."

Nigel sped up. "Thanks." Nigel flew down to the basement.

"She's a bit unsteady, attacked two of our officers." Beckworth called after him.

This was it, this Lorna woman must have something, some clue.

Nigel entered the cell.

"Did you find her?" Godiva leapt forward and grasped at Nigel's jacket, pulling him toward her. Nigel pulled her hands away and loosened her grip. Her breath was foul, she wasn't at all what he had been expecting.

"No. I'm sorry, Mrs. Muller. I need to ask you some very important questions."

Godiva marched toward the back of the cell. "Questions, questions, can't you people look for her and ask questions at the same time?" She turned to face him.

Nigel sat down on the board fashioned as a bed.

"You're Elise's mother, is that correct?" The disbelief in his voice was apparent.

"Her name is Victoria; her sister's name is Michelle."

It clicked. Lorna Muller. The mother of the dead child, Mademan's victim. The more things came together, the more concerned Nigel became.

"We've searched for her family and records of her, but we found nothing and there was definitely no mention of her being Michelle's sister."

"I gave birth to Victoria and Michelle. They're my children. And that, that man is pure evil. He'll get her, too. He doesn't even know…"

Godiva's voice trailed off, a look of shame coated her face.

"Doesn't know what? That Elise—sorry, Victoria—is Michelle's sister?"

"He's a fucking monster, evil he is. Evil to the core. The darkest heart I ever knew."

"Mrs. Muller, where do you think she might go?"

Godiva rolled her eyes incredulously.

"If I knew that, I wouldn't be here, now, would I?"

"You were arrested, weren't you?"

"The only way for someone to listen to me; no one listens anymore."

Nigel's voice tone softened. "I'm listening. I have to know, I'm interested. Do you think she's capable of killing? Do you think she planned to take his life?"

"She's an angel. Not a spiteful bone in her body." Godiva's eyes lit up, and Nigel witnessed her true beauty. Godiva pressed her back up against the wall and allowed her legs to give way beneath her.

"But for what he did to Michelle. Yes." Godiva lowered her face into her hands. "He raped me."

Nigel leaned forward. "I didn't get that."

Godiva threw her head back, her face contorted in rage. "He raped *me*! Evil, dirty, scum of the earth. He raped me!"

Lorna recounted her past, reliving every painful second of her existence. Stefan and her husband had been childhood friends; Stefan had always been the leader, the instigator, the fire-starter, and Gregg, her husband, the follower, the sheep, doing everything that Stefan ordered. Lorna and Gregg had fallen in love and Lorna had hated Stefan from the moment she had clapped eyes on him.

"Full of himself, the world owed him a living. He thought Gregg owed him. I told Gregg, over and over, I told him, that man is trouble from the strands of his hair down to the crusty nail on his big toe. Bad news."

Nigel listened, seeing the truth of Lorna's life being played out before him. She described the night of their simple wedding. After the registrar's office ceremony, they'd gone on to their local, where they'd all drank and eaten too much. Stefan as usual followed them back their bedsit.

"He couldn't leave us alone for one bleeding minute not even on our wedding night."

Stefan plied Gregg with drink until he passed out and Stefan's attention turned to Lorna. He had taken her forcefully, violently, and all the time Gregg had slept like a baby, snoozing peacefully.

Gregg hadn't wanted to believe the truth. Stefan denied any wrongdoing, claiming that Lorna had come on to him and he had declined. Gregg defended Stefan, assuming that Stefan hadn't meant any harm. Perhaps Lorna being as drunk as she was had somehow imagined the whole sordid experience.

"We were never the same, me and him after that. I didn't even know I was pregnant till I was four months gone."

Gregg had insisted that a paternity test wasn't necessary, but Lorna had needed to find out; she had planned an abortion when she received the results, but when Gregg had begged her to keep the child, she had succumbed.

"I knew it wasn't her fault, she was just an innocent coming into an 'orrible cold world. I couldn't do it."

Gregg vowed to bring Victoria up as his own and disassociate with Stefan altogether. They never uttered a word about Victoria's true parentage to another living sole. There had been times when they had both believed they had witnessed Victoria was undeniably Stefan's child. The obsessive behavior, out of control temper tantrums, and if anyone crossed her, her actions were uncontrollable.

"She's mine, my baby, my angel, and it's all our fault. Our world fell apart. Gregg started drinking and when I fell pregnant with Michelle. I actually thought we could turn our lives around."

Godiva's head fell again as she sniveled into her coat.

"So you never told her, Victoria, who her father was?"

"E's not her father, never was. Gregg's her father."

Nigel remembered hearing that Gregg had taken his own life. Theirs was a tragedy, one catastrophe after another had befallen them and now this. Nigel didn't want to think about whether Victoria had somehow discovered that Stefan was her father. Either way she had motive for sure and there was no way Stefan could have known that Michelle was her sister.

"Are you going to let me out of 'ere?"

Nigel nodded, his mind racing ahead. He could track her down find her; she needed help more than anything.

"I can't guarantee they'll drop the charges, but I'll put in a good word for you."

Nigel's heart went out to her. She was harmless: he'd seen her many a time, roaming the streets, not causing any fuss, minding her own business. She had no associates as some of the homeless he'd seen. They tended to have their little groups, but Lorna was different, a loner. He wanted to help, but how? What could he do to heal the years of turmoil that Lorna had lived through? What a life.

CHAPTER FIFTY-NINE

Nigel found nothing noteworthy at Elise's home. The place was bare. No clothes, belongings, or ornaments. There were a few scatter cushions on the sofa, the bed was neatly made. The remote control for the TV appeared brand new. The kitchen cupboards were in order, everything clean, tidy, spick and span. There was no warmth here, it was as if someone had come in and cleaned the place up. If Elise and Stefan had intended to return surely there would be some personal affects, something that showed this was their home or at least Elise's home. Nigel felt it was all staged and the only reason for Elise to stage anything would be because it was a setup, a plan.

Locations Estate Agents returned more of the same. Elise was a hard worker, meticulous, earned good money, had a great reputation, had no known friends, rarely socialized with her team, no one knew anything about her. The receptionist stated that Elise had looked unwell on her last day, but she had put that down to the fact that she was about to hand in her notice. Of course they were all shocked and mortified when they'd heard the news. Most of them in the office simply didn't believe the story that Elise had been writing to Mademan and was planning a life with the infamous and convicted pedophile. They simply refused to believe that Elise of all people was able to keep that a secret. There must be more to the story and so they carried on, waiting for further news, news that somehow there had been a mix-up and Elise would return to work and explain everything. Nigel found their reaction extremely odd, yet it gave him a little insight to who Elise actually was, or rather the person she wanted to be known as.

Mike Turner, Elise's boss had been the most disturbed by Elise's sudden resignation. Nigel sensed there was more to Mike's feelings for Elise than a concerned boss; he was visibly shaken and seemed glad that Nigel had come to the office. Mike wanted to talk.

"She's intelligent and focused. Never had any problems with her at all. Never any signs of, well you know." Writing to, falling for, and planning a life with a convicted pedophile, possible murder suspect, yes, Nigel knew. He knew that Mike Turner knew nothing about Elise but then who knows anything about anyone?

"Where did she work before here?" Nigel couldn't believe she had lived under the radar for so long, only surfacing and becoming Elise Miles just five years ago.

"This was her first job as far as I know, after university that is. It isn't true is it?"

Nigel shook his head. "We won't know the full facts until we get a chance to speak to her and we do need to speak to her. If she makes contact." Nigel passed his card to Mike.

"She's a lovely, lovely young woman. I just hope she's alright, wherever she is."

A lovely young woman? Nigel thought not. He headed back to the station, he would locate those files and was determined to find out why critical information had been deleted. There was bound to be a justified reason, he admonished himself for jumping to the conclusion that something more sinister had taken place. It was beginning to feel more like tracking the invisible woman. Elise Miles was a figment of Victoria Muller's imagination. He had absolutely nothing to go on, no one knew Victoria Muller, everyone claimed to know Elise Miles. He would not be defeated.

CHAPTER SIXTY

As Nigel pulled into the car park, he spotted Octavia. She was driving a black Audi S3 from the car pool. Nigel became immediately suspicious. She didn't notice him. Nigel's instincts alone alerted him to follow her. He had no reason apart from his gut guiding him, and he always followed his gut.

"It is a wise father that knows his own child."

—**William Shakespeare**

CHAPTER SIXTY-ONE

MAY 9, 2005

Octavia had booked out the Audi S3, wanting to remain inconspicuous. She had a couple of hours before the biggest, most important meeting of her life. Octavia had never felt as nervous as she did then and so decided a drive would do her good.

Ten minutes and she found herself outside a small row of identical council-owned terraced bungalows. The curtains of number seven twitched. She stepped out of the car, strolled over, and lightly knocked on the door. Before she could knock a second time the door gradually opened.

"Hello, Dad." The brightness in her voice didn't fool her father.

"You get fired yet?" He left the door ajar and reversed in his wheelchair.

Octavia stepped in and closed the door quietly behind her.

Head bowed, she followed her father into the kitchen. Robert Arnold pulled up at the small round kitchen table, lifting a mug, still warm from his last cup of tea and handed it to Octavia. She went to the sink, rinsed the cup, and switched the kettle on.

"I don't know what I ever did to deserve this life." Robert began his soft-toned sermon.

Octavia inhaled deeply. She visited once or twice a week, paid all his bills, ordered his groceries, and made sure he never did without, yet it was exactly the same routine every single visit.

"I worked hard, I loved your mother, I took care of you and look. Look at me. I don't deserve this." He opened his hands, palms faced upwards.

Octavia poured the boiling hot water into his cup, added a tea bag and three sugars with a drop of milk.

"Do you think I deserve this life?" He genuinely wanted an answer.

"No Dad." Her voice mechanical. If he wouldn't change the record, she most certainly would not.

"All those years of taking care of you and for what, eh? Sometimes I wonder why I even bothered."

It cut deep, but Octavia kept her resolve. There was so much she wanted to say, could say, she wanted to retaliate but she never did. Let him believe that he was the greatest father on the planet, the best husband, what did it matter to her?

She knew better.

She would usually cook him something, make herself a coffee, listen to his self-pitying ramblings. But today was different. She simply couldn't stand it. She even questioned why she had bothered to drop in on him.

"I'm off, Dad."

"What about my dinner? You just come and going again?"

"Yeah."

"Just leave me to fend for myself. I'll be alright." Robert laid on the guilt thick.

"I know." Octavia answered too quickly. Their eyes met for the first time in years. They always made a point of avoiding eye contact. Octavia held his hard stony gaze, the lump in her throat threatening to rise. She held it down. He took her by surprise, and his eyes became glassy and saddened.

She turned away and headed for the door.

"I tried my best for you." He called after her.

Octavia opened the door.

"I know it wasn't good enough."

Octavia stood still, her hand trembled a little on the door handle. She knew that this was her father's apology. She was stunned, she had never heard him apologize for anything to anyone. He had always been the injured party, the victim, the sad case. She didn't believe that he ever looked within himself but how wrong had she been.

She turned and nodded, forcing a smile.

"You coming back?" His voice soft.

Octavia nodded again, She couldn't speak, she didn't trust her voice to follow through, so instead she stepped outside and closed the door behind her.

CHAPTER SIXTY-TWO

Nigel saw Octavia leave and instantly felt guilty. Why was he following her? Yes, he was jealous of her success and reputation, and, yes, he wanted her to want him, see him as more than a mate and a colleague, and, yes, something about her intrigued him to the point of disbelief. Something about her simply didn't fit and he wanted to know, had to find out even though he was fully aware his behavior was abnormally stalkerish.

CHAPTER SIXTY-THREE

Octavia pulled into the Bournbrook estate, the estate where she had grown up.

Her journey down memory lane, the final trip. Her heart heavy, the place hadn't changed, in fact it appeared to have been left out of the area's regeneration plans. She didn't really know what she had hoped to find but it wasn't what she had expected. It remained the same desolate and hopeless place.

The street names all but covered up by graffiti, those who walked the streets were either elderly or children with no better place to go. Rubbish piled up outside of houses or covered the patches of what was supposed to be grass but resembled dirt pits. Her generation was missing. It was eerie, a ghost town, the past lived on here, there was no room for the present, only what had been.

Octavia hadn't been back along the streets where she had once played and roamed in over twenty years. This was a place that she avoided, there was no need for her to visit, she no longer knew anyone, she had no attachments except for one and it was neither pleasant nor fond. That attachment would be broken today.

She had one place that she was supposed to be, and this wasn't it. She had driven so close, she had to just take a peek, see the area through new eyes, maybe there'd be closure but she wasn't holding her breath. She pulled up outside the first home that she knew. The bungalow.

The windows of the bungalow were coated in condensation, the wooden front door showed signs of once having been painted red, now showed years of decay, weathered and beaten, neglected. By the looks of the place no one lived there. In her mind's eye she could see the bungalow as it had been. Bright red shiny door.

The same door that her mother had slammed shut on her way out, never to return. The same door which she had to pause before entering, preparing her for her father's depression and dark moods. The same door that held all her heartbreak and disappointments. The whole place gave her a sense of a time that she was glad was behind her. She pondered the idea of being able to turn back the clock. Everyone she knew had this utopian image of their childhoods, "the good old days," "remember when..."; if there ever came a time when people would be able to go back to their childhoods, she would firmly decline the offer. The thought of her childhood left her feeling cold and unloved. She wanted nothing to do with her past.

The net curtains that her father was forever peeking from behind, in the hope that her mother would somehow miraculously walk back into their lives. She had once lived in that very same hope. Every Christmas, she had written secret letters to Santa, right up to the age of ten when she no longer believed in the fairy tale, asking him to get in touch with her mom and send her home. Beyond that, she simply wished that her mother would get in contact just to show some modicum of interest in what she was doing and who she was.

In her early training days on the force, she had sought out her mother, tracked her down to West London where she was living a very nice life indeed. Her mother had remarried. Her new husband was a senior partner of an architecture firm and they had two children who attended a private school. Cleaned up good and proper. Octavia had watched from a distance and despite herself, found that she admired her mother. Being able to pick herself up, go out into the world, and seek the life she most desired. Her mother was a winner. She wanted to be a winner too. She never told her father, she didn't want to break his heart yet again, although she knew he would never believe her and would find a reason to accuse her of lying, yet again.

She was a new person, she had a job that she loved, a life that she loved, she didn't want to go visiting the ghosts of the past, holding onto what ifs and maybes. She liked where she was now, AND she was grateful for her present and held onto her bright future, the past was for deadbeats. The past had nothing to do with her, and after today she would never have to look back over her shoulder.

If she had had a choice, she would have chosen never to step foot on the Bournbrook estate ever again, but there was one last thing that she had

to do and she promised herself that after today, she would never do anything she didn't want to do again.

CHAPTER SIXTY-FOUR

Shauna's memories coursed through her mind as she made her way through the fields. The council had held onto this oasis in the middle of the dank and darkness of the Bournbrook estate. The sun beamed down on her back, and she knew her shoulders would be burnt scarlet red.

Letting go of Kent had been too damn easy. She had not shed a tear. She realized after walking out of his life that she should have walked a long time ago. Kent was a good man, but they wanted different things, a different life and trying to gently coax him along her path had taken some doing but he was his own man and she had known that at some stage he would try to guide her his way.

She was selfish, there was no give and take with her; it was her way or the highway. Kent was the type of man that would never give up on her and would spend a lifetime of energy and love showing her, pushing and prodding her in his direction. It was better to dig her heels in now rather than later when things would get decidedly messy. Marriage, kids. No, she had made the right decision and her shoulders felt lighter. It was over and now she had to make a life for herself. She was excited to forge her own way, not following someone else's path.

Once today was over, she was going to get to grips with what she really wanted and as she walked through the tall grass she wasn't even sure she knew exactly what that was just yet. She had butterflies floating around in her stomach. She hadn't seen her friends for over fifteen years. She knew she would recognize them straight away, but this wasn't a typical reunion. This was something else entirely. She was ready to release the shackles she had drawn along with her almost her entire life and then she would truly be free.

Elise lay back on the grass shielding her closed eyes from the sun. Her skin tingled from the heat and a nervousness that had visited her many times before in her life. It was the nervousness of elation, joy, and power that overtook her body, a natural high. She knew she needed to allow the feeling to wash over her and it would leave her as swiftly as it had come.

She felt strong and empowered. Right now there were only two other people on the planet that knew exactly who she was and what she was about. There was a deep connection that had held them bound together for most of their lives and today, they were uniting for what would be the last time. She didn't want this to be a final goodbye, more than anything she wanted this to be a new start for all of them. Would they allow that?

Elise was lonely. She had never allowed anyone into the stratosphere of her life before. Even though the only two people who truly knew her had been missing for a big part of her life, she could feel their energy and she knew they could feel hers. As a child, the only other person she had felt a connection with had been Michelle. She spoke to Michelle often; Michelle's memory had often kept her company and helped guide her through difficult times. Elise tried to imagine what Michelle would look like now, how she would dress, where she would work. She'd definitely be married with at least one baby boy called Earl. Michelle had told her so.

The entire direction of their lives would have been substantially altered. She herself would not have made the same choices, she knew that for a fact. Elise liked to imagine Michelle as a fashion designer. Michelle had loved clothes and making stuff, inventing new ways to wear a scarf, sticking plastic letters and glitter on her jeans. Michelle had been the creative one. Elise thought she herself would perhaps have been in sales of some sort. She had always had the gift of the gab, could sell sweets to the sweet shop, a hostel worker had once told her.

Many a time the two of them had lain in that exact spot, allowing the sun to soak into their skin, relaxed and happy, at times in silence sharing the moment, at other times chattering away ten to the dozen. Elise had listened to Michelle's dreams and aspirations, knew her plans for her life, her wishes, and wants. As Elise lay there, she felt the space, the gap where Michelle should be in her life. The hole was all encompassing. Elise fell into that hole and drifted through time and space, grasping on to a bunch of Michelle's buttercups, allowing herself to float and drift, breathing easy, free as a bird. It felt good, too good.

Elise felt Shauna's thigh against hers, felt her ease herself to the ground beside her, holding out her hand. Shauna's slipped easily into hers.

"Can you feel her?" Elise's voice entered the atmosphere as a small whisper.

Shauna nodded. "Yes." Shauna was choked. This was an ending as well as a beginning and as dark and dangerous as it had all been, she still felt torn. This was their spot, their place, their home. It still hurt that even this small tiny thing that they had and shared had to be taken away from them.

Shauna closed her eyes, feeling the baby softness of Elise's hands, warm and comforting, yet strong and powerful. Shauna embraced the calmness and stillness. "I can hear her."

"Me too." They lay there side by side, holding onto the remnants of their childhood and preparing to let go for one last time.

Octavia cast a shadow over the two of them.

"I'm in the middle." Neither opened their eyes, they simply scooted sideways, allowing Octavia to slip in the between them. Octavia looked down on either side of her, overwhelmed, happy, yet desperately grief-struck. She had known that going there, on that day, would open up wounds that she had plastered over years prior. She knew that seeing her friends would remind her of that night, the night that changed all of their lives. She had not shed a single solitary tear since that night. She had ploughed all of her emotions into fighting for her life, fighting her way through university, and fighting her way through her career. Now as she lay back, she felt the hot stinging of tears, pooling in the corners of her eyes.

"What the fuck." She whispered, lifting her hands to stem the tears. Shauna's and Elise's hands clamped in hers. Understanding, feeling, allowing her the freedom and space. Identical images of that night, the aftermath, Michelle, Dane, blotting out the face of Mademan. Their hearts heavy with grief, the relief of knowing that Mademan could no longer harm or haunt them or anyone else for that matter.

"We did good." Elise had so much to say, choosing her words carefully so as not to stain the moment with the reality of that they had all been involved in. The lack of response irked her.

Octavia's eyes flashed open. "I think we all know what needs to be done now."

"We stick to the plan and get the fuck on with our lives." Shauna was firm, and both women knew that Shauna's words were spoken in warning. Octavia wanted to stamp out any further connections or meetings that Elise may have on her mind. She had waited too long for this day; there was no way she was planning and plotting further with her longtime friends.

"You have a life?" Neither Shauna nor Octavia had the energy to respond. They remained still, eyes closed.

"Working all the hours, no social life, no husbands, children, even hobbies to speak of?" Elise desperately wanted their union to continue. What had it all been for if naught? They were the only people on the planet who knew what they had been through, the years of pain and torment that they had endured. How could they simply let go?

"Jeremy Clark, a close associate of Stefan's..."

"No." Octavia and Shauna shut Elise down in unison.

Elise paused for a second and continued. "Known to the police for forty-two offences of child abuse, but we all know there'll be countless more. He's being released in twelve days' time and..."

Octavia sat up. "No Elise, this ends today."

"Why? Because we've ended Stefan's legacy? Because we're the only victims who needed an end, closure?" Elise needed to be heard.

"Because we have broken the law. Because we have taken the law into our own hands. Because we are all responsible for a man's death." Octavia saw what they had done and knew that if they were found out, Stefan would win the entire war. She couldn't let that happen; they couldn't let that happen. Hadn't they suffered enough?

"And?" Octavia's reasoning did not wash with Elise.

"There has to be an end. We cannot spend the rest of our lives fighting the cause. We all have dreams, we all have goals, we need to live without his shadow and darkness hanging over us. We got what we wanted. We have to move on. That was the plan, the plan that you put in place." Shauna choked back her tears. She was tired, worn out emotionally and the idea of going back to square one with yet another abuser turned her stomach.

"My dream was always to stop child abuse, not just Mademan. He's just the tip of the iceberg, you both know that. There are hundreds, thousands of people out there, right now as we sit here bickering, causing pain and hurt to defenseless children and you two want to go off and live your lives, which wouldn't be so bad but neither of you can live, carry on, move forward. I know for a fact I can't. He did that to us, he ruined our lives, our families, we don't just get to turn the last page and close the book. We don't. Stop lying to yourselves. There's work to be done."

Octavia stood and brushed down her jeans. "I've got to go."

"You know how to get hold of me when reality gives you a wakeup call."

Elise shielded her eyes from the sun, looking up at Octavia. Shauna stood then.

Elise wanted to grab them both and give them a good shake. Elise knew they wanted to pretend that their lives were on track and that there was a chance for them, but she knew different. She had given up on her dreams of a real life, making connections, having friends, marrying, settling down. Although she felt she had dealt with what had happened, there was a gaping hole within her that could never be filled, she had accepted that. She had accepted that she couldn't have a normal life and had decided that Michelle's death would not be in vain. She was going to make good.

Every abuser that she knew about would feel her wrath. She would continue the good fight until her last breath of that she was sure and she wanted her allies by her side. They made a good team. She also knew that it was going to take time for them to recognize the truth. What Mademan had done to them and their families was final. There was no healing, getting past it, moving on. He had planted seeds of doubt, pain and disgust within them and those seeds had flourished, no amount of therapy could wipe it away. The only way to end it was death and she was not about to take her own life and let scum like Mademan win. Absolutely not.

"I love you both, you know that." Elise reached out her hands toward them.

Octavia leant and kissed Elise on the cheek. "Right back at ya."

Shauna took Elise's hand and opened up her other arm wide, Elise stood and joined the huddle, they embraced. They held on to each other tightly, not wanting to let go. Lost, abandoned, alone in the world, the only connection and real love they had experienced was from each other, yet they had to break it. It was the only way.

Octavia loosened their grip, turned, and walked away, never taking a peek over her shoulder. Shauna strode in the opposite direction, back through the fields.

Elise turned to watch each as their figures became dots in the distance. Her heart was breaking all over again. How many times would she have to endure this feeling? She knew trying to persuade them further would fall on deaf ears. All her life she had taken action, and that was all she knew: she was a fighter and that was the only way to get results. That's what she would continue to do.

"For not an orphan in the wide world can be so deserted as the child who is an outcast from a living parent's love."

—Charles Dickens

CHAPTER SIXTY-FIVE

Nigel sat motionless in his car, not believing what his owns eyes were seeing. This was the first time in his life that following a hunch, and getting the answers he expected, didn't bring about a sense of achievement and satisfaction. Instead, he felt sick to his stomach. Being right meant that these three women had been victims of Mademan, that they had plotted and planned his murder, and gotten away with it. It also meant that his job was to make the three arrests and report to his superior.

He had solid evidence and proof. He'd taken pictures of the three together, talking and embracing. He could link the three of them back to the children's home. Shauna ensuring Mademan's release, Elise the murderer, and Octavia, his Octavia, crime fighter extraordinaire, closing her eyes to it all and making sure that no one else on the force took a blind bit of notice. Deliberately omitting and tampering with statements and documents. He had been right all along: she was smart, savvy, devious, ambitious, and manipulative. Just like him.

Nigel knew that Octavia's only interest in him was his interest in the Mademan case. That was it, the long and short of it. She probably didn't even find him attractive. Why would she? She was way out of his league.

As Octavia pulled out of the car park, his heart sank. She was the reason he was about to break the code of ethics, something he hadn't planned on and would never have considered, not for any reason. Was it time to leave the force? His best mate had asked him to bend a rule, he had bent it and then some, now he had to question who he was, his actions. He didn't know if he was in love with Octavia or whether he felt great pity for her, what she had been through and survived and still reached the top of her game. And Shauna and Kent, his actions hadn't caused their break up, but he knew what had, and he couldn't share that with Kent ever. Kent would never forgive him for keeping schtum—he would never understand, and why should he? If the tables had been turned, Nigel knew for sure that he would've wanted the low down at any cost. The tragedy that was Elise Miles, or Victoria Muller. Where would she go now? Could he really go and arrest the three of them, knowing what he knew?

Nigel knew that Mademan's blood was on all of their hands and Elise appeared to be the ring leader, the one who had carried out the harrowing and brutal dismemberment of Mademan. Nigel was disgusted with himself: he understood and almost wanted to congratulate her on what she had done; he got it, and that alone hurt him. He hadn't had to question his morals before in his career but here he was, glad that Mademan had met a gruesome end, glad that they had planned his demise and bought him down. He was glad. Relief washed over him as he admitted that fact to himself. He was glad, he was proud of what they had done. What did that make him? Worthy of promotion?

CHAPTER SIXTY-SIX

Elise headed down the motorway in a small navy blue Vauxhall Corsa. Despite herself, she was excited. There was so much to do. The weight had been lifted from her shoulders. She had taken action and made change, change that didn't just affect her, but the lives of her dearest friends and thousands of others. Adrenaline pumped through her body in waves, and she at times noticed that her foot rested a little too heavy on the accelerator.

The smile plastered across her face showed joy, accomplishment; she was a champion. Visions of Stefan, pleading, begging her forgiveness, flashes of his surprise and dismay. Her heart pumped hard. Her father, her sister's murderer, could they really be one and the same? She had taken great pleasure in every moment of his torture and she would do it again. If the police ever caught up with her, plan B, she would admit it and give her reasons, she would make sure every single person in the country knew why she had done what she had done, and she would happily do the time, but plan B was not required. She had got away with it. The whole country knew that Mademan was dead; people could rest easy in their beds.

She had been playing with the idea that those evil abusers, life wreckers, love poisoners should get a head start. She wanted to find a way to let them know that she would not rest until she had taken the life of each and every one of them and she would. She would meat out punishment where the law failed. That's what was required, real punishment. Prevention was the answer, she knew this, as things stood, a child abuser could commit his crimes and go undetected for years before getting caught and punished for a fraction of their true crimes.

Prison was no prevention; this scum was an infestation on society: they were everywhere, in every nook and cranny, high society to crack dealers, everywhere. If she could somehow let them know that she would end their lives, end their lucrative operations, that may serve as a deterrent. It made perfect sense to her.

Elise pulled into to a small local train station one hundred miles away from her childhood home, Removing a small carryall from the back seat, and slinging it over her shoulder. Everything she required for her new life was contained in the bag. A driver's license, passport, and seven thousand pounds in cash. A brand new boxed mobile phone with a sealed phone chip, a pad and pen. A few clothing items and toiletries. Dressed in black skinny jeans, a chunky black sweater, and black knee-high Timberland boots. Only the laptop would be discarded once she had completed the final part of her plan. Her jewelry, mainly chunky silver and heavy. She found the new piercings irritating her eyebrow, cheek and nose but it was an irritation she would have to bear. This was her new life, her new identification, and she liked it. Tired of the prim and properness of her past life, regular manicures, hair dressers appointments, and facials had become tiresome. She was pleased that her choices would now allow her to grunge down, revel in her naturalness and fuck all those who were offended by her new look.

Before entering the train station, she pulled out a black Nike cap and slotted it onto her head. There was a coffee shop within the station, and Elise sauntered in and ordered an Americano, her new coffee of choice. Sitting down at a table tucked away to the rear of the coffee shop, next to the bathrooms, she slid the laptop from the bag and connected to the coffee shop's Wi-Fi.

Accessing the dark web, she entered "the real news dot com" into the search bar and waited for the website to load, searching the site for the article written on Mademan's release and subsequent stories she typed.

Mademan received the punishment he deserved. Prison was not a punishment, prison only served as an incubator for a degenerate. I know this because my name is Victoria Muller, a.k.a. Elise Miles. I am the one with whom he confided his darkest desires, I know what he was capable of and what his intentions were. I may not have acted within the bounds of the law, but I don't believe the law understands, or will ever understand, a criminal of Mademan's caliber.

The only way to stop him was to end his life, so I did. I need others like him to understand that I will not stop there. Mademan was simply one in a line of many hundreds and thousands across the world who need to be stopped and, as no one appears to be up to the job, I shall take on the task of ending this sickness that is ruining the lives of millions of people. Not everyone was abused as a child, but everyone had been touched by this evil. It should be treated like a cancer, yet there are no funds to eradicate child abuse, there has to date been no attempt to stop these perpetrators, so I will. I see it as my duty to myself and society at large. I will not stop.

Satisfied with her ranting confession, she hit the publish button. She blew on her steaming cup of coffee. Within minutes, people began to respond. Elise skimmed through: every single comment congratulated and cheered her on. There were no judgments, only support, which is exactly what she had hoped for. In her heart she knew that people had had enough. The only part of her plan that had not panned out was Octavia and Shauna joining her, but she knew they would someday.

Next, she unclipped a small compact mirror from her keyring, opening it revealing a small silver USB stick; she slotted it into the computer. Elise opened the terminal navigated through to an online forum on the dark web. She copied and pasted the exact statement with an addition.

Join me in bringing justice to the abusers. Know of an abuser? I will remove them. I will do my own research of course. Looking for genuine people who believe in real justice. This isn't my cause, this is a worldwide cause and together we can delete child abuse from our futures.

Elise was expecting to be inundated with messers and pranksters, but she knew that the majority of responses would be genuine and she was ready.

Draining her cup, she made her way to the awaiting train. She didn't look back, only ahead.

Once seated comfortably, she made a call, the last call she would make as Elise Miles. Telling the switchboard that she needed to speak to someone who was dealing with the Stefan Mademan murder, she was quickly put through to Nigel.

"DCI Pemberton speaking." Nigel caught his breath.

"Yes, you'll find Stefan Mademan's body at Buttercup cottage, off Granthock Road, the Peak District."

Nigel interrupted. "Victoria, is this your revenge?"

Elise hesitated, her mind raced. "My name is Elise Miles."

"I've spoken with your mother, and she explained everything but she's worried about you. She thinks you're in danger, that Stefan is a threat to you."

"Stefan is no longer a threat to anyone. I'm sorry, I have to go."

"Wait. Was it revenge for Michelle or for your mother?"

Elise paused.

"I understand he destroyed your family, your life." Nigel took a beat before continuing. "Him being your father…"

Elise ended the call. She sat, stunned for a moment. Her mother had gone to the police. What else had she expected? She considered her mother's reaction to hearing the news; she hadn't really thought about it till then. Her mother and Stefan together; she shuddered.

Elise removed the chip from the phone, walked to the end of the carriage and pulled down the window. She stuck her head out slightly, allowing the gusty wind to ravage her hair. She drew back and threw the phone and the chip out, watching them disappear down the stony embankment. That was it. Elise Miles's life was over. Ivy Cadeau's life was just beginning.

"You may shoot me with your words,
you may cut me with your eyes, you
may kill me with your hatefulness,
but still, like air,
I'll rise..."

—Maya Angelou

CHAPTER SIXTY-SEVEN

Ivy didn't realize how tired she was until she awoke and checked her watch. She'd slept straight for two hours, and she'd only meant to catch twenty minutes or so. She was happy to see that nobody had taken any of the other three seats. She looked around; the train was half full, yet her new look was having the desired effect. As Elise, at least one of those seats would have been taken by some deluded man with the need to start a conversation.

She dug into her bag and rooted out her flask of soup and popped one of her tablets. The soup was lukewarm, but she was ravenous and enjoyed every drop. She pulled out her A4 lined writing pad and pen.

Dear Jeremy,

I know this may seem very odd, me writing you a letter, you receiving my letter, and I'm a complete and utter stranger. I understand if you do not respond, but if you're still reading this, you must be intrigued. I've been following your story, your case, and in all honesty, I feel as though you have been treated unfairly. Your alleged connection to other criminals does not make you a criminal and the fact that your wife chose to divorce you and your children have disowned you is a tragedy in my eyes.

I'm familiar with feeling all alone in the world and I just wanted to reach out to you. Perhaps you need a friend, someone to talk to, and I want you to know, I'm here. Everyone deserves a second chance and you deserve complete vindication.

A little about me: I'm twenty five years old, I'm an accountant, single *smiley face* and would love to get to know you.

I've been thinking about writing you for some time, but could never find the courage to actually put pen to paper. I've written nine letters or so, and I've thrown them all away. It's difficult to find the words to say that I feel a strong connection to you, I'm drawn to you. I hope you don't think I'm some crazy woman.

I hope to hear from you.

Love

Ivy Cadeau

Ivy carefully ripped the page from the pad and folded it neatly in three. Sliding it into an already addressed and stamped envelope, she sealed it, and kissed the back of the letter, leaving her bright red lipstick print.

Satisfied, she laid her head back in the seat and closed her eyes. She had another forty minutes of her journey, so she could sleep easy and awake in a new city, with a new identity, ready for her new life.

THE END.